The Dead Commando

They drove in out of the desert and took the isolated
fortress before the Italian garrison could resist. Then the
operation went wrong and the Germans moved in. With
the Allied armies on the move to El Alamein, Rommel
could not risk an enemy-held strongpoint in his rear.

But no one on the British side was going to lift a
finger to save the seventeen men of John Offer's
Glasshouse Gang. They had only one hope of survival:
they'd be dead men or prisoners if they held out in Fort
Telatha, but if they could slip away before the balloon
went up, who would know if they were alive or dead?

John Offer had overlooked one factor. Hauptmann
Braunschweig of the Afrika Korps was learning his
enemy's ways, and the Glasshouse Gang would have to be
very, very dead before he gave up the hunt.

Like the earlier novels in this series, *The Glasshouse
Gang*, *Desert Marauders* and *Benghazi Breakout*, *The Dead
Commando* tells a thrilling story against an authentic and
detailed background.

The Dead Commando

Gordon Landsborough

Allan Wingate · London
A Howard & Wyndham Company
1977

Copyright © 1976 by Gordon Landsborough
This edition, 1977 ~~ORMSKIRK~~

This book or parts thereof may not be
reproduced in any form whatsoever
without permission in writing

Printed in Great Britain by
Fletcher & Son Ltd, Norwich,
for the Publishers, Allan Wingate Ltd,
44 Hill Street, London W1X 8LB
Bound by Richard Clay (The Chaucer Press) Ltd,
Bungay, Suffolk

ISBN 85523 321 4

It was like something out of Beau Geste. Fort Telatha stood isolated in the hot, shimmering desert, brutally square and solid, a short tower at each corner, and with the thick walls pierced for riflemen.

The flag of Italy dropped disconsolately from a flagstaff. That could be seen through binoculars. Those powerful glasses also revealed a machine-gun mounted on the flat roof of each tower, though for the moment only one was manned. No doubt, too, men paced the catwalks within and kept watch through the rifle slits.

Also to be seen were the Arab civilians who trekked daily with their camels and asses from the oasis a mile away over the rolling, wind-sculptured dunes. They'd be doing trade with the garrison, bringing meat, vegetables, eggs and fruit. But not water. An army tanker maintained a steady run between the springs of the oasis and some cistern within the fort.

When they had learned all they wanted to know, the distant watchers put aside their binoculars and prepared to attack. After eleven in the morning would be the best time; then the civilian traffic dwindled away, the Arab traders returning to their cool green oasis to meet the heat of the day. The garrison would not be at its best by that time, either, the ferocious heat from the desert sapping initiative, and making men find excuses for not staring too hard over the glistening sandy wastes.

The officer leading the party, a man rather on the short side, tanned by exposure to the desert sun to little less than Bedouin blackness, his nose flattened as if by contact with

5

boot or fist, at length stirred and walked over to his Jeep. Seven Jeeps stood together, their occupants crouching in the dwindling shade thrown by the toy-like vehicles. A Browning machine-gun was mounted in each Jeep.

'Okay,' called the officer, and at that the men dragged themselves erect and took their seats. No order was given; they all knew the parts they had to play in the next few minutes.

One Jeep only moved off at first – the officer's. His driver, a runt of a man with steel-rimmed army-issue glasses and a mouthful of curiously tiny teeth, headed without hurry for the fort. The third man in the Jeep was a lean private who sucked on the dead tab of a Woodbine, but his hand never left the butt of the Browning.

The big double doors of the fort were still open. They were always kept open while civilian traffic came and went within the fort, but the British raiding party had noticed that around noon the doors were closed for the rest of the hot day. Eleven o'clock – still plenty of time.

A sentry lounged in the shade between the massive doors, his rifle propped against the guardroom built on to the thick outer defence wall. He was a sensible man, hating this uncomfortable desert, hating the war and pining for the cool green slopes of his native Piedmont. Not so sensibly, because his life was at stake, he was giving scant attention to his duties as gate sentry.

So it was that the Jeep came within four hundred yards before his apathetic eye encountered it. It created no alarm. The distortions from the rising air currents over the hot dunes rendered the vehicle unrecognizable at that range. All he knew was that a vehicle was approaching from the direction of Telatha Oasis. For a moment he thought it was the water tanker, then remembered it had made its last run for the day and was even now emptying its load into the underground tank across the square.

He should have come alert at that, but his mind was heat-dulled and worked slowly. Anyway, the vehicle was

6

approaching at a most sober pace, so there was little to alarm him.

But suddenly he did stir, suspicion coming to him. The vehicle was taking shape and it was unusual thereabouts; it was one of those little American cars the enemy had started to use, cars used by Allied desert raiders who did so much damage to isolated Axis installations. They had all been shown pictures . . .

Abruptly he kicked the stop away from one of the big doors and it started to close under its own weight. Then he grabbed his rifle and went across to shut the other door. Still he did not move at any great speed, for he could not believe that here, two hundred miles behind the front line at Alamein, there was any danger. But if this was some superior Italian officer making his rounds in a captured enemy vehicle he wanted to show he was on the alert.

The officer in the Jeep saw the door begin to swing to. 'Now!' he called, and his driver rammed his foot hard down and the Jeep roared into top speed. The laconic private settled himself behind his Browning.

A suddenly startled sentry heard the revving of the Jeep engine and paused to look towards it. In that pause he died. The Browning thundered and the bullets hit the sentry and dropped him. Above, the machine-gunners on their sand-bagged tower heard the heavy Browning and leapt to their weapon. Too late. The Jeep was too close for them to have time to bring their gun into action.

One big door was still open, wide enough for a Jeep to get through. It raced within the entrance. As they passed through the gateway the officer tossed a grenade against the hinge of the open door. When it blew up the hinge would shatter and no one would be able to close that door in a hurry. The other Jeeps would be able to get through.

Those other Jeeps leapt into movement the moment their officer's car accelerated. They came racing in, bouncing at recklessly high speed over the desert sand, and the machine-gunners on the tower saw them approaching and were momentarily demoralized – which enemy to tackle first, the one within the fort or the approaching vehicles?

The solitary Jeep shot through the gateway on to a sandy parade ground, around which the fort was built. The occupants had a momentary impression of low, flat-roofed buildings running around the base of the thick fortress walls, glassless windows looking out at them. The flat roofs were firing platforms for the rifle slits, with catwalks above them, and two Italian soldiers were up there, rifles lifting to aim at the Jeep.

The Jeep slammed on its brakes and skidded to a mad halt, sand showering in a wide spray, a dust cloud rising immediately. Officer and driver seemed to hurl themselves out of the vehicle. The officer had a tommy gun, the driver a rifle which seemed too big for him. A burst from the tommy and one of the sentries collapsed and came head first off the flat roof. The rifle swung to the shoulder of the little driver, fired once and the other sentry spun round and died.

The Browning caught the machine-gunners on the tower before they really realized there was attack from behind. A thunderous roar, cordite fumes rising and making their stink, tracer darting swiftly up towards the sandbags. Neither of the flustered Italian machine-gunners had had sense to get down, and they died at their post without firing a shot.

Startled faces had appeared at the open windows. The Browning depressed and raked them; the officer and his driver went running the length of the buildings, tossing grenades through the windows.

The guard came tumbling out by the big gate, at which moment the grenade blew off against the hinge and sent them back reeling, stunned. From roof hatches Italians began to pour up on to the catwalks, and other men were frantically scaling the towers, trying to get at their machine-guns.

Six Jeeps began to roar through the gateway. One halted just inside the heavy doors to cover any need for retreat; the

8

other five took up positions around the first Jeep.

Bullets were beginning to fly, Italians with rifles firing out from one building which looked as if it were the administration office. Six Brownings got to work. The noise echoed and re-echoed within those high walls; the stench of cordite grew stronger; dust and smoke drifted over the miniature battleground.

Concentrated firepower smashed all resistance inside the admin office. Wild-looking bearded desert raiders swiftly deployed from their Jeeps and with their rifles picked off the climbers as they raced up the scaling ladders. Bodies fell into space, dying men screaming before they hit the sandy parade ground. The Brownings turned on other Italians who suddenly appeared on the high exposed catwalks. They hadn't a chance.

One minute twenty seconds after the attack had begun all resistance ended. Short, swift and savage. This wasn't fighting, it was murder. From the moment that Jeep surprised them and gained a position within the fortress, the defenders hadn't a chance.

Now they stopped running and stood with hands raised above their heads. The Brownings quietened. A great silence fell over the square. Still the raiders held their positions against the sheltering walls, while the gunners crouched behind their machine-guns, fingers ready on triggers. The officer stood alone, Thompson sub-machine-gun swinging from its sling, as alert as his men and ready to come into action at the first sign of renewed opposition.

None came. After a while a white cloth waved from the admin office. The officer walked slowly towards it. Twenty yards away he halted and called, '*Avanti!*' and for a man who had just led a murderous and bloody raid, his voice sounded pleasant, good-natured, and not at all intimidating.

Men began to emerge from the building, hands aloft, blinking as they came into the bright sunlight. A few officers – a major, a captain, some lieutenants – and some clerkly-looking soldiers filed out. They appeared most dejected and woebegone.

A lean red-faced sergeant-major came up alongside his captain, as if to give him protection in case of attack. Sweat was pouring down his face, and he still panted from the exertions of the last hectic moments, yet he was a happy man. He said so, in effect.

'We did it!' His voice was jubilant, yet soft so that only his officer would hear. 'We took the bloody fort, just as you said!' And then he said something curious, his voice bewildered. 'But why? Why do we need this Christ-awful place?'

His captain appeared not to have heard him. He had begun to pace before the line of officers. Big brown eyes regarded him with apprehension. The major opened his mouth to speak, but a gesture from the British officer silenced him.

He had come before an Italian captain and now he halted and seemed to examine the officer carefully. The Italian was a short man, only a few inches above five feet, barrel-bodied and fleshy. His face, blue-chinned, was soft and rounded with too much good-living; fear-distended eyes met the grey ones of the British officer and the Italian seemed to quail before them.

The British officer slowly wagged a finger before the face of the Italian captain, a gesture which seemed curiously admonitory. 'You,' he said reprovingly, 'are called Musso-lini.' Then he half-turned and rapped out an order. 'Sergeant Walker, put a guard on this man, *and I'll have your guts for garters if he gets away from you!*'

Bizarrely, Fort Telatha was assaulted and a captain taken prisoner because of Sergeant Walker. Walker, that big and amiable man, knew it and would for ever afterwards be grateful to the man who had led the raid, John Offer.

But then Walker was Offer's comrade, a man who had shared a cell with him during an unforgettably brutal period in one of His Majesty's Glasshouses on the Sweet Water

Canal. Also he had shared Offer's hazardous existence in the desert ever since, and such things are binding, to some men at least.

One such hazardous foray had been a daring raid on Rommel's oil supplies at Al Agheila on the Bay of Benghazi. Nearly half of Offer's Glasshouse Gang had lost their lives or been taken prisoner. Walker was one of them.

The S.S. had treated him as a special captive, and he had suffered terribly at their hands until John Offer's commando came to his rescue some weeks later. But Walker, army deserter on the run, was by now too far gone from starvation and brutal torture to resume their desert wanderings, and to save his life the Gang had had to fly him to Cairo for hospital treatment. There he had been recognized, court-martialled and given a ten-year sentence for desertion, bank robbery, and for taking part in a celebrated raid on that same Glasshouse months earlier.

John Offer and the surviving members of the Glasshouse Gang Commando Unit had come to Cairo in the hope of staging a rescue bid. It was done brazenly, of course, typically Offer. They had rented a villa up the Nile (knocking off a French bank to provide themselves with funds), and were so open about their presence there they knew no one would suspect them. After all, who is to suppose that army deserters would take a villa and maintain a smart sentry, day and night, on the pavement outside the gate? And there were many such villas in Cairo's suburbs, legitimately rented to house some odd department of the Allied armies, so that no one looked twice at Offer's temporary H.Q.

But being so near to their comrade brought no inspiration to Offer to get his sergeant out of the hands of screws who wouldn't forget the hiding they'd taken that day of the riot. That is, until he opened his bed to visitors.

The best thing that had come to John Offer's bed at that time was a charming nursing sister in Cairo Main Hospital called Angela. The bed was in the Continental Hotel, much favoured by officers on brief leave from the desert war, for John Offer could hardly have brought her to his own bed in the Nile villa. For one thing, she knew him as Captain Roger Tansley, R.A.M.C. Another, his villains would have given the game away in no time.

Angela was a soft touch for men wounded in defence of King and Country. Injured warriors, silently suffering, brought tears to her eyes and a passionate desire to console and comfort them. In Offer's case she had done this on earlier occasions in bed, he posing as an M.O. wounded in battle, having got her there without much trouble, and she finding that generosity had its moments of compensation.

'Your limp's gone,' was Angela's first observation, though, when they met this time, and she seemed ever so slightly to regret it. A wad of paper in his brothel-creepers had given him the limp at their first meeting, but this time he had forgotten to put it in his desert boot.

'Hate limping,' said the rogue, Offer. 'Try not to do it, y'know. But it still gives me gyp if I put too much strain upon it,' and he looked very noble as he said it. Angela brightened immediately. Her Roger still had need of her generous instincts. She gave them.

And when she had given them twice, and they were relaxing, very cheerful and enjoying a meal brought to their room by a smiling Egyptian room-waiter, who knew a good jig-a-jig when he saw it, Angela gossiped. Angela, lovely girl, liked to talk, and her talk was always shop.

In the course of time she began to talk about a young S.A.S. second-lieutenant who had been flown in wounded from some distant spot in the desert. So young to be at war, so dreadful to have been blown up and have a leg shattered. So handsome, lying there against the bed sheets, thought John Offer good-humouredly. He knew his Angela. Her heart would have gone out to the dashing young officer from that glamorous outfit. Indeed, she seemed to blush a little as she talked about the warrior and her eyes were very bright. Offer wondered if she had thoughts on consoling the lad in bed, for one never knew what went on in a nice girl's mind. He was not a bit put out, not so long as Angela was there when he wanted her.

'He was on a very important mission,' he heard Angela prattling, for she did prattle on. Offer was wondering how soon after the meal he could pop her into bed again. 'It was to some oasis I've never heard of – Fort Telatha.'

John Offer knew the place from his desert wanderings. Bloody dump; the enemy was welcome to it, all flies and heat. The wine made him feel warm and benevolent and he thought Angela looked most fetching, using his bush jacket as a dressing gown and not bothering to button it. No, they wouldn't dally when the meal was over.

'And what sort of a mission was it?' Offer said, quite idly, not interested. No planes to blow up at Fort Telatha.

Angela surprised him. 'They were on a kidnapping expedition. Mussolini's son's there with the garrison.'

'Mussolini's son?' Suddenly John Offer was alert. 'What do they want with Musso's offspring?'

Angela was vague. Something to do with P.O.W.s in Italy, a hostage for their better treatment. John Offer put two and two together.

'Your young hero is rather talkative, isn't he?' The mildest of reproof for the second-lieutenant.

'Oh, it doesn't matter now. The thing's been called off.'

John Offer kept her talking, pulling out the items of information he required. When he knew as much as she did about the abortive expedition – which seemed to be everything; her blue brimming eyes had kept the subaltern talking – he had her out of his bush jacket, then into the bed which she was reluctant to leave when it came time for her to report for night duty.

Offer returned to his Nile villa a thoughtful man. After a while he called Sergeant-major O'Keefe to his room and said, 'I think I've got the answer.'

O'Keefe didn't ask what the question was. He knew it.

13

John Offer said, 'I think I know how to get away from Sharafim when we've rescued old Walker.'

O'Keefe looked startled. His mind couldn't keep up with Offer's. 'Stone the bloody crows, but first how do we rescue him?'

John Offer dismissed the question as if it hardly required an answer. 'Getting him out of Sharafim is easy. No problem about that.' O'Keefe merely continued to look astonished. 'It's getting him away from the damn' place that's been bothering me.'

This time they'd have road blocks everywhere and no one would be able to bluff their way easily through them when they knew Sharafim had been assaulted yet again.

The sergeant-major said, 'Pardon my thickness, sir, but would you mind telling me this easy way of springing Walker?'

'My boy –' Offer was indulgent '– there's nothing to it. Always remember prisoners vastly outnumber screws. Any day on that square there are several hundred prisoners and a mere handful of screws drilling them. And the screws are unarmed except for their boots and sticks.'

'There are armed sentries all round the square.'

'And who would they fire on?' Offer's eyes were glowing; he could see it all happening. 'Sergeant-major, the way we do it is to cause confusion. We must have every prisoner there in on the act. You can get word through to Walker and the others?'

No problem there. O'Keefe nodded.

'Then here's my plan.'

O'Keefe was shaken by the utter simplicity of it. 'It's so damned easy, it can't go wrong, sir.'

So Offer called his signaller, lumpy Art Weybright, and dictated a signal to a certain major-general in G.H.Q., Cairo. It was a request for a meeting. From a man on the run the request was audacious and impudent, but it wouldn't be the first time Offer had got what he needed from that big, elderly general.

When Weybright went off to his transmitter John Offer said, 'Bless Angela and her bedside prattle!' Now Sergeant Walker stood a chance of escaping from that terrible Glasshouse.

The atmosphere in the big bare office inside G.H.Q. Cairo was relaxed and even tranquil. Overhead the punkah fans rotated steadily with a pleasing soft whirr of electric motors. At one desk sat the big major-general; at another, discreetly distant, was his aide, Captain Roger Tansley.

A hatless corporal came in bearing a signal for the general. The big man was humming when he started to read it. When he had finished he uttered a remarkable invitation.

'Well, bugger me!'

Tansley looked up, interested. The major-general had abruptly taken on that purple hue associated in medical minds with apoplexy.

'You appear, sir, somewhat upset,' Tansley, the young smoothie, said.

'Upset? Ye gods, the cheek of that rascal, Offer!'

Tansley rose and crossed to his superior's desk. 'And what has your protégé, the resourceful Captain Offer, done to annoy you this time?' He appeared to enjoy the general's choler.

'He's not my protégé,' snapped the major-general. 'Neither is he a bloody captain, and you know it.' He mouthed almost silently to himself, 'Damned Glasshouse con! The nerve of the young bastard!'

Without invitation Captain Tansley took up the offending signal and read: 'Request meeting urgently. Can assist considerably re Operation Threedom. Require your pledge of temporary immunity.' It was signed Captain John Offer, Glasshouse Gang.

'Well, it is a bit cool,' admitted Tansley. 'But then Offer's a cool customer.' He did not disguise his admiration for John Offer and that annoyed his major-general.

'What the devil are you looking so satisfied about? Anyone would think you approve of this damned rogue of

15

a Glasshouse-wallah.'

'Well, we do, don't we?' Roger Tansley looked amusedly at his C.O.

The general avoided a direct answer. He had picked up the signal again and was re-reading it, deliberately to stoke up his annoyance. 'The hell with him, a man on the run saying he'd like to have a chat with me! Who does he think he is? Give me a safe passport and I'll come and tell you how to run the war. Damn it, we can't do that!' he exploded.

'Why not?' A very calm man, young Tansley. 'You've done it before –'

'Can't keep on doing it.'

'It proved profitable for the war effort –'

'Agheila, yes. Not the last time. Didn't spring our generals from captivity.'

'But they must have shaken the enemy in Benghazi. A bold man, Offer.'

Grudgingly the major-general agreed with the last sentiment. He brow furrowed. 'Roger.'

'Yes, sir.'

'What does a deserter know about Operation Threedom?'

'Well, it's off, sir.'

'But does he know that?' The big, heavy general gnawed at his moustache, then shot a glance through spiky eyebrows at his aide. 'I'd like to know how much the young sod knows about that particular do. The only thing –' he hesitated '– the Big Boys wouldn't like it, me having further truck with the rascal.' The Big Boys were down the corridor, his fellow generals within the War House.

So that's why the signal's so upsetting, thought Tansley shrewdly. There was impudence behind the message, of course, but irritating to the major-general was the knowledge that his superiors at G.H.Q. were scandalized by his meetings with the army deserter, and he'd landed himself into quite a lot of trouble as a consequence.

Tansley thought, still amused, 'All the same, the old boy's going to invite Offer here.' He knew his superior officer too well. The major-general would do a lot of bellowing, but in the end he'd defy opinion at the War Office and get Offer to call on him. Whatever the m-g said, he had a soft spot for Offer and did tend to regard him as his protégé.

And so it was. After sufficient time for the major-general's bile to settle a signal went off over the air: 'Immunity granted. Some day your nerve will land you into trouble. Request inconspicuous arrival.'

When he'd dictated the message the major-general said, 'Now, I wonder in what oasis he's lurking now? How long before the blighter gets here?'

The 'oasis' was less than two miles from Cairo's G.H.Q.

When John Offer received the signal from the major-general he smiled with satisfaction. 'I thought Operation Threedom would hook the fish.'

Signaller Weybright had brought the message, and Squadron Sergeant-major O'Keefe happened to be with Offer at the time. O'Keefe's eyes shone. It looked as if the resourceful Captain Offer was going to land them in another hectic adventure, and he was glad: the villa was too quiet for him.

This time O'Keefe didn't ask, 'Are you going?' That promise of temporary immunity would take Offer to the War House in no time. Once, all would have sworn it was a trap, but by now they had acquired a confidence in that growling, ferocious-looking major-general and accepted that if he gave his word it would be kept.

John Offer said, 'It's almost tiffin time. We'll lunch, then I'll drop in on the old boy.' Not before three, though, in case the old boy was taking his time over lunch in the W.O. mess. Offer was very casual about it, as if unperturbed by the thought that he, the most wanted deserter in the Middle East, was about to shove his head right into the lions' den.

Weybright, who joined in on any planning conversations, now referred to one sentence in the signal: 'What's he mean, sir – "Request inconspicuous arrival".'

Offer shrugged. 'I've to go incognito.'

'The Big Boy doesn't want anyone else at the War House to know you're visiting him?' O'Keefe was a shrewd man.

'Looks like it.' To an ex-actor disguise was easy. He'd use the old Elastoplast-over-the-bumpy-nose trick to change his face, and would elevate himself to the rank of colonel, just for the hell of it and to make young Tansley keep his place. A colonel of what? Offer decided to join the Royal Corps of Signals, Pomegranate Face, his batman-driver, he knew, having the appropriate badges in his untidy kitbag.

So they lunched in luxury on a balcony which caught the breeze off the Nile, John Offer sitting with his men at a long white-clothed table, for he believed in civilized behaviour when he had the opportunity to practise it. His men showed a hearty preference for Canadian canned beer, but Offer, Weybright and Palfreyman sipped of a good white table wine brought down from the sunny slopes north of Haifa.

Later, Lashley, the Australian, drove him right up to the doors of the big brown house that was Cairo's G.H.Q., set him down, then brazenly parked in the official car park for senior officers across the road. Colonel John Offer sauntered into the cool, shady building. No one looked twice at him. Colonels were ten a penny here, and the plaster across his bent nose guaranteed him against recognition.

He sent his name up to Roger Tansley. The name wasn't his own but was sufficient to have young Tansley coming down the broad staircase in a hurry. The name he gave was Colonel Tansley, R.C.S.

John Offer greeted him with – 'Hello, son. How's tricks?'

'Son be buggered,' said Tansley wrathfully. 'And you stop using my name, see?' But he wasn't as wrathful as he made out, and led the way to the general's office.

The major-general said, shoving himself back in a chair which creaked under his bulk, 'You'd better have something good for me or you'll never get out of this place alive, Offer.'

John Offer was not moved to fear by the threat. The old

boy had given his word. And he had something good for the m-g, too.

'There's been a big disappointment in your life recently.'

'Are you reading my palm? Come on, get on with it.' That was to show this damned upstart that he was a great major-general whose time wasn't to be wasted.

'You had planned a very important raid on a place near Bir Hakim called Fort Telatha.' Telatha, three in Arabic. 'You gave it the code name of Operation Threedom.'

'That one's off.' The major-general spoke impatiently.

'I know it's off,' the bogus colonel told him calmly. 'The S.A.S. patrol which was to mount the raid ran into trouble. They got in a minefield south of Sollum. Two of their five trucks went up, killing three men. One was the lieutenant in charge of the patrol. They had to call off the operation and return to base. The wounded were flown down the desert to Cairo Main Hospital.'

'You seem to know a lot about the do. Where d'you get this gen?' The old boy was very interested. How the devil did a man on the run get to know so much? Offer did not answer the question, so the major-general decided to try him further.

Sarcastically, 'Of course you know the object of the mission?'

'Of course.' The calm, very sure answer made the major-general blink. 'You wanted to kidnap young Mussolini.'

The general said, 'I've given up being surprised by you, Offer. Now, reduce my tension by telling me everything. Roger.' Captain Tansley was hovering in the background. 'Rustle up some char for all of us. I'm sure Glasshouse John's going to do a lot of talking.'

While Tansley was out of the room ordering tea, John Offer piled surprise upon surprise. Settimo Mussolini – the Italian Fascist dictator's seventh child – had got himself into trouble in Rome. Young Sett – that was the way John Offer referred to him – had been given a commission in the Italian army, with the rank of captain. He could hardly be described

19

as an exemplary officer, and in fact it became a scandal that their War Leader's son hardly ever bothered with the army except to draw his pay. Instead he lived the soft life around Rome with a dashing set of young people who had parties reported as little better than orgies, until finally even his father had had enough of him.

'So Mussolini ordered his son to join his regiment, now in North Africa, and told his C.O. to post the lad away from the temptations of any big city. Young Sett's now sweating it out in Fort Telatha, no doubt wishing he'd been a bit more discreet back in Rome.'

Tansley returned, followed by an Egyptian bearer with cups of strong tea. 'Milk? Sugar?' The usual hostly questions, the major-general very courteous.

'Milk.' John Offer patted a waistline thickening already in that short time at the villa up-river. 'No sugar. Thanks.'

'And why do we want young Mussolini? He isn't exactly a prime military objective.' The major-general was probing, testing the extent of Offer's knowledge.

'No, but he's Mussolini's son, and by all accounts his father dotes on him. That's the fate of all last sons, to be doted over. For instance, Mussolini wouldn't want him to be hurt.'

'No?'

'Or suffer like, say, our P.O.W.s suffer in Italian prison camps. And that's young Settimo's value to our side – he can be used as a piece of barter. Mussolini could be told, "Give our men in your prisons more humane treatment or your precious son will have a rough time in ours".'

'That's all? Merely a piece of barter? And we were going to risk lives just for one particularly useless Italian?'

'You've already lost a few lives.'

'True.' The general suddenly shot another question at him. 'You know so much, tell me, do you think Mussolini would be influenced by Settimo's capture?'

Offer shrugged. 'I don't know. But it's worth a try, isn't it? Isn't that what you think?'

The general didn't tell him what he thought. Instead, 'What are you getting at, Offer? Telling me you'll hop over to Telatha and oblige by bringing back youn Mussolini? Big-hearted suddenly, aren't you?'

'Big-hearted,' admitted Offer, unabashed. 'Look, you haven't time to mount another expedition.' Not if the big battle at Alamein broke out before the end of the month, as everyone was pretty sure it would. 'And here we are, just the job for you, right on the spot and ready to shove off up the Blue within two or three days. Worth a thought, isn't it?'

The major-general stopped pretending that young Mussolini and Fort Telatha were pieces of Offer's imagination. 'All right, I'll admit you're right about Operation Threedom. And if you can go and fish out Mussolini for us we'll have some feeling of gratitude towards you and your men.'

'Sufficient for a King's Pardon for our crimes?' John Offer smiled whimsically, knowing the answer.

'You'll never get that. The army isn't a forgiving institution. But —' he held out a scrap of bait '— it wouldn't go against you when you have that inevitable court-martial.' That was all he would offer.

'Well, we might as well do something for King and Country as sit on our backsides here on the Nile.'

'You'll take it on?' The major-general was suddenly pleased with the day's work. Operation Threedom had seemed a fair idea for his department. Now it could be on again.

'Provided we have the usual conditions.'

'Which are?'

'An authority from you guaranteeing us immunity from arrest for the next four weeks.'

Watching John Offer the major-general thought, 'Something odd about the way he said that.'

'Why four weeks?'

'Two or three days beforehand to get kitted out.' Loads of petrol, water, food and equipment to be picked up. They'd also need a few more Jeeps, the last foray knocking up some of their vehicles beyond their powers of repair. 'Two weeks or so up the Blue on the job, then a bender in Cairo as our reward. You'll have to lift us all out from Telatha by plane, of course.'

Silence. The major-general sat hunched in his over-burdened chair, suspicion in his old eyes, chewing the end of his moustache. And Offer sat stiffly erect, hanging on to the decision, and again his manner seemed wrong to the general. Finally the m-g made his decision.

'Roger. Get it typed out. You know what to say.' Captain Tansley slipped out to find a bod with a spare typewriter and willingness to do a bit of active service for him.

While he was away the major-general said, 'You're a remarkable fellow, Offer. Pity we meet under these circumstances.'

'But for the circumstances, would we ever have met?' Offer spoke lightly, relaxed from the moment the general sent Tansley off for that letter of immunity.

'What beats me,' growled the old boy, 'is how you get so well clued up. You know too much – our Security must be lax if a man on the run can learn what you seem to know. Now, do tell me, where do you get your information?'

'It comes to me in bed,' said Offer without smiling, and the major-general had to be satisfied with that answer. Tansley came back with his bit of army bumph, which the general signed and handed to Offer. Again the shrewd major-general was sure Offer was disproportionately relieved.

John Offer rose to go, but he had another request to make. 'I'm getting tired of having your bloodhounds tail me when I leave your office. Let's have a gentleman's agreement, shall we? If I visit you, you don't try to have me followed when I depart.' Offer shrugged. 'They only land in trouble, anyway.'

'By God, they do,' thought the major-general, but aloud he said, 'You've got a gall, Offer. All right, then, you won't be followed. My word on it.'

Offer was satisfied. He left then. After he'd gone the major-general seemed almost to chuckle, back in a good mood. 'I like that rascal, you know, Roger.'

'I think we all know,' Tansley said, 'and you lose popularity in some quarters for it, sir.'

'The hell with popularity.' There were times when the m-g could be highly contemptuous of the opinions of his fellow generals. Yet he frowned. 'Roger, I'm a bit uneasy about Offer, all the same. That fellow's up to something.' He'd seemed to set great store by that letter of immunity. A week or so's bender in Cairo after risking his life up the desert? Something very odd about Offer, volunteering for such a mission. 'And what did he mean by things coming to him in bed?'

That Thursday was like any other day at Sharafim. Occasionally the gates opened to allow time-served prisoners under escort to be driven out to their units; about as frequently trucks came to decant unhappy men under escort to begin their sentences.

The truck which rolled up to the grim gates about three o'clock that hot afternoon, October though it was, appeared no different from the others. In fact it had been knocked off only a couple of hours before, and had been escorted by seven Jeeps to a point almost within sight of the prison. There, in a dip in the dusty track which led from the Sweet Water Canal road to the Glasshouse, the Jeeps halted and the truck rolled on, alone.

At the gates a sentry halted them, then shouted for the duty sergeant who came popping his bullet head through the wicket. By this time no less than six handcuffed prisoners, fully equipped even to filled packs and awkward kitbags, had alighted over the dropped tailboard of the truck. A driver, small and with tiny teeth, remained at the wheel, but two sergeants got down with the prisoners.

The screw, a bright new bastard who'd learned his stuff

at Armley Jail near Leeds, did his top when he saw six prisoners with only two sergeants in charge. Bloody irregular, he mouthed. Didn't their O.C. know the fuckin' rules?

The full-sergeant in charge of the prisoners said he fuckin' did, but the rest of the escort had got the fuckin' squirts back along the Alex road and had to be dropped and they'd come on alone. He seemed a nasty-tempered full-sergeant, not giving an inch to the screw, who did not like being talked to like that and said so, and the two snarled at each other for a few seconds like bad-tempered alley cats.

It ended, as it always did, with one of the big gates being partly opened to allow the squad of prisoners to enter the jail. The screw bellowed and got them in step, giving them their first dose of prison punishment, marking time and having them lift their knees to a painful altitude. Then he shouted, 'For – ward! At the double, you –' He made the inevitable slander on their ancestry. 'S'arnt-major, six more for you!' A bellow to a distant strutting, important figure, Sergeant-major Jack Fry. The eyes of the lance-sergeant with the party, a shortish man with a flattened nose, seemed to glow with particular hatred when they alighted on the distant sergeant-major.

The six swaddies went doubling off at frantic pace to where squads of prisoners drilled at the double while others made the dreaded Walking Wall crawl around the perimeter of the parade ground. At the gate the screw said, 'Sign 'em in and get your receipt.' His head jerked towards the guardroom to one side of the gate.

The full-sergeant followed him. He seemed somehow reluctant, though, hesitating as he stepped inside the prison compound. The armed sentry stood in the open gateway, while another guard prepared to close the big door.

. . . something was happening on the parade ground, no one at first quite knew what. Sight of those six double-marching figures seemed to have an effect on the squads of prisoners drilling there. They kept on drilling, but now it

24

was without response to the bellowed commands of their screws. Astonished, the staff-sergeants took seconds before they realized that their squads had stopped obeying them.

The squads now went racing up and down across the square in any old direction, at first in formation, then beginning to break up into individuals. Even then no one stopped running. Men ran from one corner of the parade ground to the other, criss-crossing each other's paths, hundreds of men suddenly all in motion, kicking up a dust, a moving pattern of illogical human behaviour. Bellowing screws found themselves isolated with men stamping at the double in every direction around them.

On the Walking Wall the prisoners dropped to the parade ground, to the astonishment of their screws, and added their presence to the drill squads. Confusion reigned.

And through it all the six newly arrived prisoners ran in perfect step and formation across the crowded parade ground, the other running prisoners parting to give way to them. As they ran the new men dropped their kitbags and the mouths were open and from them spilled packets of fags, boxes of matches and satisfying blocks of chocolate, the contribution of a Naafi robbed the night before. Now the doubling prisoners swerved towards the bags, swooped without stopping and grabbed what they wanted, cigarettes or chocolate, so that a minute later that demented medley of running figures ran with cigarettes smoking from their lips, or chewed ecstatically upon Cadbury's fruit-and-nut bars.

At the gate it was quite a time – a good half-minute – before anyone noticed that anything untoward was happening on the parade ground. Bellowing commands weren't new to Sharafim guards, and men doubling weren't a rare sight, either.

It was the chap deputed to close the gate who first spotted something out of the ordinary. He looked back, frowning. He had never seen men racing independently like this before. Like scalded cocks was his unoriginal thought.

'Hey, Staff,' he called to the screw, bad-temperedly

making out a receipt for this lean, red-faced sergeant who talked back to him. 'Staff, something's bloody up. I mean, they gone mad or somethin'?'

Staff turned, and what he saw brought his jaw dropping in astonishment. Only one small squad moving as a body on the whole of the parade ground, everyone else beetling about on their jack, their screws lost to sight by the running mob.

That solitary squad, keeping perfect time, was running straight for the gate now, but there were seven in it, suddenly. The lance-sergeant was doing something with a long slim canister. Outside the gate, the driver of the truck was busy turning his lumbering vehicle.

The screw at the gate shouted in sheer amazement, 'Well, stuff me!' but got no further than that because the lean, red-faced full-sergeant clouted him hard across the face and dropped him, stunned, to the ground.

A dense black smoke was issuing from the canister. The lance-sergeant tossed it into the guardroom. All at once no one could see the gate because of a smoke screen. The lance-sergeant grabbed the lad holding the open door and hurled him into the smoke. The lance-jack was coughing too, unable to see anything now, but holding open that big prison door.

Seven smartly doubling prisoners went running past him through the dense smoke. The lance-sergeant called, 'Okay, sergeant-major,' and the red-faced sergeant came running out into the open where the truck was waiting for them. Everyone clambered aboard. A thump to say they were okay, and the truck ground into speed. And everyone shook Eddie Walker's hand and said, 'Welcome back, you old so-and-so.'

Looking behind they couldn't see much of the prison for smoke, and the guard on the wall wouldn't be able to see them in turn, Lance-sergeant John Offer pointed out to Full-sergeant Angus O'Keefe, a very satisfied tone in his voice. Inside the prison compound the men were cheering,

26

cheering them for the presents they had brought and wishing them well on their way.

Three minutes later they abandoned the truck, took their places in the waiting Jeeps, then in convoy headed for the Sweet Water Canal road and the highway which led towards Alexandria.

Before they hit the main Cairo–Alex road, however, they began to see signs of military agitation. Truck after truck shot past them, loaded with grim-faced Red Caps. John Offer wondered if the prisoners in Sharafim had taken this opportunity to go on the rampage once again. It looked a bit like it. Behind him his men in the following Jeeps began to cheer as each Military Police vehicle tore by.

Then in the vast tented area that housed an army of men along the Sweet Water Canal, carefully sited beyond the flying range of the female, malaria-carrying mosquito, they ran into a road block. M.P.s were stopping all traffic heading away from Sharafim. The barricade looked to have been recently installed; only a few trucks were ahead of Offer's Jeeps, so the Gang was up to the check point in no time.

A Red Cap came perfunctorily saluting the captain in the laden Jeep, good-humouredly taking his turn at the post. 'Identity papers,' he rapped, nothing subservient about this busy cop.

Captain Offer silently handed him the War Office letter signed by the major-general. The Red Cap looked at it, glanced swiftly at the bearer as if wondering what the hell was special about him to warrant such an authority, then handed it back. 'Okay,' he said. 'Drive on.'

They were through. Jubilant, the Jeeps went scooting off along the Alex road. O'Keefe in his vehicle, second behind Offer's, said admiringly, 'You've got to hand it to the Old Man. If he says a thing will work, it'll work. But where does he get these ideas!'

He was talking to Sergeant Walker, seated beside him. At the halt at the post O'Keefe had asked him how he had been treated in the Glasshouse this time. Eddie Walker was

27

short about it, not wanting to remember those weeks. But they'd had a special go at him, O'Keefe gathered, and he guessed what that meant.

'Well, you're back with the lads. Now you're going to convalesce for a couple of weeks.' O'Keefe was serious. Two hard weeks' travel over the hot desert, with an enemy-held fort to storm at the end of it, was routine stuff to the sergeant-major.

On the Alex highway there was another road block. The authorities, it was most apparent, were determined to capture the men responsible for this second outrage on H.M. Prison at Sharafim. 'They'll guess who's done it,' Offer smiled to himself. Who else but the Glasshouse Gang? By now their descriptions would be out, especially his. He thought of again muting the shape of his profile with a strip of Elastoplast, but decided against it. It wouldn't help much, and anyway he had confidence in that letter of immunity.

At the second barricade he saw the care here with which they inspected troops and their identities. At first they'd have been looking for a 3-ton truck and a load of men; now they'd have guessed there'd been a switch to other vehicles so that everything mobile came in for their sharpest scrutiny.

When the M.P.s saw the seven Jeeps and their loads of tough humanity someone got suspicious right away. Offer saw an M.P. halt, regarding them for a second, then he called something over his shoulder. Immediately all the other M.P.s detached themselves from their inspections and began to close on Offer's Jeep. A lieutenant Red Cap came pushing through and halted beside Captain Offer. He didn't speak, hard eyes probing, memorizing the details of that brown face in the passenger seat. His hand was out, fingers impatiently gesturing for identity documents. Offer handed over his precious War Office authority.

The lieutenant read it carefully, but made no move to hand it back. 'I think you'd better get out, sir, and wait here while I do some phoning.'

'You think so, do you?' John Offer climbed out of the Jeep and stood resolutely before the taller, younger officer. 'I don't. You've read that note and you know what it means. We're on such special duty that we cannot afford to have our time wasted. That's why we were given that authority. Now, give me that back and we'll be on our way.'

His tone was hard and incisive. He reached out and took the immunity document from the lieutenant's hand. The subaltern said, roughly, 'A few minutes won't hurt you –'

'You're putting us under arrest?' – very sharp.

'No, but –'

'Of course you are! What else is it but arrest?' Offer tapped the letter of immunity. 'This says no one's to arrest us. Hold me up and you'll have to answer to a major-general who won't like his orders questioned.'

That got the M.P. wavering. John Offer did not turn and remount his Jeep. Turning would have been weakness, fostering suspicion. He just stood there, insisting on the lieutenant capitulating, which abruptly he did.

'All right.' The Red Cap gestured and stood aside. His hard-eyed suspicious men reluctantly pulled away from around the leading Jeep. Without hurry Captain Offer climbed back in his car and the column slowly pulled away from the check point.

His face sombre with anger the lieutenant caught the eyes of tough men who sat in the following Jeeps. Every face was expressionless, yet in some way they conveyed a feeling that he was being jeered at. He turned. 'I'm going to phone. That's Offer, all right.' The description fitted. 'And he's No. 1 suspect tonight.' But while he held a major-general's passport ... 'There's time to put up another road block if we can get over that damned m-g's letter.'

When the news was phoned to the major-general he did his nut properly, thumping his desk and roaring, 'I knew that young sod was up to something! That's why he was so anxious to get hold of an immunity from arrest. God help him if he ever falls into my hands again!'

He gave an order to ignore his warrant of immunity, and tersely told the Military Police they were on to a roasting if they let the Glasshouse Gang through their clutches again.

A snarling voice assured him they'd be picked up at a new road block twenty miles along the Alex highway.

Five miles along the road to the delta John Offer said, as if the thought was highly amusing, 'You know, they'll try to hold us again somewhere towards Alex. That wouldn't be nice. I think we'll turn off now.' The open desert was a piece of cake to his hardened roamers.

They struck off and headed towards the terrible Qattara Depression, south of the village of El Alamein. It was an area as big as Ireland, several hundred feet below sea level, a treacherous salt marsh surrounded by seemingly un-climbable cliffs. According to the cartographers it was an impassable barrier, but the L.R.D.G. had found a way across it, and now John Offer proposed to follow that secret trail.

At their first halt, Sergeant Walker came up to his com-manding officer and in his way expressed thanks for his release from jail. 'We all knew you'd come,' he said. 'Even the screws.' He shook his head. How easy it had all been, the rescue.

Walker could speak with the familiarity of an old com-rade, one who had once shared a cell in Sharafim with Offer. 'It was a cracker, getting that warrant of immunity.' All the boys were still chuckling at the impudence of it. 'But why are we still going on?'

'To Fort Telatha?' Walker nodded. John Offer looked surprised. 'But that's part of the bargain. I couldn't pull out now, not without earning that passport.' He shook his head. That wouldn't be cricket. Besides it would be letting the major-general down, and he had quite a liking for the ferocious-sounding old boy.

So they went on to Fort Telatha where John Offer saw

how simple it was to capture the place if only he could get one Jeep inside before the garrison took alarm. Now they held Fort Telatha, and with it that unlovely piece of human barter, Mussolini's seventh sibling.

The fort taken, immediately there was a scene of intense activity. O'Keefe and a few men went foraying round the buildings and turfed out a surprising number of Italians. When the final count was made they held fifty-eight dejected prisoners. Additionally they had seven dead on their hands and fourteen wounded.

It always surprised Offer how few casualties there were in any battle considering the amount of bullets and high explosive hurled about. His own party had suffered just one casualty. A ricocheting bullet had burnt a furrow across the fleshy seat of one of his men. Because it was the little loud-mouthed Pom, the Gang thought it very funny and he got the great ha-ha from them, so he sulked and wouldn't do any work.

Captain Offer's first act was to get Signaller Weybright to transmit a message announcing their success to G.H.Q. Cairo. That should please the old boy, he thought, and they'd have a transport plane out to them without delay. One Dakota would be quite big enough to lift prisoner and Gang back to the Nile Valley. It would have to be done quickly, though, because when Fort Telatha failed to come on the air the enemy would become suspicious and send planes over the desert to investigate.

Offer ordered a couple of look-outs on watch. The prisoners were shepherded into the shade where a roof projected from the battered admin block, two Jeeps facing them, Brownings pointing and menacing. He went to look at the wounded, to see if he could do anything to make them more comfortable, and saw that the Gang's medical orderly, Arab Ward, was helping the Italian M.O. and his medical staff.

He came out into the sunshine in time to see the lean

figure of his sergeant-major loping across the dusty parade ground. O'Keefe was again sweating copiously, as if he had been doing something energetic, but his face was one big grin and he seemed jubilant. 'Sir, see what I've found!'

There was a concrete stairway by the big sunken water cistern. Descending, they found themselves in a low, concrete-ceilinged vault of such remarkable extent that Offer thought it must run the length and breadth of the sandy square overhead. Neatly racked in bays were cases of ammunition in staggering quantity, spares for vehicles especially for tanks, equipment of all sorts and any amount of food. At one end were lozenge-shaped storage tanks – two of them full of petrol.

'A supply dump,' was Offer's immediate thought. When the big battle started these supplies would be required for Rommel's motorized columns operating on the right flank of his army.

Gleefully O'Keefe said, 'When we get lifted out, sir, we'll blow the bloody place up! What a bang!' His mind delighted at the thought of such destruction.

John Offer nodded. They certainly weren't going to leave all this equipment and supplies to help the enemy. 'That'll be your job,' he promised his sergeant-major, and they climbed from the coolness of the underground stronghold back into the strength-sapping sunshine of a Libyan midday.

The Italian cooks under close supervision now made food and drink for Gang and prisoners alike. Offer was a humane man and did everything to make his prisoners comfortable. He even gave reassuring words to the Italian fort commander. 'When we fly out I'll turn you loose.' He'd give them food and water and set them marching towards the coast. It was only fifty miles away, and though they'd hate the slog the fit men would make it in time.

'What about the wounded?' asked the major. Offer said they could use two of the Italian trucks.

Not much more than an hour after they had taken the fort, a shufti kite came buzzing over. Offer manned all four

Bredas in order to make a show of strength. He wondered what to do about the Italian P.O.W.s. There were so many of them, and with eight men now up on the Bredas it didn't leave enough of the Gang to maintain an efficient guard.

Then he thought of the underground storeroom. There had been one large empty room which looked like an air raid shelter. 'Sergeant-major, there's a funk hole down below. Get these prisoners under lock and key there.' He felt quite a relief when he saw the prisoners being rounded up and taken below.

The shufti kite, an obsolete Fiat CR-42 biplane, was drifting round the fortress but out of range of their Bredas. Plainly the pilot wasn't taken in by the Italian flag which drooped above the west tower.

Weybright said, watching that tiny plane, 'He'll be calling up the fort on his wireless and getting no answer.'

Well, it wouldn't be hard for anyone to deduce that the fort had fallen into enemy hands if no one responded to wireless signals. How long before the pilot whistled up bombers?

In time the shufti kite sheered off. Half an hour later planes came whistling up, but they weren't bombers. Instead they had sent fighters, two Macchi C-200s, Italy's best. Offer was disturbed, seeing them. Any moment now an unarmed Dakota might show up over the skyline and it wouldn't have a snowball's chance against such swift adversaries.

The two pilots made a distant circling reconnaissance, then started to climb. 'This is it,' grinned Sergeant-major O'Keefe, and seemed pleased to think they were going to see action. They saw the Macchis begin to turn, hover, and then the dive began. The roar of aircraft engines began to louden.

When they were within range the Bredas swung into action, tracer leaping up to greet the Macchis flying one behind the other. The pilots seemed to ignore the danger and just flew through the curtain of bullets unharmed. The

Macchis came flashing over the walls of the fortress, their noise sending men crouching instinctively, twin machine-guns raking gouts of sand across the deserted parade ground and chipping splinters out of the masonry of the buildings. Two swift shadows flitted overhead, then the pilots were pulling away madly, climbing into the sun, a diminuendo of sound, only to circle again when they had attained a great height and begin another power-dive.

Four Bredas again met them with a converging fire. Perhaps this time it was disconcertingly close, perhaps the aircraft were even holed in places, for both aircraft pulled away before quite reaching the fortress and skipped out of range very hurriedly. And now there was a change of tactics, as if they recognized that fighters weren't the thing for dislodging their enemy. This time, thought John Offer, they will be bringing up the bombers.

He watched the two fighters circling menacingly above them, and thought, 'I don't like that.' His glasses combed the distant desert for sight of enemy troop movements, though it was a bit early to expect them if they were to come all the way from the coast road. 'While they're there the Dakota can't come in.'

His binoculars paused and he stiffened. 'Dear God!' Weybright heard him say. He dropped his glasses. 'The bloody Dakota's heading straight for us!'

He could see it, flitting low above the desert. A Dakota? But hadn't this one twin fins and rudders?

Weybright cheered ecstatically. 'Caught the buggers!' he yelled, pointing. Five escorting Hurricanes had dropped out of the sun just as the Macchis spotted the low-flying plane and turned for an attack on it. Suddenly the Macchi pilots realized they were outnumbered, out-gunned and with no better speed than their assailants. Five R.A.F. pilots took them on, harrying them as they flung their aircraft into evasive action while trying to climb. For a few minutes everyone watched the dog-fight over the desert, but it was too one-sided to last. A Macchi streamed out smoke and

34

began a long shallow dive which ended near the horizon in an explosion quite clearly heard miles back at Fort Telatha. The second Macchi kept going with five aircraft on its tail and Offer and his followers didn't rate his chances of making the coast in safety.

But now that low-flying aircraft was coming in, and it wasn't the expected Dakota but a Lockheed Lodestar. Offer was aghast when he saw it. A little plane like that couldn't lift them all out. What was G.H.Q. doing?

There was a dirt landing strip which ran quite close to the fort, and the Lodestar came settling down between the parallel rows of upturned oil drums, then ran almost up to the main gate before closing the throttle.

Offer said, 'I'm going out. Take over, sergeant-major.' He got into a Jeep and drove across to where the Lodestar stood, propellers idling. He was a very disturbed man. An officer was dropping down from the tiny cabin. Offer thought, 'Now, he looks familiar!'

It was Captain Roger Tansley. He greeted Offer with his usual smooth smile. 'Congratulations, old chap. I don't know how you do these things, but you seem to pull them off. Everyone's so pleased back in Cairo.'

But John Offer wasn't going to be soft-soaped by young Tansley. His brooding gaze was on that tiny Lodestar. 'What's the idea? We can't all get in that damn' thing.' The aircraft wouldn't take more than three or four passengers in addition to Tansley and young Mussolini.

'That,' agreed Tansley, beaming, 'is the idea.'

'We're not going to be lifted out?'

A shake of the head, amusement on Tansley's face. 'Musso, yes. But I've a message for you, from the m-g.'

'And that is?'

'Try using your immunity letter to get out of this.'

Offer said, 'The bastard!'

Tansley reproved him. 'That's a court-martial offence if I report it.'

John Offer was lurid about what he could do with his

report. But he was bewildered and aghast. No nice, easy airlift into Cairo. Instead he was being told to slog it back the way he had come, over the desert. The trouble was, this time the enemy was alert to their presence, the desert would be lousy with hostile patrols, and the skies black with Stukas.

Tansley continued to look amused, but then he wasn't going to risk his neck in the desert. 'The m-g thinks you'll come in useful, just at the right time.'

John Offer, still smouldering, said, 'Come again?'

'The Big Bang starts any time now, as you must well know.' The break-out from Alamein. 'The enemy can't afford to have any British force operating behind their lines while that's on. So they'll have to divert precious troops to round you up, and the m-g says in that way you'll be making some atonement for all the trouble you've caused us. He also thinks you're unlikely to come out alive, but –' Tansley shrugged. '*C'est la guerre*, you know.'

Offer thought, 'So we're expendable again.' Put into this position for their nuisance value, in their tiny way helping the Eighth Army in their drive against Rommel. Christ, what a trick to play on a man! Offer regretted now being so honourable in keeping to his part of the bargain. Next time he'd double-cross the fat old bastard! Next time? Was there ever going to be a next time?

Tansley's voice, just a little impatient. 'I've no time to lose, old chap. Hand over the prisoner and let me push off.'

He got into the Jeep and Offer grudgingly ordered Lashley back to the fort. Inside, Offer found his men silently staring down from the ramparts. They'd guessed they'd been double-crossed and weren't going out by aircraft. Offer said, 'You and you, escort Captain Mussolini to the plane.'

A scared seventh sibling was packed on to the Jeep. Tansley said to Offer, 'Well, it's been nice meeting you.' He shook his head, though, as if to say this would be the last time they'd set eyes on each other. Then he drove off.

Sergeant-major O'Keefe came up to his commanding-officer. 'What's the score, sir?'

'You know bloody well,' snapped Offer, and stalked away, furious. His sergeant-major went back and told the men there'd been a change of plans, no airlift for them this day, so they squatted in the shade and watched their commanding-officer pacing a solitary beat out on the sun-drenched parade ground.

John Offer's thoughts weren't pleasant. They were in a hell of a mess, and this time he couldn't think how to get out of it. Such a sweet idea, knocking off the fort, picking up young Musso, then flying off to Cairo before the enemy knew they'd paid them a call. But the plan had gone sour, the old fox in Cairo getting his own back over that Sharafim do. Grudgingly Offer had to admit he *had* pulled a fast one over the old boy, but stranding them up the desert!

He felt wretched. He'd let his men down. His job wasn't to put them in impossible places but to think for them, and keep them from dying nastily, and this time he'd really dropped the poor bastards in the pan. If any of his men were killed or hurt now he would be responsible for it; and responsibility weighed heavily upon John Offer where his Gang was concerned.

Under the shade, his men sensed what was going through their C.O.'s mind, especially O'Keefe and Walker. Walker said, 'He's giving himself hell.' And all over me, he added to his thoughts.

O'Keefe, who thought the world of his superior, said, 'Let's get him a drop of char. We can't have him like this.' Sure, they were in a jam, but while Offer was in this mood they'd never get out of it. 'Calm the Old Man down and he'll think of something and have us out of here before you can say Burkha Street.' That was the brothel area in Cairo. O'Keefe's faith in his captain was endless and sublime. Even now he remained unworried. Just get Offer to cool off . . .

The sergeant-major himself brought the tea out to where

his C.O. paced, oblivious of the eyes watching him. 'This'll do you good, sir.'

'Nothing will do me good.' Offer allowed pessimism to run riot. 'Sergeant-major, I feel bad. I've dropped us all in the excreta.'

Comfortingly O'Keefe said, 'Of course. Really deep down in it, too, sir.' Cup in hand, John Offer was startled to hear such agreement. 'But there's not a man here blames you for it, not one of us but isn't damn' sure you'll dream up something to get us out of the shit.'

It did the trick, just as O'Keefe, crafty sod, knew it would. John Offer could hardly have failed to have been moved by that curious vote of confidence. He swallowed the hot sweet tea, almost instantly snapped out of his mood, and said, 'Right, let's start planning, sergeant-major.'

'It's no good scarpering now, sir.' O'Keefe was helpful.

'No.' They could hardly leave the protection of Fort Telatha while daylight was with them. It wasn't hard to guess that very soon there'd be hostile aircraft galore very interested in this area, and from now on there'd be no Hurricanes to give them cover. 'I can't see us making a run down the desert today and coming out of it alive.'

'Maybe tonight, when it's dark.' The usual hope of the hard-pressed desert-raider – hang on till darkness, then we'll give 'em the slip.

'We'll see.' That would depend on the strength of any ground force sent to relieve the fort. For certain they'd shuttle troops out, for Fort Telatha with its supplies must loom very importantly in Field-marshal Rommel's planning. Offer cheered up a bit, then. If the troops were thin on the ground they could find a way through the cordon after dark.

He looked towards the main gate, with its sagging door. 'Better get that door repaired so that it can be closed, sergeant-major. Dig out some Italian chippies to do the job – they're sure to have some.'

'Yes, sir.'

'And keep the men rested as much as possible. Man one Breda only, the men to keep close watch. Relieve them every hour. The rest, bring 'em down into the shade.'

The R.S.M. went off bellowing and men came sliding down the ladders for a cooler. John Offer thought what a pitifully small garrison they had to defend such a large fortress. Not much chance against a determined attack, yet if they were to live they must last the day out until nightfall. He would need to come up with some very bright ideas, he told himself, and that set him to browsing around the fortress, seeking inspiration and finding none for the moment. Finally, some fifteen minutes later, John Offer again came out on to the parade ground and walked over to where his off-duty men rested.

They had dragged a table out under the shade before the admin office and were quite happily playing pontoon, as if without a care in the world. Offer felt an affection for them, looking at them. It was partly inspired because he knew it was reciprocated.

A bottle of wine was on the table. That made Offer frown. Alcohol and his men could be an explosive combination. He spoke to Sergeant Walker about it. Walker was looking a more solid man than he'd been when sprung from Sharafim jail. 'Go easy with the grog, Eddie. We're going to have some action shortly.'

Walker was reassuring. 'Sarn't-major said they could have one bottle only.' Captain Offer nodded approvingly. 'He's locked up the rest because he doesn't trust the bastards.'

'Neither would I.' John Offer was looking at the card players. Jimmy Wilborn had his elbow resting on the thickest pile of notes his captain had ever seen in the possession of a swaddy. They were huge notes, at least twice the area of sterling, and colourfully printed. Italian banknotes.

'Where'd you get that money, Jimmy?' Offer's voice was sharply suspicious. His thought was that the former safe-cracker might have been through the prisoners' pockets and he didn't approve of that.

Jimmy closed one eye against the curling smoke from his inevitable Woodbine, studying his two cards. 'Musso gave it me.'

'All that?' John Offer was incredulous. 'Why?'

Wilborn hesitated but it was over his next move with the cards. 'Musso? He wanted an ignition key for a Jeep. He was going to scarper. Offered me all he had for one.'

'You gave him one?'

'Sure.' The tab was now too short to be comfortable, so Jimmy spat it out. Laconically, 'It was for the Jeep which ran out of petrol, remember?' Just as they got on to the parade ground, O'Keefe had given the driver a bollocking for neglecting to fill up at the last halt.

John Offer shook his head sadly. 'You're nothing but a horrible con man, James, my boy.'

'But it pays,' grinned Jimmy, then made up his mind. 'Twist,' he said to the dealer, and Offer thought, 'You're a twister, all right,' but Jimmy was a good boy, at any rate within the Gang.

They brought bombers as well as fighters this time. When they heard the droning engines and saw the dark specks lifting above the horizon, O'Keefe put every man up on the Bredas.

They were all Italian aircraft, Caproni medium bombers with an escort of Fiat G-50 fighters. For some time they did a lot of circling high above Fort Telatha, while one of the Fiats came in at lower altitude and, they guessed, inspected them through glasses. Perhaps they were counting the men on the defences, Offer thought. An idea began to stir in his mind.

The fighters came in, line astern quite suddenly, as if on some radio command from the spotting Fiat. Twin machine-guns spat at the Breda gunners on their towers, fighter after fighter hurling itself down on the fort then zooming away to circle and come in again. The Bredas fought back with venom, skilled gunners, even on unfamiliar weapons, intimidating with the accuracy of their fire, yet somehow never damaging those swiftly evasive Fiats. Dust flew and bullets spanged in line along the high walls above the cat-walks where riflemen contributed their fire to the Bredas'. Yet no one was hurt by those attacks, the defenders so few and too dispersed to be easily hit.

John Offer thought, 'It'll be the bombers' turn next.' And time a ground force showed up. He let his glasses roam over the desert towards the coast. Sure enough he saw a tiny cloud of dust on the far horizon. The ground forces were closing in; they'd be at the fort within half an hour he guessed. He sighed. They did seem right up the creek this time.

The bombers came in at a height of about eight thousand feet. The Bredas wouldn't do any damage to them at that range. Each made a run and conditions were perfect for precision bombing. Constant height, constant speed, steady course, Offer quoted to himself, then saw the bombs detach from the leading Caproni and began to whistle down. Couldn't miss.

But the first ones did, overshooting the mark by fifty yards. Beyond the high fortress wall two fifty-pound bombs blew holes in the desert, cracking the eardrums of the Telatha defenders with the explosive sound and hurling sand and stones up at them along the ramparts.

Another bomber. A direct hit in the corner by the cistern. Dust and fumes everywhere and one of the buildings sagging and looking as if about to collapse. A third bomber. Screaming bombs hurtling down, the world seeming to rock before their disruptive power. Everyone reeled before the blast and covered their eyes against the debris that flew everywhere. The fourth bomber coming over.

Captain Offer started to run. He found O'Keefe. 'Find out if any of the men have been hit.' He thought they'd been lucky, so far, no bomb directly hitting a wall. He could hear the Bredas still belting off – useless to fire at that range, but it helped keep up morale so he wouldn't stop them.

He kept on running towards the stairway and the air raid shelter. Pom appeared from somewhere and Offer grabbed him. 'I need you.' That idea had suddenly blossomed in his mind.

They had to crouch while the fifth and sixth bombers unloaded in quick succession. Both missed, bombs again ploughing up the desert north of the fort. So far the garrison had been lucky, but it couldn't last. The bombers were circling away before making another attack. The fighters were coming in again to strafe the gunners. That would please the boys, he thought, dropping down the concrete-lined stairway, Pom hard after him, creased backside forgotten. Fighters would come within range of their Bredas.

As Offer unlocked the prison door he heard the swift roar of a fighter diving overhead, then another, another, and another. Hardly any interval of sound, and the passage shook and dust rose and got up their nostrils. He'd have to hurry, Offer thought, and threw the door open.

The room was packed with prisoners. Startled faces turned towards him. Offer stood in the doorway, Pom covering the Italians from just behind his C.O. Offer spotted the fort commandant and beckoned to him. The major came reluctantly. Inside the air raid shelter the noise of the aerial attack was deafening. Offer had to shout.

'Your radio operator. I want him.'

'You're going to surrender?' The Italian officer bucked up at the thought and smiled.

'Maybe.' The major gestured and a small thin Italian came quickly over to join them. Writing in Italian, Offer was printing a message on a pad. 'Pom, get Weybright.' He wanted his wireless operator to supervise the despatch of this signal and see that no tricks were played. 'Take this fellow with you.'

He was about to hand the signal to the Italian operator but the major got his fingers there first. Grimly Captain

Offer watched as the major read the brief message. He saw the man's face blaze with indignation and anger. Offer had written: 'I hold 58 Italian prisoners. There are also some wounded. I am going to put the prisoners up on the walls and the wounded out on beds on the square. If you make any further attacks you will kill your own countrymen.'

The Italian was incensed. 'You can't do that!'

'I can and I am doing. Back into the room, major; I want to lock the door.'

'It's against the Geneva Convention. Prisoners of war cannot be put into any position of danger like this –'

John Offer told him, tersely, 'I didn't write the Geneva Convention.' Tell Mussolini about correct treatment of prisoners; weren't they in this jam because the Duce didn't seem to subscribe to the Geneva Convention, either? 'If this is the only way to survive, I'm damn' well taking it.'

He slammed the door, then raced after Pom and the small Italian. Above, the dust was settling, the walls ceasing to reverberate to the sound of over-taxed aero engines and gunfire. For the moment there was a lull in the attack. Offer spat out the dust, saw Weybright come down a scaling ladder on Pom's shrill call, and raced over to where O'Keefe was hauling on Breda ammo cases to be hoisted in a sling to the top of the towers.

'Forget that, sergeant-major,' he told him. A few Bredas weren't going to save their lives, but his plan might. 'Pull half your men down.' For all the good the others were doing up there he could bring the lot down; until the ground forces came within range, the machine-guns weren't very effective.

O'Keefe showed the gap in his teeth with a big, sweaty grin. 'What have you dreamed up now, sir?'

'I'm going to save our lives by being a bastard.' When the Italian H.Q. knew what he proposed to do he'd be a man as much wanted by their army as by the Afrika Korps after that Lake of Sand tragedy. 'Sergeant-major, get your men to bring up the prisoners.'

'All of them, sir?'

'Every damned one of them.' The more the merrier. 'Get them up on top of the walls. Get them to sit with their legs hanging over, right?'

'Right,' said O'Keefe, but he seemed a very startled man. 'We keep 'em covered?'

'You do. And after that you put beds out on the square, fit a shade over 'em, and bring out the wounded.'

'Sir, I agree with you, you're being a bastard.' But O'Keefe appeared happy with the thought. 'Still, it gives us a chance.'

He raced off, shouting. Men came sliding down the scaling ladders, picked up guns and ran rowards the staircase. In seconds, it seemed, apprehensive Italians were flooding up on to the sandy square. Their officers protested vigorously, but menaced by the Gang's tommies their men began to climb the ladders set against the walls. On top they were made to sit with their legs dangling over the edge, prime targets for the next hail of bullets.

There were only a few Italians in position, however, when the next bomber attack was mounted. The Capronis came droning high overhead. Offer watched their approach, follow-my-leader, his eyes on the bellies from which the bombs would tumble. Apparently no signal had yet come through to stop them. They were on course, steadying on the bombing run preparatory to unloading. Or, Offer had a sudden thought, had a signal come through and was it to bomb and not bother about their own countrymen, for wasn't this war?

Everyone crouched. The Italians on the wall, helpless men, were white-faced, staring up. Now was the moment when the bombs should begin their fall . . .

The leading bomber passed by overhead, nothing detaching from it. John Offer heard a great sigh of relief from those around him. The signal had got through in time; his plan *had* worked. The other bombers travelled harmlessly on, then peeled away and began their distant circling of the

44

fort again.

John Offer said, 'I think we'll have some char, sergeant-major.' Take it easy and relax while they could. He guessed there'd be a lot of agitated wireless messages flashing from Command H.Q. on the coast to aircraft and back again, nobody knowing quite how to handle the situation. 'Nothing's going to happen for some time,' he told himself, and proceeded to make everyone as comfortable as the situation permitted, even the Italian prisoners.

Now he ordered one in three of the Italians to remain on the wall, the others to descend into the shade. No sense in keeping all of them in the hot sunshine. 'Treat 'em like a guard, sergeant-major,' he ordered. 'One hour on the wall, and two hours off.' He reduced his own gunners grilling in the sun to two Bredas manned only.

Tarpaulins had been stretched over one corner of the square. Some beds had been dragged out, but so far no wounded were there. John Offer said, 'Cancel that order about the wounded.' No need to put the poor devils in danger. Recce-ing aircraft would spot the tarpaulins and would assume he'd carried out his threat and had the wounded lying beneath. Instead he let the Italian prisoners sit there under the shade.

All the time they could hear the drone of circling aircraft, but it remained a distant sound, still no attack being mounted.

Then Pom came up from the underground storerooms with a useful contribution to the war effort. He'd been on the scrounge, looking for something worth filching, and he'd found a locker full of sporting equipment, mainly golf clubs, so it looked as if it were for officers only. But with the golf clubs were a couple of dozen umbrellas. Some were ordinary ones, sombrely black, and probably brought out in winter when at times it rained so hard and so long that men wondered why it was called a desert. The others were over-sized gaily-coloured affairs such as golfers use. Offer wondered where the golf course was. Probably somewhere in Telatha Oasis.

Offer beamed at Pom's find. 'Now, they'll come in real handy, Pom, old scout,' he said and sent a party down to fetch them all to the surface. Then they were distributed to the gunners behind the Bredas and to the slowly frying men disconsolately seated with their legs dangling in space over the high walls. It looked a bit ridiculous, men perched on those fortress walls shaded by colourful umbrellas, but Captain Offer wasn't bothered by appearances. In that sunshine the brollies must seem a godsend to men on watch.

The day dragged by. After a while the fighters flew away towards the coast, and later all but two of the bombers disappeared over the horizon, too. Somewhere some Italian commander had said he wasn't going to take the responsibility for bombing his own men clearly seen on the walls of Telatha. They've passed the buck, thought Offer; they're waiting for Higher Command, probably as far back as Rome, to make the decision for them . . .

The ground force had rolled up long ago. From on top of a tower John Offer had watched their arrival through his glasses. There were truck loads of infantry, the inevitable armoured cars, and field guns on tow. Offer spotted some howitzers and didn't like the look of them at all. As if on orders from some distant commander, the ground force did not immediately come in to the attack. They parked in folds of ground roughly a mile distant from the fort, and deployed their forces so that within an hour Fort Telatha was surrounded.

It was a thin line of besiegers, all the same, with such a huge perimeter to man, and Offer, cheering up, thought, 'Bet we can slip by them after dark without much trouble.'

Once or twice the Bredas opened up on the platforms above them, bringing Offer and O'Keefe running, sure that at last an attack had been mounted. But they were only warning bursts to deter Italian infantry who were worming their way as close to the fortress walls as possible.

The ground force appeared to be all Italian, and Offer

thought that might be in their favour. Italians would be particularly reluctant to fire upon the fort if it endangered the lives of their own comrades. The Germans might not have been so constrained.

The Italian commandant came over to him once and said, very hopefully, 'You were going to send us off to the coast.'

John Offer looked at him pityingly. That was when they thought they'd be flying away from Telatha, blowing the damn' place up behind them. But the crafty old sod back in G.H.Q. had properly buggered that deal, and with it the idea of turning their prisoners loose on the desert.

'Not now, my friend,' he told the major. 'Now you're necessary to me.' Without his P.O.W.s the bombers would soon be at them, and the ground force would mount an attack that would over-run the fortress in quick time. 'That's the idea in your mind, isn't it? If we let you go your people will soon have Fort Telatha back in their hands.'

The major grinned a little sheepishly, as if caught out. Offer shook his head sadly. He wasn't such a chump as to fall for that one. The major walked away.

Offer jerked his head towards Pom, and the little man came reluctantly over. 'Pom, my lad, I've got a job just right for the walking wounded. See that Italian commandant? I want you to keep an eye on him from a distance. Make a note of who he talks to.' John Offer had suddenly got the sniff of danger; there was something sharp about this Italian, a feeling that he was a restless man who would try anything to get away.

'Right, sir,' and Pom walked stiff-legged away.

Captain Offer made all preparations for a break-out after dark. When the day became cooler, his men gave the Jeeps a good going over; their jerricans were topped up with Italian petrol and water, and food supplies were replenished. An hour before dusk the Gang was ready to take to the desert.

47

Offer and his sergeant-major had spent much of the afternoon on the flagstaff tower, examining every yard of the surrounding terrain through their powerful binoculars. After a time and much discussion of possible routes through the thin line of besiegers, Offer thought he knew the best way of escape.

'They'll expect us to head for the open desert, if we try to make a run for it.' A natural thought, with men who were accomplished desert raiders. 'But that's the place for us.' He indicated the drooping palm trees of Telatha Oasis, grey-looking and drab in the heat of the afternoon. The oasis was only a mile away. 'Once inside we'd have good cover, and we could dodge anyone on our tails and pop off into the desert in any unexpected place.'

The sergeant-major said, 'Yes, I think you're right, sir.'

They kept watch until the sun set and a breeze came and with it a gathering darkness. Then they went down to the men. Now the Italian P.O.W.s were brought off the wall, and all were marched below and locked in their air raid shelter for the night.

Offer thought, 'If they're clever they'll anticipate this.' The ground force might set up an attack if they guessed that the prisoners were out of harm's way. He ordered gunners up to man all four Bredas, and posted an additional look-out man on the catwalks against each of the high walls. Even so he had an unpleasant feeling that the enemy was beginning to move silently forward, right up to the fortress walls, and that his look-outs wouldn't be able to spot them.

Abruptly the dusk changed to light. Offer heard an engine start up, then electric lamps began to glow, quickly, building up to brightness – lamps in the barrack rooms and bigger, shaded lamps illuminating the square. John Offer had seen the electrical fittings earlier, but hadn't given any further thought to them. Of course a permanent garrison like this would have its own electrical generator.

Weybright would be responsible for giving them light. Offer decided to send for him, but before he could do so the big wireless operator suddenly appeared from beyond the admin office, his face suffused with a pleased smile.

'Good man,' Offer congratulated him. 'But have someone stand by to switch off in a hurry.' They wouldn't want any light behind their backs when they opened the big gates leading on to the desert.

Weybright said, 'They've got angled floodlights built into each tower, sir.' Weybright must have been exploring, following cables.

'Floodlights?' Useful in case of attack upon the fort, lighting up the desert close to the high walls. 'Well, we shan't need them. We're going out when it's completely dark.'

That would be within an hour. He wondered if the enemy, in anticipation, would bring up a detachment to cover the big gates.

John Offer had a momentary picture of the gates being silently opened, of the Jeeps creeping quietly out into the night. Even with the headlights switched off, they'd be able to follow the trail which wound across the dunes to the oasis. With luck they could reach the palm trees without alarming the enemy, but if the gate was covered they'd have to put their foot down and make a race for the oasis. Not all of them would survive.

O'Keefe came up with a problem. 'Sir, my job was to blow up the fort when we left.'

Captain Offer saw the trouble right away. They had prisoners down below and quite a number of wounded. The original plan could hardly be followed now.

'We can't turn the Eyeties loose before we do a bunk, sergeant-major.'

'No, sir.' That would tip off the enemy there was to be a break-out.

'And we can't blow up the fort with them in it.'

'No?' O'Keefe seemed less sure of that statement.

'No.' Offer was firm about it. It was illogical, he knew; they were spending their years trying to destroy their enemies, but he wasn't going to blow up helpless men. 'I'm afraid we'll just have to leave them to be rescued by their comrades when they take the fort. And that means we shall have to leave all those stores for the enemy.' A pity.

O'Keefe said, 'There's an aircraft approaching, sir.'

Offer cocked his ears and heard the distant drone. He wondered why they were sending a plane to Telatha that night. They heard it come cruising overhead. It was not a big plane, and Offer thought it might be the Fiat biplane they'd seen earlier that day. They stood together, he and the sergeant-major, puzzling over it, trying to understand why a potty little plane like that should be sent against them.

Abruptly there was an explosion of light overhead and a brilliantly bright flare swung below a parachute. The fortress was revealed in the hard blue-white light, and just as vividly the surrounding desert was starkly illuminated for many square miles.

Around him men stirred in consternation, Offer feeling it and more than sharing it. To himself he groaned, 'Oh, Christ, that's torn it!' No break-out from the fort while that swung overhead. It was one thing to run a gauntlet of fire in the darkness, but another to do it under such conditions of brightness.

Captain Offer stirred. He wasn't going to let his men see how that flare affected him. He merely said, 'We'd better wait until they stop dropping their fireworks.' But if they kept it up all night? 'Sergeant-major, I saw some perfectly good brandy in the officers' mess. I think a tot each wouldn't come amiss.'

That cheered the men, the drink was brought up and everyone had a good stiff bracer and felt better.

Out in the desert someone fired a shot. Behind their sand-bagging up with their Breda a machine-gun team heard a bullet whine away into the darkness. As if it had been a signal, now other weapons opened up from the desert, machine-guns as well as rifles. The enemy must know the P.O.W.s had come down from the walls. Down on the sandy square they could sense that a lot of metal was flying around high above them. Then their Bredas opened up in short bursts, and Captain Offer and his sergeant-major shot up the ladder to find out what was happening.

The enemy wasn't advancing, that Captain Offer quickly learned. They were keeping up a steady fire at the machine-gun posts on the fortress walls, doubtless in the hope of silencing them, long-range stuff but infinitely more sensible than advancing over a desert illuminated by that parachute flare. Offer's gunners were firing back wherever they saw enemy fire.

Offer, crouching behind the protection of the sandbags, saw that here was a danger. Every time his gunners opened up they were slightly exposed, and there was so much muck flying against the Breda posts that in time some of it would find targets. Offer stopped his men from firing, and when he could be heard he said, 'That's what they want. They want you to fire back, and that gives 'em a chance of nailing you. So stop firing. Keep down. Let the look-outs on the catwalks keep an eye on things, and if they see an attack developing, then you can open up with your gun.' Much less chance of look-outs being hit through a rifle-slit.

Each Breda post was connected by telephone. O'Keefe cranked the box and relayed Offer's orders, and the other three Bredas stopped firing. The volume of enemy fire, however, did not diminish. From across the desert small arms fire kept up a furious fusillade.

The light was dimming, the parachute flare coming too low and drifting off across the desert. John Offer stared up at the sky. Much depended on the next minute or so. Would the enemy drop another flare? If so it looked as if the idea was to keep the Gang from slipping away while the enemy cooked up some plan for overwhelming them.

The light aircraft was still cruising overhead. Abruptly there was more great light as a second parachute flare was dropped overboard. Offer sighed. He was pretty sure he had his answer – the flares would keep descending while ever

51

there was darkness.

He said, 'Sergeant-major, for the second time now we must revise all our plans.' There'd be no sliding off to Telatha Oasis this night. 'Looks as if we're penned in here.' For how long? That would depend on how much water they had in the cistern. When that was gone they would have to surrender. Listening to the flying bullets overhead Offer thought, 'Long before that happens they'll have picked us off one by one.' His men wouldn't be able to keep out of harm's way all that time.

'Sergeant-major, we're going to have accidents if we don't do something about those bullets.' He rubbed his chin. Time he had a shave. 'I think we'll again persuade the enemy to stop firing on us.'

'Yes, sir,' said O'Keefe hopefully, but without a clue as to what was passing through his C.O.'s mind.

'I'm afraid that once more we must use our P.O.W.s. Get me eight of them, two for each Breda.'

While he was away John Offer sent Sergeant Walker off to the cookhouse with an order to prepare four delicious picnic baskets. 'Plenty of fruit, the best of everything to eat, and a bottle of plonk in each basket.'

When eight Italian soldiers were paraded before him Offer addressed them in their own language. 'I'm sorry to drag you away from your comrades, though it couldn't have been very comfortable down below. Now, I want you to help me. It's this silly business of firing guns at each other. Some of us – your men out on the desert as well as my own – are sure to get hurt, and why hurt each other?'

From being cagily apprehensive the Italian prisoners relaxed, listening to Offer's good-humoured voice. One of them agreed that it did seem useless, firing away at each other.

'Good,' said Offer. 'Between us we'll stop our private little war, shall we? I'm going to put two of you to sit in front of each Breda. You'll go out with a white flag, and your comrades won't fire on you. I want you to make yourselves as comfortable as possible on the wall, and I've got a nice basket of food and drink for each of you.'

He showed them the picnic baskets and his P.O.W.s became very cooperative. Sergeant-major O'Keefe with an escort took the first pair of prisoners up the ladder, while Offer called Weybright over to him.

'You said there were floodlights set into the walls. Do you think they can be angled to illuminate the Breda gun positions?'

Weybright said it would present little difficulty, so Offer sent him off with a party to do the work.

O'Keefe himself went out on to the wall ahead of the prisoners, very cautiously at first, holding aloft a big white sheet on a long spar of wood. The firing on that side of the fort dwindled away. At that the two P.O.W.s were pushed forward and encouraged to sit on the edge of the wall right under the muzzle of the Breda. O'Keefe's escort now came up with the picnic basket and this was set between the prisoners. Abruptly a light beamed upon them from the opposite gun position. Weybright did things with a screwdriver and finally the floodlight steadied upon the prisoners and the gun position behind them.

From out in the desert the besieging force would see, clearly illuminated, those two men in Italian uniforms sitting in front of the sandbagging. They must also have seen them dig enthusiastically into the picnic basket, pull out a bottle of wine and pour it into glasses, and then reach in for food. It must have staggered the watchers, seeing a happy little picnic brightly illuminated high along the fortress wall.

Then a second picnic party was ushered into place, and floodlight was turned upon them. A third and fourth followed. Over the desert now was silence, no guns firing. Floodlit picnicking parties in the middle of a battle took some assimilating. They'd be wondering what the devil to do about the situation, Offer thought, and doubtless the Italians would be relaying reports back to the coast, once again passing the buck.

When they came down into the square Sergeant-major O'Keefe said, 'By God, it's working, sir.'

Offer shrugged, then decided they all could risk another brandy. Of course it was working. How could men fire upon their own countrymen? It was all in breach of the Geneva Convention, of course, as the major had pointed out, but he thought, 'Now, that's damned silly. Here am I most sensibly keeping men from killing each other, yet will I get thanks for it?' Not likely.

Offer took a glass of good Stock brandy and said, 'It's working, but it doesn't solve our problem.' It looked as though, for the moment, at least, he'd got the measure of the enemy, but that wouldn't send them away. Maybe after all their freedom depended on the amount of water in the cistern.

Another flare was tipped overboard high above them. Stalemate. Both sides using lights and neither side able to do anything effective as a consequence.

The night wore on. After a couple of hours the sergeant-major put new men on watch and brought the Italian P.O.W.s down. They appeared to be satisfied and merely reluctant to have to go underground again. Eight more prisoners were sent aloft with baskets of food and wine. Before dawn there were further changes of personnel.

Only when the first light of day crept over the horizon did the enemy stop dropping parachute flares over Telatha.

Offer was a tired man after a night of wakefulness on the ramparts. He should have been despondent, because their position was undoubtedly precarious, and yet he wasn't. John Offer was an optimist; they had survived one night, and they would survive many more.

He ordered the Italian cooks to put on their best breakfast. Nothing like a good meal for putting heart into a man, he thought, and he saw to it that the Italian prisoners shared the good meal, also. They were brought up from the air raid shelter and fed in a messroom, first cleared of debris

54

made by an exploding hand-grenade thrown the previous day by either Offer or Pom. The Italian officers breakfasted with their men, so that not too many of the Gang were employed in keeping guard over them.

John Offer went in to the messroom during the meal to see that everything was all right. The Italians were very cheerful this morning, as if they had lost their fears of the desert raiders – or perhaps it was that John Offer radiated such bonhomie that he was reassurance himself. Some of the P.O.W.s even made jokes with him and he responded, and there was a lot of laughter when a prisoner, a sergeant, complained that one bottle of wine was insufficient for two men on the wall. To prove it, he said, not one man had fallen off.

The Italians did not exactly volunteer to go on the wall again, but Offer felt there was some preference for it if only to get away from the crowdedness of the air raid shelter below. Well, he thought, we'll have to keep on using them, and just then O'Keefe came bustling in to pick out eight P.O.W.s to relieve those up top.

'Everything okay, sergeant-major?'

'Not a squeak out of 'em.' O'Keefe seemed very satisfied. Then he threw in his own opinion: 'The Italian Command isn't going to order Italians to take Telatha, not with these ginks in the way.'

'You think we'll have a holiday? For how long?'

O'Keefe was vague. 'Days,' he said, but John Offer didn't share his optimism. Fort Telatha was a sore in the side of the enemy, and they wouldn't allow it to remain unattended much longer. Still, enjoy the respite while they could.

He went out to his own breakfast. This was being served to the off-duty Gang under the shade across the corner of the square. The beds originally brought up for the wounded Italians were now occupied by his Breda gunners, grabbing sleep before their next turn of duty in four hours' time.

John Offer set off to inspect the wounded, and on the way ran into Pom. 'How's the major, Pom? Up to anything?'

Pom shook his head. The Italian commandant seemed to keep with his fellow officers most of the time.

Offer seized upon the remark. 'Most of the time? What did he do in the other time?'

Well, said Pom, thinking back, he'd talked for a while with a couple of his men. Which men? Offer wanted to know. Sparks, said Pom, the garrison wireless operators. Offer went off very thoughtful.

Arab Ward, wearing shorts and Arab headdress, greeted him in the tiny garrison hospital. Captain Offer was relieved to know that none of the Italian wounded were badly hurt, and their own M.O., a first-rate man, was doing wonders to make them more comfortable.

John Offer came back into the sunshine wondering why an Italian commandant should seek out wireless operators for conversation. After a while he had Pom brought before him. He gave new orders. 'Pom, I want you to drop the major. Instead, watch the wireless ops.'

Pom had to do his usual bit of rabbiting. He didn't want to watch anybody with this heat growing over the fort. 'Well, what can they do? I mean to say, they're prisoners –'

Offer said firmly, 'Watch 'em!' And equally firmly he added, 'And watch your big mouth, too – you yap off too much.'

Pom mooched away disconsolately. His 'war wound' wasn't keeping him out of unwelcome duties.

The hours dragged by. The heat increased the higher the sun rose. It was the usual airless day, and with nothing to do time hung heavily on everyone's hands. Still, out across the desert the enemy stayed under cover and not a single shot was fired all during that day. Offer felt that the situation was bordering on the uncanny. Still, better this than trying to kill each other and tossing high explosives over the wall into their midst.

He allowed the Italians to come and rest in the shadow of the walls, and most of them curled up and went to sleep or curled up and looked as if they were sleeping. Offer didn't know the difference. All he knew was that he had a Jeep facing them, with a Browning machine-gunner vigilantly on watch for any hostile move.

'They won't move,' said Sergeant Walker confidently, but Offer thought, 'We'll take no chances.'

Most of the day Offer spent up in a Breda gunpit. He passed the time with his glasses out, carefully examining the desert before him. After a while he was able to spot where men had dug in with machine-guns, and then solitary figures lying under bushes keeping watch on the fort. Behind them, not altogether concealed by folds in the ground, the enemy transport was in leaguer, and sometimes he saw movement as men crossed from one position to another.

But no one made any sign of attacking the fort. The enemy had gone to ground and didn't seem inclined to shift. 'They'll stay like that until they get orders to do something,' Offer thought. But what? He shrugged. After all, what was the urgency? Let the problem resolve itself was a good maxim even in time of war.

By ten o'clock that morning there was so much shimmer across the baking desert that spotting for detail was hopeless. Captain Offer came down and had a talk with his sergeant-major.

'Let's make it an easy day, sergeant-major,' he said. 'Post a man on watch in each Breda post but fully man only one of the guns. If there's an attack we can be up there before it has a chance to develop.'

'What about the prisoners, sir?' They were still sitting along the wall under those incongruous shades.

Offer made a decision. 'Bring 'em all down.' No good subjecting anyone to unnecessary discomfort and if there was an attack they could have the P.O.W.s in position in a matter of minutes.

So the P.O.W.s were brought down with their bright sunshades, given as much to eat and drink as they wished, and then marched off to rest with their comrades in the shade of the high wall.

And the day grew hotter and hotter and dragged and dragged . . .

Quite suddenly the air became appreciably cooler. That was about five o'clock, and after all, thought John Offer, it was October and early winter. The fort, so somnolent during the day, all at once appeared to come to life. Men rose and took showers, P.O.W.s, too, under supervision. Offer wondered if he ought to permit this lavish use of water, for if they really were in for a siege their supplies ought to be carefully husbanded. He decided to permit it this day, but from tomorrow, depending on the situation, there'd be no more baths.

The Italian commandant suddenly detached himself from a group of his men and came over to where Offer was knocking back his umpteenth tea of the day. He seemed in a brisk mood, and his first words were almost hearty. 'I challenge you,' he said, 'to a game of football.'

He said his men would like a match with the British, because weren't they the masters of the round-ball game? John Offer gave it a moment's thought, as usual trying to probe beneath the surface to see if there was anything ulterior behind the proposal. Finding none, he agreed and the square was cleared and two teams set to with a will to kick a rather shapeless football between goalposts chalked upon the fortress walls. The British side consisted only of nine men because guard duties restricted them to that number.

It certainly enlivened the evening. The non-playing P.O.W.s were all lined up down one side of the pitch where Sergeant-major O'Keefe could cover them with a gun. John Offer did not play but took a turn on a Breda so as to permit Jack Redpath, who fancied himself as a centre-half, a chance to go below.

Occasionally looking down, Captain Offer thought there was more noise than skill. Everybody on the Italian side seemed to shout all the time, telling the man with the ball what to do next. In fact they did very little, being too selfishly intent on scoring themselves, so that Offer's nine men, with a greater idea of teamwork, began to rattle up the goals and the opposition in the process.

Still, everybody thoroughly enjoyed themselves . . .

Someone was climbing a scaling ladder. When he crossed the flat roof before making the final ascent Captain Offer saw that it was his batman-driver, Pomegranate Face. He thought, 'Now, what's Pom doing, dragging his sore backside up all these steps?'

Before Pom's sweating face appeared level with the gunpit John Offer knew there was something wrong. Pom came over the edge panting and moaning about his arse killing him. Offer said, sharply, 'What is it, Pom?'

Pom blinked through his steel-rimmed glasses. He had that cagey look of swaddies sure they're in for a bollocking. His approach, typical of his kind, was oblique, so that Offer had to guess what he was trying to say.

'Them sparks, sir. The Wops. Scarpered. One minute they were there. Next they wasn't – wasn't anywhere, sir.'

Offer's first reaction was to look out over a desert fast losing heat as the sun dipped below the horizon. If he expected to see a couple of Italians legging it for the enemy lines, he was disappointed.

Offer said, 'How could they disappear?' Only one exit from the fort, and the gate hadn't opened all day.

Pom's story was that he'd been keeping an eye on the pair and they'd been on the touchline, with their comrades. Then he lost sight of them, as if they had been jostled from their positions.

'– or deliberately stepped back among the crowd,' interposed Offer, his mind racing. That sharp garrison commander had been seen speaking to the wireless operators, and immediately John Offer connected it with their disappearance. 'What did you do then?'

Pom had watched for a while, expecting to see them reappear but they hadn't, so Pom had gone among the P.O.W.s looking for them. The wireless ops weren't to be found among the spectators. 'So I came up to you right away, sir.' Pom hadn't the kind of mind to rise to any emergency, and thought he'd done his bit by reporting the matter.

John Offer cursed. Perhaps it was too late, if they were up to something. 'Take over, Pom,' he snapped and left an aggrieved Pomegranate Face to do his first stint on the wall.

Offer shot down the ladder. He was thinking, 'They were on the touchline backed by the staircase.' 'They' were the Italian spectators; the staircase led down to the vaulted storerooms below. Offer was sure that was where the Italian operators had disappeared, for there was nowhere else for them to go. If Pom had had his wits about him he'd have been down in a minute and seen what they were up to.

Captain Offer came running out of the long black shadow of the west wall. He called to the Italian lieutenant who was acting as referee, 'Stop the game!' And to his sergeant-major. 'Line 'em all up against the wall. Two men, follow me.'

Wise and Tiffy Jones grabbed tommies and came running after him. Offer drew his pistol before dropping down the concrete stairway. They made a lot of noise, descending, but it could hardly be avoided. The thing was to rout out the Italians and stop them doing whatever they were doing.

Offer had forgotten the generator wasn't running, so there was no electric light below. No good hunting for men in the dark. 'Hop back and get a torch,' he ordered Tiffy Jones, while he and Wise stood guard at the foot of the stairs, their eyes peering into the blackness ahead.

Ears cocked, both heard sounds. Someone certainly was down there and moving around. Offer called, 'Stand still, there!' He had an awful feeling that he and Wise could be seen silhouetted against the grey light at the foot of the stairs, and here amid these many supplies must have been plenty of lethal weapons with ammunition. Then Tiffy Jones came down the stairs three at a time, a torch waving.

The light beamed down the long storeroom. It fell upon

two Italian soldiers, both standing docilely there, hands above their heads. Offer rapped, 'Come on, get upstairs!'

They mounted to the sandy parade ground. Every eye was upon them, P.O.W.s' and the Gang's. Seeing the two prisoners being hustled before the guns of the British, instantly the Italian major came hurrying across. 'What are you doing with them?' he was calling in Italian. 'They haven't done anything wrong.'

'How do you know?' snapped Captain Offer, then ignored him, turning instead to question the scared-looking Italians. 'What were you going down there?'

There was some hesitation, then one of them spoke, his voice surly as if he didn't expect to be believed. 'We were tired. We did not want to watch any more football. So we went down to have a rest in the air raid shelter.'

'But you weren't in the shelter when we found you?' They were doing something among the stores.

'It was so dark; we could not find the room.'

'Hooey!' thought Offer. Anyway, men didn't voluntarily leave daylight to take a rest underground in a room devoid of light at this time of evening. 'Come on, out with it. What were you up to?' He waved his pistol threateningly.

Again the major interfered. He was determined to protect his men. 'These men have done nothing wrong. You heard them. You have no right to threaten them. The Geneva Convention –'

He was hot on the Geneva Convention. John Offer said, very distinctly, 'Bugger the Convention. I want to know why they slid away like that.'

Yet they stuck to their story, unlikely though it sounded to everyone there, and the major kept arguing and protesting and hurling the Geneva Convention at the British officer. The light was fading. There were urgent things to do. Offer had the Italians searched but found nothing on them.

'Sergeant-major, lock these two men in a separate room. Then get all the P.O.W.s down to the shelter except eight of them. Man all the Bredas and shove eight P.O.W.s up like last night.'

He walked off, thinking hard. What would wireless ops be looking for in a storeroom? Weapons? Perhaps. His guess was it would have something to do with their trade. John Offer was willing to bet there would be plenty of radio material downstairs in that storeroom.

'Maybe there's a spare transmitter, or they had hopes of building one secretly.' He couldn't see what information a pair of wireless ops could transmit to the besieging force which would be of help to them, but he thought that might be the idea. Of course the damned Italian major had put them up to it. Well, locked up they couldn't do much harm. Probably they hadn't had time to do anything adverse to the Gang's safety.

All the same Captain Offer spent an uneasy night.

There were no parachute flares that night; in fact no aircraft came over at all. Instead a powerful searchlight suddenly switched on from the desert far beyond the range of their guns and settled on the massive main gates of the fortress. 'They must have brought it up during the day,' Sergeant-major O'Keefe said to his C.O. Much more economical than aircraft. The use of light in this battle was taking another curious turn.

Offer said, 'They're making it obvious, sergeant-major.' The Italians could not storm the fort while Offer used P.O.W.s as human shields, but they were going to make sure the British party did not escape during the night. 'No more showers, Angus, old son.' Now they must eke out their water supplies as long as possible. Offer fretted. He didn't enjoy being cooped up in this fortress – 'Reminds me too much of Sharafim,' he told himself – and sighed for the freedom of the open desert again. Still, all they could do was make the best of it and hope the affair would take another turn before long.

Electrifyingly it did, that same night. John Offer had got

his head down for a few hours kip, completely whacked. His bed was one of the tables under the shade in the corner of the square, hard but thoroughly comfortable to him. Shortly after three in the morning Sergeant Walker came sliding down the scaling ladder and wakened him.

'Sir, I think you should come and see what's up.'

Offer mounted the ladder after him. When they reached the Breda gun position it was still difficult to know what was going on. In every direction across the desert headlights were flashing and moving, sweeping in wide arcs low across the sandy wastes. Quite clearly, too, they could hear the sound of powerful engines roaring.

After close on an hour of manoeuvring a pattern began to emerge. It appeared as though vehicles were converging from distant points around the fortress to a position close by where the searchlight beamed silently across at Fort Telatha. Then the headlights swung away, pointing north, and the engine roar began to die away.

John Offer said, amazed, 'Good God, I think they're pulling out!' Or was it a trap?

It was a curious trap, if so, for the searchlight continued to focus on the fortress gate. Sergeant Walker said, 'That shows they've left someone behind.' But how many? And was it safe for them to brave the searchlight and make a dash for the oasis? Against that, if the enemy *had* pulled out was there any need to leave Telatha in a hurry? Maybe they could still pursue the original plan, turn the P.O.W.s loose and blow up the fortress behind them.

But why had some of the enemy pulled away in the night? John Offer sighed. Nothing for it but to wait till dawn and see how the land lay then. Abruptly he had a thought.

'Where's Weybright?' Weybright was doing a turn on one of the Bredas. 'Get him relieved and tell him to listen in for news.' Sergeant Walker shot away.

Just about the time that the eastern horizon was paling Weybright sent a runner up the ladder to his C.O. Captain Offer took the signal, positioned himself in the light of one of the big floods and read: 'B.B.C. news from London. A brief report that a big offensive has been launched by the 8th Army at Alamein.'

Offer silently handed over the signal to Sergeant Walker, then took a turn along the ramparts. How did the news affect them, and what connection had it with the Italian troop movements out in the desert during the night? He puzzled over it but for the moment was baffled.

Sergeant Walker saw it in much simpler terms. The big push had started; that meant the Eighth Army would drive up the coast and in a matter of days there'd be no enemy around Telatha and the Gang could wander off happily into the desert again. Offer heard his sergeant softly cheering, and turned and saw the big ex-palais bouncer looking mightily pleased with himself. Perversely Offer decided to be sour.

'What's filling you with joy, Eddie? I don't see anything stupendous about that signal.'

'Why, sir –' Walker had patience with his captain '– don't you see, the Eyeties have been pulled back to try to stop Monty's lot. We'll be able to shove off from this flea-hole any time we like.'

Offer shook his head sadly. 'Eddie, my old cell-mate, things don't work out easily like that, not during a war.' He gestured towards the unblinking searchlight, the beam paling, though, as the morning light grew brighter. 'If they've pulled out, why didn't they take that thing with them? No, Eddie, they're up to something and my guess is it's not something that's going to be nice for us.'

Then up came the runner with a second signal. Weybright had tuned in to G.H.Q. Cairo and had picked up a signal addressed to Captain Offer personally. 'Report instantly if still at Telatha. Captain Roger Tansley.'

John Offer whistled soundlessly as he re-read the signal. It said 'instantly' but Offer wasn't going to hurry. The instinct of a man long on the run was to examine everything carefully for hidden snares. So Offer waited until after sunrise before replying, for first he wanted to know what was happening on the desert.

His glasses soon satisfied him that not all the Italian force had been pulled away in the night. Under cover of darkness some earthworks had been made about five hundred yards into the desert directly in front of the fortress gates. Possibly cannon as well as machine-guns dug in there. Offer's binoculars slowly traversed the desert around it, but finally came back to rest on that gun position, uncomfortably close. By the look of it, all other Italian troops had been withdrawn from the area. This appeared to be the only gun position left.

Offer thought, 'If we want to break out, now's our chance.' Jeeps were elusive things. The trouble was, they were only elusive where they had space for manoeuvre. The open gateway of the fort did not constitute space. They would have a chance of dodging bullets out on the desert, but how were they to get safely clear of the gate in the first place?

As soon as the big doors began to swing open, that would alert the enemy gunners facing them. It took time to get seven Jeeps through a narrow gateway, and all the time heavy fire would be laid against them. Offer thought, 'One or two might be lucky and slip through, but for certain they'd get one of the Jeeps and put it out of action and that would block the way for the others.'

The more he thought of it, the less he liked the idea of a break-out. He rubbed his chin, stubbly again, and wondered at the Italians' manoeuvre, pulling out most of their troops. If he and his men dropped from the rear wall next night after dark, they could storm that position and put it out of action. His pulse stirred. He'd like to have a crack at it. And why wait for darkness? Perhaps, though, they'd posted the odd rifleman on watch around the fortress, anticipating just such a manoeuvre, and he'd fire off a warning to alert the machine-gunners.

So what? John Offer would back his men anywhere.

They'd deal with those riflemen and knock out that gun position. Of course they would sustain casualties, and that was something Captain Offer tried hard to avoid. He wondered if there was another way . . .

His roaming glasses picked up a dust cloud rolling up fast and he thought, resignedly, 'There isn't going to be another way.' In fact no way of breaking out at all. Here was another force racing in to invest the place, and this new enemy would be upon them long before they could tackle the gun position close by and make a getaway.

Sergeant Walker had spotted the dust cloud, too. Optimist, he said, 'That might be our men, sir. A scouting party ahead of the Desert Rats.'

'Come off it, Eddie.' Offer wasn't a man to kid himself. 'You don't throw scouting parties a couple of hundred miles ahead of your army. They're enemy, Krauts or Eyeties.'

Walker said, 'What I don't understand is why they bother to pull out one lot then bring up another.'

John Offer thought he knew the answer. 'They're Germans.' The approaching column, now visible under the rising dust. 'Don't you see, Eddie. The Italians weren't getting anywhere, not while we kept the P.O.W.s between us and them. Perhaps they flatly refused to attack us, knowing they'd kill a lot of their own men if they did. So Rommel's pulled them out and my bet is he's sent in his Afrika Korps with orders to take the place regardless of P.O.W.s.'

Sergeant Walker looked a bit bleak at that. 'They mean business?'

'Why go to the trouble of sending a column all the way from the coast if not?' Especially with Alamein starting. Rommel must have a powerful incentive to detach any troops to storm a distant desert fortress at a time like this. Yet again John Offer thought he understood.

'My guess is Rommel knows he can't hold the Eighth Army. He's going to fall back, but put up a defensive battle. What he can't afford at such a time is to have us occupying

66

Telatha, a menace to his rear. He must have wondered why we bothered to capture the place, and probably now thinks it was deliberate, part of the plan for the Battle of Alamein.'

And then two thoughts occurred to him. 'You know, I'll bet Rommel doesn't know how few of us are holding Telatha. For all he knows we might be a very strong force, and what general wants to fight with a dangerously strong enemy tucked away in his rear? For all he knows we might come out at some critical moment and create havoc.'

He snapped his fingers, sure of his reasoning and suddenly seeing daylight, too.

'That's what those Italian ops were up to!' They were intent on laying their hands on a spare transmitter so as to signal their H.Q. that a mere handful of men occupied Telatha at that moment. Well, they hadn't got through . . . Or had they? The thought jolted Offer. Pom, stupid git, had given them time enough to put out a call if a transmitter had been ready for use down below. But what about current? He remembered the generator hadn't been running, so they'd have had to use batteries. Where could they have laid hands on charged batteries in such a short time?

Offer gave up worrying. Either the enemy knew how many they were or he didn't. One thing was certain, while the ops were under lock and key they wouldn't get another call through.

The Germans came up at a spanking pace and finally came to a halt a mile back in the desert. Offer guessed there'd be much conferring with the officer left commanding the Italians. Now he looked at the signal from G.H.Q. and thought he'd better do something about it.

'All right,' he said to Walker, 'we'll tell 'em we're still here and see if that agitates them.' He wrote a signal and sent it below to Weybright.

An hour later another signal came from G.H.Q. 'Battle of Alamein has started.' Late news, thought Offer sardonically. 'Imperative you hold Telatha as long as possible.'

Sergeant-major O'Keefe came up for a word with his O.C. at that moment, so Offer drew him into a conference with Sergeant Walker. He showed them the signal. 'We've suddenly become important.' He didn't want to feel important, not under circumstances like these.

'Accidentally we're occupying a key position in G.H.Q. planning.' That major-general had stranded them in Telatha on the eve of Alamein. Now G.H.Q. was trying to turn the situation to advantage.

Walker was perplexed. 'I don't get it. How can we be important, sir? Fifteen of us here, while a million men slog it out over there.'

'All right, minor importance, then, but important enough for Rommel to send quite a strong force to winkle us out.' He explained his theory, that for all Rommel knew he might have a big hostile enemy presence right in his midst. 'Rommel can't stand that. We're only fifty miles from the Med, and think what damage a force based on Telatha could do if he has to retreat along the coast road.' Besides, Telatha had been planned as a refuelling and re-equipping base for Rommel in case of need.

'He's sent a Panzer column along with orders to drive us out p.d.q.' John Offer wrinkled his nose thoughtfully. 'Anyone good at mathematics? How long can fifteen bods in a dirty great fortress hold out against a Panzer regiment?'

Neither of his men essayed an answer. Offer took one look across the desert before descending to the parade ground. The Panzer force was already deploying east and west of the fortress. The Germans were in a hurry. Offer saw armoured cars scudding across the desert, throwing up long trailing clouds of dust, clearly defined against the early rising sun. Field-guns were jolting more slowly over the rough ground, and Offer saw a howitzer on tow and liked that least of all. It wasn't going to be long now.

At ground level he began to give orders. Every man would be needed on the ramparts; but they had enough machine-guns in those Bredas, and what he wanted were some mortars mounted up top. Shells dropping in on a closing enemy would shake them a bit. 'But not hold them back altogether.' Offer, the realist, knew there could only be one end to this fight.

He sent some men down into the big storeroom to seek for mortars. 'There's sure to be plenty,' he told them. 'And bring up a good supply of ammo.'

Then he went into the messroom where the P.O.W.s were having breakfast. He called the Italian commandant over to him. 'I'm afraid it looks as though we're in for a hot time.' He told the major how the Italians had been pulled out, leaving the way for the Afrika Korps to storm the fortress. The major's eyes widened and he looked disturbed.

'My men –' he began quickly.

'I'm pulling them down from the wall right away. You're all going to be packed into the air raid shelter where you won't come to any harm.'

'That is very good of you, captain.'

Offer shrugged. He didn't want anyone to get hurt unnecessarily. Italian P.O.W.s weren't going to stop Germans, anyway. He told the major to take ample supplies of food and water into the shelter, in case the battle went on a long time. The Gang would be too occupied to look after prisoners. 'Sorry I must keep you locked up, major.'

It was the commandant's turn to shrug. It was no more than he expected.

The prisoners were brought down from the ramparts and marched into the air raid shelter with the others, the two wireless operators with them. Offer felt better when he was told they were all safely locked away. Later he remembered the wounded and thought, 'I'll need Arab Ward' – he'd have need of every man – so he had them borne below on stretchers under supervision of their M.O. They'd be safer in the shelter when the shelling started, anyway, and Ward was a good man with a rifle.

A stirring of his stomach reminded him that though the P.O.W.s had breakfasted, none of his men had, so he ordered them down in relays and got a sulking Pom to make up the grub. Sergeant-major O'Keefe phoned once from the look-out that the Panzers were still manoeuvring into position, and he didn't think it would be long before the dirt began to fly. The whole of the Italian contingent had now pulled out and was heading north for Bardia. As an afterthought O'Keefe added that they'd taken their searchlight with them.

'That sounds a bit final, sergeant-major.' O'Keefe said he didn't get his meaning. 'The Germans reckon they'll dig us out before dark.'

Down the wire came O'Keefe's thoughtful voice. 'I wouldn't think they'll be far out, sir.'

'No?'

'Not unless you come up with one of your bright ideas.' Offer replaced the phone.

He called Weybright down from the wall. Weybright had gone over to mortars. 'I want you to send a nicely heroic signal to that major-general in G.H.Q.' He made several attempts before finally, satisfied, he passed it over to Weybright.

His signaller read: 'Situation bad. Surrounded by Panzer regiment. Resolved to fight to the end. We die for our king and country. Request posthumous pardon to clear our names of all crimes laid against us.'

Weybright said, admiringly, 'This is one of your best, sir. But you don't mean it. I mean, about dying.'

'Not likely! If there's no chance of escape, out we go with our hands up.' No bloody heroics for him. The idea of going into the bag was damned depressing, but better that than a gory end. Still, they would put up a bit of a fight.

Weybright was still charmed by the message. 'You think the major-general will swallow this guff, sir?'

'Not bloody likely!' That old cynic would probably chuckle over it, but he wouldn't be taken in. The m-g had the measure of John Offer by now, and the captain knew it.

He passed a second signal across to Weybright. 'I want

you to wait a while – half an hour, say – then put that out.'

The signal was also addressed to the major-general. It had the merit of simplicity. It began, 'Add to previous signal –' And then gave profound advice: 'Get stuffed.' The m-g was going to chuckle over that one, too.

Something whistled over the fortress and exploded beyond the north wall. A howitzer was starting to find their range. John Offer went up the scaling ladder like lightning, and crawled out on to the rampart beside O'Keefe. Across the desert smoke drifted. As they watched the howitzer belched into smoke again and another shell lobbed over the fort, still punishing that long-suffering desert north of them. Simultaneously from every depression and from behind every screening bush German infantry opened up with all the guns they'd got. Bullets whined within inches of the defenders crouching on the towers, or spanged against the breastworks and went ricocheting noisily off into space again. The Bredas came into action, deafening them, crouching there.

Offer heard his sergeant-major shout, 'Just one thing we can count ourselves lucky on, sir.'

Lucky? At a time like this? Offer looked at O'Keefe in astonishment. That lean warrior seemed remarkably unperturbed, harassing though the situation was. 'What's lucky about today?'

'No aircraft.'

Their absence had been noted by Offer earlier. For a time he had confidently expected the bombers to come in and reinforce the ground troops, but now, a couple of hours after daybreak, still they hadn't appeared. Evidently Rommel could afford to detach a Panzer column – probably part of his reserve – but had need of every aircraft possible for the Alamein battle.

'For such little mercies, let's be thankful.'

Field guns were coming into action now. With commendable economy the Panzer commander wasn't wasting shells

71

on the thick walls of the fortress. He had two field guns drawn up facing the main gates, and each systematically sought for range and bearing, found them, then began to blow the gates to hell. The whole place shuddered as the shells exploded against the woodwork. Stout though the timbers were they weren't proof against high explosive. Peering down, Offer saw whole sections of gate being blown on to the parade ground.

O'Keefe said, 'They're coming!'

Across the desert stooping Panzergrenadiers were running, seeking cover as they went. After only a few strides they hurled themselves down out of sight, then seconds later were up again, making another quick run before diving into cover once more. When they went down to ground they opened fire, and the combined effect was to produce a hail of bullets which never ceased and had the defenders shrinking behind the breastworks.

O'Keefe said, 'They're within mortar range. Lay down a barrage before the gate!' Weybright and his mortarmen went into action, and the little shells rose into high arcs, then dropped to the desert below. There was so much noise, though, no one even heard them exploding.

The howitzer was making the most row. It was also the most formidable weapon ranged against them. Looking down at the damage it was causing, Offer thought, 'I'll have to make a decision quickly.' That howitzer would do for all of them if it kept on firing, particularly if it shortened range slightly. What was the good of hanging on, hoping for a miracle to happen? Better quit now while they had a whole skin.

But John Offer didn't quit. Just a few minutes more, he kept telling himself, while around him his men fought back, spraying the desert with Breda bullets and making the advancing Germans move cautiously. But they were coming on. Nothing would stop that advance.

He kept in touch with his Bredas on the north wall. 'What's happening on your side?'

Palfreyman's voice. 'Nothing much, sir.' A very calm young man. A solitary machine-gun had been mounted out in the desert, he reported, but its purpose appeared only to keep the defenders' heads down.

'No sign of attack?'

'No, sir. Are you being troubled?'

Offer felt like saying what Wilborn, Wise or Pom might have said under the circumstances: 'Cor!'

Troubled? The Germans hadn't been at it more than a few minutes and the end already looked pretty near. At least one howitzer was almost on target. The shells came lobbing out of the sky, exploding now against the north wall. It must have been shattering for Palfreyman and his gunners, in the gun positions above.

Dust was rising, dust and smoke burning their eyes and choking them. The noise was tremendous, the field guns belting off non-stop, firing through the open gate now and doing damage to some low buildings against the east wall. One of them was the messroom and kitchen. No one was going to eat out of those places ever again. But the howitzers were doing most damage.

Fascinated, screwing up his courage to surrender, John Offer saw the north wall begin to disintegrate before the exploding force of those howitzer shells. For the moment all seemed to be landing about the same spot. If the howitzer had been slightly more elevated shells would be exploding along the top of the walls, killing his men and himself at the same time.

O'Keefe wriggled close to his C.O. and shouted, 'Doesn't seem much good, sir.'

'No good at all.' Offer recoiled as another howitzer shell landed smack against that north wall. Smoke and dust and the whole place trembling. Offer said, suddenly, 'Good lord, look at that!'

The concrete face of the north wall had seemed to peel off. Behind it was a brick wall. 'Christ, that was a bit of jerry-building,' thought Offer. Some corrupt contractor must

73

have made a packet, building native-brick walls and facing them with concrete. But then he had never expected war to come seriously to this dusty, distant desert outpost. 'It wasn't designed to withstand modern howitzer shells,' he thought, and then another shell landed against the exposed brick and the whole thing simply collapsed.

When again the dust began to clear John Offer saw a hole in the wall like a big window. His first thought was one of alarm. If the enemy simultaneously mounted an attack on the gate and from the north side, there wasn't much to stop them romping in both ways now. Then he remembered Palfreyman saying there was only one machine-gun covering the north flank, no assault troops there . . .

O'Keefe heard his captain say, 'Jesus!' And then some words which sounded like – 'Can still do it!'

Then Offer was shouting to Weybright. 'Quick! Follow me! No time to lose! Bugger your mortar!'

Captain Offer went sliding down the scaling ladders like a madman. Weybright couldn't keep up with him. He saw his C.O. dodge across the square, another shell exploding as he did so, sand hurtling up at him and sending him staggering. Next time Weybright saw him he was running on towards the staircase by the water cistern.

When Weybright, panting, reached the head of the stairs, John Offer already had the air raid shelter door open and was shouting in Italian to the men inside. Promptly two men came hurrying out, Offer locking the door behind them. As they came running up the stairs Weybright saw who they were. The Wop ops.

Offer came up hard on their heels, urging them on into speed. 'Get them into the wireless office. See if the set's still capable of transmitting.'

When they were inside Offer began to work out a message in Italian, writing it down on an odd scrap of paper. Weybright looked up from the set. 'Nothing wrong here, sir. If the aerial's okay you'll get through.'

'Good.' Offer hustled the operators into their seats and

placed the signal before them. In Italian he said, shouting because of the roar of battle outside, 'I want that message to be sent to your Command H.Q., wherever that is. *Presto! Subito! Rapidamente!*'

They leapt to it, shaken by the force of his command. Yet Offer had something else to tell them.

'Don't get up to any tricks, either. Just send that message, nothing else, understand?' To Weybright: 'Watch 'em, and if they try anything, belt 'em.' Though how Weybright could spot tricks in a language which he didn't know . . .

The place seemed to be falling down over their heads. Dust rolled in great gusts on them as shells exploded outside the wireless office. The rattle of his Bredas seemed non-stop. The enemy must be coming very close now, the mortars and machine-gun fire only slowing them a little, but not halting them. The Gang couldn't hold out much longer.

The Italian operator was tapping away: 'Fort Telatha Commanding Officer to Officer Commanding Italian Army in North Africa. I ask for a truce of one hour in order to save the lives of Italian wounded and prisoners. Cease firing and I will march them out. Attacking force must not advance beyond present positions during truce or regretfully we shall open fire on P.O.W.s.' Strong stuff, but it had to be to be effective.

Offer thought, suddenly suspicious, 'That op's taking a long time!' As if suspicion had come to Weybright, too, Offer saw him rise from his chair, a big lumbering man, wrath upon his heavy face. Weybright swung and hit the Italian operator across the neck, and it was a mighty blow and the fellow just collapsed to the floor. The other operator ran in fear to the back of the room and stood there, watching in apprehension.

Weybright was furious. 'Under my nose,' Offer heard him shout above the din. He was waving the signal. 'He kept on going and I couldn't follow the Italian.' But Weybright knew his morse and he did know a few words of Italian, particularly numbers, and when the Italian tapped out '*diciassette*' Weybright knew it was a word not in the signal.

'It means seventeen, sir. You know what I think?'

Offer didn't have to be told. 'Sod it!' he was saying to himself. The major had put these fellows up to it some time ago, he guessed. 'If ever you get a chance,' he must have ordered, 'signal the strength of these Britishers.' And he, John Offer, had given them this opportunity to get their message away! Once the enemy knew they were faced by seventeen men only they'd come along at a gallop. Offer felt pretty sure the information had gone out before Weybright tumbled to what was going on. Well, it was too late to do anything about it now . . .

Not too late for everything. There was still this idea that had come to him, an idea to make use of the hole in the north wall.

He said nothing of his plan to Weybright, who must have been curious about that signal but didn't ask questions, perhaps because the Italians were there. The one with the brutally used neck was sitting up and looking very injured.

Offer said, 'You –' to the other operator, still looking wary against the back wall '– get your harness on.' He indicated the headphones. 'Keep listening for any reply.'

The Italian took the chair and fiddled with the receiver. Minutes were passing. Every half minute or so a howitzer shell fell inside the fort, hurling sand in a blinding rain everywhere. At times little could be seen for the dust cloud which swirled up with each explosion. The field guns were still pouring in shells through the open gateway, though they weren't doing much harm. Still, the German gunners probably thought they were keeping the defenders occupied in some way, dodging the blast. Above his head the Bredas and mortars fought back ferociously against the relentless advance of the enemy.

John Offer thought, 'I ought to be up there with them.' Perhaps they had even noticed his absence and wondered why he wasn't with the guns. But this was more important, being down here, trying to save their skins. The dust cleared and again he had a picture of the desert through the gaping hole in the crumbling north wall. That was the way they'd take their skins . . .

Why the bloody hell didn't the Italian H.Q. pull their finger out and give an answer! Offer realized that he was very tense, unable to sit down and take the waiting time calmly. But so much depended on the Italian reply. Ten minutes had gone by. He supposed that ten minutes weren't a long time for the Italians to make their decision. Probably they were exchanging signals with the commander of the Panzer column . . .

Captain Offer caught a bright metallic glitter across the square. The Jeeps were parked there, protected by the south wall, and by a low concrete wall which formed a series of parking bays. Offer, very alert now, thought, 'Someone's back there, behind the Jeeps!' Who could it be? All his men were on the guns.

That movement again, a flash of light. Then a figure moved forward slightly and Offer saw a face. It was Pom, very lugubrious behind his steel-rimmed glasses. Between shells Offer went to the doorway and bellowed across at his driver. Pom looked up at the sky as if he might learn something from it, then put his head down and broke a few records for a dash across the parade ground. Offer dragged him into the passage, then slammed the metal door to just as another shell came and made a mess of the north wall again.

'What were you doing across there? You should have been up with the guns.'

'I just finished clearing up after breakfast,' Pom retorted, but his voice trailed off into weakness.

'You were on the bloody mike,' Offer told him roughly. He wanted to roast the fellow, but recognized that it would do no good and anyway was a symptom of his own frustration. 'Well, you might as well mike in here with us.' He'd find a use for the little scrounger in a few minutes, if the

Italians agreed to his proposal.

But the shells were still coming over and the fort seemed to rock and sway under the impact of high explosive shells. Offer wondered how many casualties they had suffered, and while waiting rang through to each Breda position in turn. 'Everyone okay?'

Two of the Breda posts were bearing the brunt of the offensive. They were the ones overlooking the main gate. Yet curiously no one had been hurt in spite of all the flying missiles.

On the north wall, however, where the firing was infinitely less intense, they had suffered their only casualties. Palfreyman had been hit in the face by a ricocheting bullet; he'd lost some teeth and part of his right cheek and big Cruiser said he was unconscious. Tiffy Jones had stopped one in his right shoulder, but was still helping to man a gun.

'We've been lucky,' Offer told himself. Or his men, wise warriors, had kept well down behind cover. But luck like this didn't last, not under such a bombardment. He told O'Keefe so, when he got through to him. O'Keefe shouted down the wire, 'They need only land one shell on top of this wall and we'll all be corpsed.'

Offer said, 'You don't need to shout, I can hear you,' and then the thought came to him that no shell had landed within the fortress for at least a minute, neither were any guns firing.

He whirled to face Weybright, his eyes shining. 'I think we've pulled it off –' he began, then realized that the Italian operator was taking down a message. Offer strode across to the table and read the signal over the op's shoulder.

'Your truce terms accepted. For one hour hostilities will cease. Your prisoners must be allowed to leave Fort Telatha immediately. You are urged to surrender, and not resist further. You cannot hope to survive with only seventeen men. If your surrender is not made by 11.32 hrs your force will be destroyed without any further opportunity for surrender.'

The Italians could talk as toughly as he. John Offer looked at the words '. . . with only seventeen men.' The operator had certainly got through with vital information. He shrugged. That was water under the bridge now. He bore no malice, for it was what he would expect any of his men to do in the circumstances.

It seemed curiously quiet, with the cessation of firing. The dust was settling over the battered fortress, and somewhere someone was shouting. Offer pulled himself together. They had only one hour in which to undertake his hazardous escape plan. First, though, he must call his men down and tell them what was happening – they must be mighty curious, he thought, wondering why the Kraut wasn't maintaining his offensive.

'Outside!' he rapped, and that included Pom and Weybright as well as the Italian ops. 'Must get rid of the ops for a few minutes,' he thought.

'Pom. Where's your gun?'

'Over there.' Pom jerked his head to where the Jeeps stood in neat array behind the protecting wall.

'Then get it.' While he was doubling away Offer used his best Italian on the prisoners. 'You're going back to the air raid shelter, but it will only be for twenty minutes or so. Tell your C.O. that next time we come to you you're going to be marched across to the German camp. Your major will be pleased to have the news.'

Pom returned. This time he had remembered his torn backside and made a great show of limping. Offer gave him an order. 'Take these prisoners down to the shelter.' He tossed a key across to him. 'Lock 'em in with the others. And keep your eyes skinned in case they try to jump you.'

'Like to see 'em try,' said Pom scornfully. 'Bloody Wop ops!'

He marched them away, a very truculent little figure, and again Offer noticed he had forgotten to limp.

They were bringing someone down a scaling ladder, a tricky

performance. That was what all the shouting was about. It was Palfreyman. The two big boys, Cruiser and Busker, were carrying him down between them. The former solicitor's clerk appeared still to be unconscious. Arab Ward, as if anticipating a need for his medical services, was sliding down another ladder, *kefir* flowing in the wind.

Offer trotted across to greet them when they reached the ground. One look at Palfreyman told him the fellow was in a bad way. Still, they were lucky, so few hurt in spite of all the bombardment.

'How's Tiffy?' Offer asked as Arab Ward came loping over.

'Not bad. I put a field dressing on him and he says all right, leave him on the Breda.'

'Good man.' Offer looked up. Sergeant-major O'Keefe was staring down at him. Offer shouted, 'Leave one team on watch. Bring everyone else down.'

O'Keefe acknowledged and began to bawl instructions across to the other gun posts, then came down a ladder in a hurry. As he strode across to where Offer awaited him, he called in perplexity, 'What's up, sir? I mean, why's Jerry stopped firing? Run out of ammo or something?' Other men were sliding down the ladders. Arab Ward had Palfreyman on a bed which had survived the howitzers and was cleaning the unconscious man's mangled face.

Offer waited until they were gathered about him. He took one glance round at their faces – tough men, he had, but even tough men can look strained and desperate when the odds are stacked against them. Then he spoke, his voice quick, urgent. Seconds were flying by; they had too little time for what was in his mind.

'Look here, I think we've a chance of saving our hides.' The men straightened and came alert at that. 'I've bought an hour's truce by offering to release our prisoners. In that hour we have to clear a way through the wall –' he waved towards the gaping hole in the north wall '– then we'll make a bolt for it in the Jeeps.'

80

They brightened remarkably at that. To their simple minds it was a piece of cake. Then John Offer showed them the problem. No Jeep could surmount that pile of brick and concrete which had fallen within the fortress. 'We'll have to move it out of the way –' the big stuff, anyway; those big slabs of concrete, for instance '– and we've got to do it without the Germans on the north side suspecting what we're up to.'

Keeping out of sight of that distant machine-gun post wasn't going to be easy, they agreed, and then Sergeant Walker raised the obvious question. 'What about outside, sir? Isn't there rubble there?'

That had given Offer a surprise when he'd first looked down through the gaping hole from the rampart above, and it may possibly have stimulated his imagination. The wall had collapsed inwards, with comparatively little rubble falling outside, yet the shell had exploded within. Still, that was how shells often behaved, dragging objects forward following an explosion, and not outwards as one would suppose.

'Some of the concrete facing's there, but it shouldn't present much trouble if once we can get our Jeeps out through the hole.' It would mean his big men manhandling each Jeep in turn across some awkward overlaying slabs, but he reckoned they'd manage it without much loss of time. Then they'd take a powder across the desert.

O'Keefe said, 'Hold on, sir. What's that Spandau going to do while we shove the Jeeps over the rubble outside. They'll see us –'

'Who says they'll see us?' Captain Offer laughed in his face.

'Something up your sleeve?' The sergeant-major brightened.

'Of course.' But he wouldn't tell them what it was. No time for more talk. Did 'em good, anyway, to make 'em try to think occasionally.

His tone changed. 'Eddie, you and two men get the Jeeps lined up. But shove 'em out: no starting engines, understand?' He didn't want an alert and listening enemy to wonder why they should be manoeuvring vehicles inside the fort in a time of truce. 'And see if any of the Eyetie trucks have survived.' They'd need a couple to take the wounded out. Pom could help his sergeant, he thought; not much good at heaving slabs of concrete, that little griper. But Pom hadn't returned from the air raid shelter. Bloody little shirker, probably having a swallow round some corner.

'Sergeant-major, take the rest of the men and get stuck into that rubble.' When they'd cleared the debris and were ready to take off they'd bring the P.O.W.s up, but not before. The prisoners weren't going out of their custody until they were all set to escape. He remembered something. 'Don't forget, sergeant-major, you're going to blow the place up when we move out.'

'Aye, aye, sir,' said O'Keefe with pleasure, going all nautical.

The men were tearing at the great heap of rubble, dragging the big hunks of concrete away, sometimes having to use bars to lever them. Again his two most powerful men, Cruiser and Busker, were invaluable, their combined strength often achieving what several other men failed to move. But it was a big job, and tiring, and every time Offer glanced at his watch the minutes were racing by.

They were trundling the Jeeps across now, lining them up for the escape. Offer glanced at them. They seemed all ready to move out, every piece of equipment neatly strapped to the tiny vehicles. Ignition keys were already inserted, and he went round switching on but not starting the engines, to ensure that tanks were full of petrol. They'd had one unaccountable lapse, but these vehicles seemed okay.

Part of his mind pondered over Palfreyman as he checked the Jeeps. How were they going to get a man, wounded and unconscious, out to safety? Arab Ward came up to ask the same question. He had his own ideas.

'We'll have to tie him in a stretcher and strap him to the side of a Jeep, sir.' That would mean getting rid of all the equipment fastened to the side.

'It'll be a rough ride for him.'

'He'll survive,' said Ward laconically. A very unemotional man, their Arab-lover. So Offer nodded agreement. 'I'll need a hand, sir.'

Offer crossed to another Jeep, just trundled up, and switched on. 'A hand?' They couldn't spare anyone for the moment. He looked round while the needle crept up and thought, 'Where the devil's Pom?' There was all this work to do and he was keeping well out of the way. He'd give the scrounging little bastard the biggest bloody –

Men were coming up the stairs across by the cistern. Not Pom among them. Blue chins, not British uniforms. Guns. They had guns in their hands. One already coming on to the parade ground, an automatic weapon swinging round to cover the gang labouring on the rubble. No one else seeing them, everyone working too frantically, time going . . .

Offer grabbed Arab Ward and hauled him into the Jeep. fingers closed over the ignition key as he rolled into the driver's seat. The engine roared. Gear in, clutch out and the Jeep leaping forward. Everyone stopping working, astonished, looking at the accelerating Jeep. Ward clawing at the Browning mounting, starting to shout his surprise, then looking ahead. With one heave Ward got behind the gun.

Men were racing up the stairs, beginning to flood out on to the parade ground. All carried guns. All were Italians.

Ward got the Browning going before the leading Italian pressed his trigger. The heavy bullets tore holes into the men still coming out from the steps. John Offer saw them falling, faces twisted in agony as they stopped bullets. He saw others panic and leap back down the stairs to gain the cover of concrete walling. But he saw others, faces level with the top of the stairs, resolutely preparing to fight back, gun barrels shoving out and beginning to fire upon him.

Offer was on top of them before they quite knew what he was up to. He drove straight at the steps, the front wheels bumping as they hit the low concrete kerb that edged the sunken stairway. The Jeep came to a violent halt, settled across the stair-head like a cork in a bottle.

John Offer got out at speed, in case any Italian below decided to fire up through the Jeep floor, and Ward wasn't slow in following him. But no one fired. They'd be too stunned to know what to do in such circumstances.

O'Keefe was racing up, grabbing a gun on the way. Behind him came the rest of the Gang. Within seconds the danger was over. Three wounded Italians writhed on the ground beside the stairs. Maybe, thought Offer, there'd be more wounded or injured men on the stairway. There was space beneath the Jeep, awkwardly suspended across the steps, for a man to crawl out if he had the right suicidal streak within him. Hard-faced British commandos covered it, and from that moment the fight was over.

'A near thing, sir,' said O'Keefe, never taking his eyes off that space. No one showed any inclination to come through.

'A damn' near thing,' agreed Offer, and was aghast to think how close they'd been to having the tables turned against them. If he hadn't turned and spotted the first of the Italians surfacing; if he hadn't been fiddling with a Jeep ignition key; if Ward, first-class gunner, hadn't been standing alongside him . . .

O'Keefe said, 'That Jeep's a write-off, sir.' It did look in a bad way, blocking the stairs.

'Can't be helped.'

How had the Italians got out of their prison? Once out, of course, there were weapons galore below for the collecting. Pom. Offer thought, 'They jumped him, cocky little show-off!'

Wireless operators never were much thought of as fighting men, but Pom appeared to have met a couple who were. He'd have been giving them mouth, being big-headed, full of courage because he had the gun and they seemed helpless. And then they'd jumped him, perhaps just when he was turning the key in the lock.

Captain Offer called below. 'Major?' A voice answered him, rather a sad voice. 'You've had your fun, now stop being silly, or more of your men will get hurt.'

Bloody silly to start a fracas just when the prisoners had a chance to march out of the fortress to freedom. But it must have been tempting, only seventeen men against them. If they could be surprised . . .

Offer thought, 'He's got an incentive.' The Italian commandant. He'd be in for a rough time, allowing his garrison to be captured by so few raiders. A great temptation then, this chance provided by resourceful wireless ops to recapture the place and regain the favour of Higher Command.

He called again, 'I want you to put all your weapons back in the armoury, then return to the air raid shelter. Do that, keep quiet, and I'll still let you march out from here as arranged.'

The commandant was silent.

Very quietly Offer said, 'If you don't I'll start rolling hand grenades down these stairs and there won't be many of you left when we've finished.'

The commandant said, 'All right.' Captain Offer heard him give an order to his men, and there was a sound of movement below and metal clinking.

Offer called again: 'What have you done with my man?'

The Italian had some sense of humour. 'Nothing much. Would you like a word with him? He's beginning to talk – swear, I think.'

'Pom!' Offer made his voice ice-cold.

'Sir!' Pom sounded scared.

'See that the prisoners drop their arms and go into the shelter. Is the key there?' A pause, then Pom's voice shouting it was still in the door. 'Lock 'em in, then come up.'

He turned. That disposed of that, though it had nearly disposed of them. Now there was such a lot to do and time racing madly.

'Back on the job.' His men doubled away, all except Arab Ward who was tending the wounded. Offer looked down on them. These were badly hurt, and there was a lot of blood everywhere. The sooner they were in German hands the better. But he needed another fifteen minutes at least.

From above the main gate Tiffy Jones called down. 'Sir, I think you'd better come up here.'

Offer didn't ask any fool questions, such as, 'Anything wrong?' His men didn't call him up scaling ladders if everything was all right. Oh, Christ, he thought, don't let anything bugger up this plan of ours! It was the only one they'd got.

Tiffy looked a bit bloody but seemed remarkably unaffected by his wound. His bare brown body, heavily muscled, had been equipped by their medical orderly with a bandage which looked like a fragile harness, all designed to keep a field dressing in place under the collar bone. By now it was well-soaked with blood which had attracted a host of flies.

Jones said, 'They're getting active out there, sir.' He waved towards the desert. Offer could see quite a lot of movement, vehicles trundling across the bare land around the fort.

'The sods!' he exclaimed indignantly. His conditions of truce were that the German force must not advance beyond their present positions, but here they were, scout cars and armoured vehicles throwing up dust as they crawled over the sand dunes. Then his anger subsided. After a few seconds he saw that they weren't advancing; changing position, true, but grudgingly he had to admit they weren't coming forward. Then what were they up to?

'When did that begin, Tiffy?'

'Shortly after the Jeep started up and the guns began to go off below.' The enemy would hear it, of course, sound travelling vast distances in that great empty wasteland. 'A scout car began to move from one position to another –' Again he gestured, showing where the enemy occupied hollows. Some sort of conference, thought Offer. 'Then the

86

armoured stuff began to come up into sight, and there they are now.'

A change of strategy, thought Offer, thinning their forces opposed to the big gate, and spreading them around. But what had dictated it? News that a mere handful of British occupied the fortress? Or, and his heart dropped at the thought, had word also come through from the Spandau on the north side that the wall had been breached and could be taken if some resolute attacking force were brought round for the purpose?

Offer thought, 'That's it. That's what all the to-ing and fro-ing's about.' They were getting ready to annihilate them once the P.O.W.s were clear of danger, and the brash occupying force refused to surrender.

He studied the armoured cars a little longer. Just right to come bustling up to that breach and with their Mgs spray inside the fort while the infantry came to take the broken main gate. Offer thought, 'Five minutes after the truce ends our number will be up.'

And then came an even more depressing thought. No longer did they have an hour's truce in which to effect their escape. The column of scout and armoured cars moving in a wide circle around the fort would be in a position to stop their break-out well within the hour.

Offer rolled on to his bottom and sat for a few seconds with his legs dangling over the top of the scaling ladder. He was trying to work out times, and just how long they had before escape became impossible. Seven armoured cars plus other vehicles were moving in line east of the fort; two armoured cars, much farther behind, had started the longer route round the west side. Offer mentally noted that if they were to escape at all they'd have to do it while there was still a gap to the west of them.

But once the armoured vehicles joined forces there'd be a cordon of steel covering the breach in the north wall, and unarmoured Jeeps weren't going to get past them against such a concentrated firepower. The Gang's only chance of getting safely away was to make the break while there was only that solitary machine-gun opposing them from the north, and Offer decided that at the most they now had a mere twenty minutes left to them.

He said, 'Report if you see anything else happening, and when I yell, come down in a hurry.' Tiffy Jones and his mate, Sally Salkirk, nodded. John Offer went down the ladder in a hurry.

He ran – there was no time for officer dignity – across to where the men laboured to move that mountain of rubble, and his heart sank as he saw the small impression their labours had made. Walker and his two helpers had now joined them at shifting debris, but ten men weren't up to the task. 'Might as well quit now,' he thought. They'd never do it before the armoured cars got into position.

Quit? Not until all hope had gone, thought John Offer, angry with himself at the mere thought. If they couldn't get away they would not fight but would surrender, he decided, but by God they'd keep on struggling while ever there was the slightest hope left.

But ten men! Jesus Christ, they just weren't enough! He looked at them. They were flagging already, the sun so hot, the weight of the slabs of concrete strength-sapping as they hauled upon them. Already they were going slower, even the big fellows, much slower. If only they had more men . . .

John Offer shouted, 'Hold it!'

Thankfully they stopped working and stared through sweaty eyebrows at him. 'No good going on like this. We've less time than I thought.' Quickly he told of the encircling armoured cars. 'Our only chance is to get the Eyeties working for us.' At least forty men.

O'Keefe said, sharply for him, 'They won't work fast, sir.' He knew his P.O.W.s. Why should they work at all to help the raiders get away?

'They'll work – hard!' retorted John Offer grimly, and his mind was racing around a whole new set of ideas. By

88

God, it could be done! 'You, sergeant-major, will make 'em work!'

He became a whirlwind of activity, inspiring men who a few minutes before had felt like dropping. 'Lift that Jeep out of the way!'

The big men leapt to it, Cruiser and Busker almost single-handed heaving on the Jeep and finally sending it toppling over the low concrete wall, clearing the stairway.

Pom was there, working with them, letting Offer see the sweat on his face to show he had been as hard at it as the others, trying to make amends for letting a pair of Wop ops jump him. 'You got the key for the prison?' Pom nodded. 'Then down you go and bring the prisoners up jildy. Sergeant Walker, take four men with tommies and if they try any tricks just let 'em have it.' This was their last chance, and nothing must stand in their way now.

Pom shot below, followed by the clattering feet of Walker and his tommy-gunners. John Offer, leaning over the stairway, heard the door open, then a lot of shouting and he began to see prisoners coming into view below. He added to the noise by shouting, *'Presto! Presto!'* and they began to run up the stairs as if in sudden panic at all the noise and the guns pointing.

They came up in a great flock and by this time Offer had all his men in a circle surrounding the stair-head, guns covering the P.O.W.s threateningly. The garrison commander was the last man up the stairs, flatly refusing to run, but mounting the steps all the same.

John Offer addressed them in Italian. 'I have no time to waste,' he told them, 'and if you want to live past the next fifteen minutes, neither have you.' That caused an uncomfortable stir among the Italians.

'See that pile of rubble.' He pointed. 'You're going to shift it to one side and you have ten minutes in which to do it.' The major stepped forward, but Offer shut him up. 'Don't start quoting Geneva Convention to me because you are going to do it. Sergeant-major!'

'Sir!' O'Keefe came smartly forward.

'I want you to go below, and I want you to put a bomb under those petrol tanks timed to go off in exactly fifteen minutes.'

'Sir!' acknowledged O'Keefe enthusiastically and went down those stairs so fast no one heard his feet touching the steps.

Captain Offer turned a cold eye upon the prisoners. 'Now do you understand why I say you will clear that rubble and you will do it fast? You have only ten minutes to do the job. Shift the rubble in that time and you will have five minutes left in which to get yourselves and the wounded out of the fort. If you're slow, we all go up when those tankers explode.'

Some of the Italians panicked and broke ranks, running to begin the work of moving rubble. Offer ordered, 'Watch 'em!' and his men took up positions where the frantically working prisoners could be covered by their tommies and rifles.

The officers hadn't moved, however. Even with this threat they weren't going to sully their hands with labour. Geneva Conventions, thought Offer, but he wasn't bothered about protocol. There were four of them. He said, 'It's up to you, my friends. You have wounded below. There won't be time to get them up these stairs afterwards, even if your men do shift that debris in ten minutes. However, there is no reason why you shouldn't start bringing them up on stretchers and putting them in those trucks over there ready to move out.'

The officers, immaculate in their well-tailored uniforms, looked indignant. Offer repeated, 'I tell you, it's up to you.' His eyes looked directly into the garrison commander's. For a moment there was defiance, then came doubt. He's thinking he and his men can't clear off leaving wounded to be blown up because the officers had left it too late to haul 'em up those stairs. Offer could read the man's mind. All at once the major cracked. Ungraciously he ordered his lieutenants, 'We will bring them up.'

Offer sent two men down with tommies to ensure that no Italian officer again decided to help himself to weapons in the armoury. Pom wasn't one of them. John Offer didn't believe in making the same mistake twice.

In a few minutes he saw the officers, very red-faced, the sweat already beginning to blacken their ritzy uniforms, come struggling up with wounded on stretchers. In fact the four officers alone would never have completed the job in time but the M.O. and his two medical orderlies were also below to give them a hand. Offer had forgotten about the medics.

He saw the stretcher-bearers beginning to hoist the wounded aboard the big Italian trucks, then went back to see how the work on the rubble was getting on. He saw that Cruiser, Busker and some of his big men had joined the Italian prisoners, as if they could not stand idly by holding guns in a time of such urgency. Good men, he thought; difficult at such times to remember what villains they really were.

Offer clambered into the opening in the wall. He could not see the German machine-gunners from where he stood, dug in as they would be, but had no doubt they could see him, surveying the desert from the gap in the north wall. He took a few cautious steps out on to the rubble beyond and looked to his right. The armoured vehicles were just coming into view. He doubted if the Gang had ten minutes left. A glance the other way was more reassuring: the two armoured cars weren't in sight. Still space for them in which to make their escape westward, he thought, then looked back and despaired yet again. For all the strenuous efforts of the Italians, there was still a lot of rubble to shift.

O'Keefe came up from the underground storeroom. 'Everything okay?' Offer asked.

'She'll go up so high they'll see it in Tobruk,' O'Keefe assured him. Now they had a time bomb ticking away beneath their feet. It wasn't a pleasant sensation. Nothing, in fact, was very pleasant at that moment, the race being on, the armoured vehicles steadily reducing their chances of a break-out, and everywhere men working at frantic pace, yet seeming to make no progress.

John Offer, 'Take over, sergeant-major. I'm going below.' He knew what to look for, and it was better he did his own last-minute shopping, he thought.

When he came running back up the steps a few minutes later, his arms full of canisters, he knew they had no more time left to them. Without looking across the desert again, he guessed the armoured pincers were closing around the fort and it was now or never if they were to escape.

O'Keefe ran across, recognizing those tins. 'So that's the idea, sir.'

'They worked well enough at Sharafim; we'll have to try 'em again here.' And their lives now depended on the contents of those containers.

'Get the guard down, sergeant-major.' O'Keefe ran off, bellowing up at Tiffy and Salkirk. Captain Offer went across to the trucks where the last of the stretchers was being hoisted aboard. The Italian officers did not look so immaculate now, sweating and harassed and greeting his arrival with looks of sullen bad temper.

'Major, get these trucks out of the fortress without delay. We have about six minutes left.' There was some wooden debris blocking the way through the gate. 'Better get that cleared so that the trucks can get through.' The commandant's officers leapt to the task, working frantically. It didn't take long under their frenetic efforts.

'Start up.' The medical orderlies clambered into the cabs and the engines roared into life. Offer said, 'Not you,' as an Italian lieutenant started to board a truck. The officers would remain with their men and march out with them. He waved the trucks on, and they got into gear and ground their way out through the shattered gateway, then accelerated madly so as to get as far from the doomed fortress as possible.

Offer said, 'Come on, double!' He took the Italian officers

back at a run to the gap in the wall. One glance and he saw that now his Jeeps *could* get out of the fortress though they'd have to be helped a bit inside the wall and even more so outside.

O'Keefe was standing there, holding a canister and looking across at him. Captain Offer made a signal with his thumb. That was all that was needed. O'Keefe began to run towards the gap, unscrewing the canister top. Behind him came Wise and Wilborn, doing things to canisters, too.

Offer shouted, 'Stop work! Get the Jeeps out!' His men leapt to the line of waiting Jeeps. One man only climbed aboard each vehicle and started the engines. The rest grouped round, ready to manhandle them if they failed to clear the remaining rubble. Engines revving, the first of the Jeeps beginning to charge the gap, men running beside it.

Black smoke suddenly poured out across the desert.

'You!' Offer pointed to the Italian commandant. 'Scram! Get your men out of here at the double!' A glance at his watch. 'You've got four minutes left.' Then everything would go up.

No one waited for an order from the major. At Offer's words every Italian there began to race for the gate, officers included. Only the commandant refused to make an undignified exit. He saluted Captain Offer. 'I hope we meet again.'

Offer's eyes twinkled. 'I hope we don't. *Avanti!*' He turned from the major, no more time to waste on him. The major trotted sedately after his men.

O'Keefe was hurling another canister out on to the desert. Dense black smoke was rolling skyward, drifting and spreading, obscuring the fortress. 'No one will see the gap from out there,' Offer thought.

The first of the Jeeps was manhandled through the gap in the wall. Offer saw it disappear, then the smoke swirled round them, highly uncomfortable, and another Jeep went bumping and roaring out on to the desert. Six Jeeps. The last drove out. Offer ran with it, giving a hand when it got stuck outside the gap.

No shot was fired as they made their escape. No enemy eye could penetrate that smoke screen. And O'Keefe in the leading Jeep would be hurling more smoke canisters out as he went, and what breeze there was would be favourable to them, drifting the smoke towards the machine-gun on the desert . . .

They ran out of the smoke within a few hundred yards. The German Mg saw the Jeeps come scudding into the open, and didn't bother about some truce time being left. It opened up and tracer came skipping low over the sand. O'Keefe's Browning leapt into action and tracer went searching back to find the German Mg.

O'Keefe, driving, used all the cunning he had ever acquired in dozens of escapes. He sought for depressions in the desert, however shallow, presenting as little target as possible to the hidden machine-gun. Every yard gained took them farther from that Spandau. Even so there were long, agonizing moments when they had to ride fully exposed on some bare, sloping sand dune, and then the tracer fairly flew after them.

O'Keefe made it, getting out of range, and for those behind it became successively easier. The leading Jeeps built up their own smoke screen, their spinning wheels hurling up the dust and creating a great spreading cloud. Yet one Jeep caught a packet just when they thought they were all going to make it.

Captain Offer, clinging on and staring through the dust ahead, saw tracer hit their fifth Jeep. It caught it low down which was fortunate for the occupants, but the bullets halted it, and a lot of metal went flying and the crew bailed out as if scalded.

Sally Salkirk manning Offer's Browning shouted, 'Oh, Christ, it would have to be that one!' and only then did John Offer realize that the stricken Jeep was the one to which the injured Palfreyman was strapped.

Offer could see the stretcher through the swirling dust.

Thank God it was on the blind side, away from the German Mg. Driver Lashley, without telling, came at a run alongside the fifth Jeep and braked hard. The Kraut machine-gun was still ripping off in bursts at the halted Jeep, and any moment Offer expected it to take fire.

The crew were frantically unstrapping Palfreyman's stretcher. Offer leapt out with Salkirk to aid them. Tracer hurtled round and the air was filled with the nasty sound of unseen bullets zipping by. It all lent speed to their hands.

Suddenly the stretcher dropped. Palfreyman moaned and tried to move but was too securely bound in. Captain Offer grabbed one end, hugging Palfreyman's feet in his arms; the other end was lifted. Palfreyman was shoved across the kit in the back of Offer's Jeep under the Browning.

'Hang on!' yelled Offer, and everyone grabbed hold of something while the over-burdened Jeep began to move away.

They lost the others then. Lashley turned at right angles so as to keep the wrecked Jeep between them and the German machine-gun. Laden as they were they couldn't get out of second gear and seemed to be crawling, an easy target if the Kraut gunner could see them.

They ran out of the lingering dust cloud. Some bigger dunes now, giving them cover. A sigh of relief as they dropped down a shoulder of sand, then started to follow the depression at the foot of it. Offer sat up and looked round for the other four Jeeps. Must divide some of this load quickly if they were to get away from this unhealthy area . . .

Two armoured cars were scooting down the dune to the left of them, intent on cutting them off.

Offer yelled, pointing, and Sally Salkirk got the warning, swung round, saw, and the Browning was hammering away in a fraction of a second. Brownings against armoured cars? Offer thought, 'Not up to it.' Even heavy Browning bullets weren't going to penetrate the thick metal hide of the German armoured cars. Speed. That was their only chance.

And Lashley couldn't get it into third.

They were climbing, the sand a bit loose under their weight, the wheels not always gripping so that there were seconds of spin and losing speed and sand and dust going up behind them. Oh, God, breathed Offer, let's get over the top!

But they weren't there; the top seemed miles away, and the car was groaning and struggling still in second. The air was filled with the sound of bullets chasing by, missing them but by no more than a cock hair. The two armoured cars were swinging across the face of the dune, trying to maintain height so as to catch them at an angle. Twin machine-guns in each turret tried to compensate for the heaving of heavy vehicles over uneven ground; bullets streaming out, almost settling on the fleeing Jeep then tantalizingly snatching away as their armoured cars hit a hollow or twisted to avoid some more formidable hazard.

But it couldn't last. The cars weren't gaining on them, but the Jeep was well within range and as sure as God made little apples those Spandaus would start to find their target . . .

The ground tremored. A shock wave hit them. The Jeep seemed to be hurled up towards the ridge, and a weight of sound assailed them that left them stunned, their ears ringing. Offer thought, 'What it must be like in one of those sardine cans!' Bad enough in the open.

He twisted round to stare back. Fort Telatha was now approximately two hundred feet into the air and much of it was still climbing. O'Keefe's time bomb had done the trick. Two huge tanks of petrol and hundreds of tons of ammunition and other explosives had been detonated, exploding almost simultaneously. Fort Telatha simply disintegrated.

Huge lumps of debris were flying above the place where a fort had been. Black smoke was tearing into the sky at astonishing speed, and a fire hundreds of feet high was fuelling everything.

Offer looked, photographing the scene in a fraction of a second, then turned towards the armoured cars.

They had come to a halt. On the side of the dune they would be more exposed to the blast than the Jeep, climbing out of the hollow. It must have been stunning to the crew inside, reverberating within the confines of their steel chamber. Perhaps for a few seconds they were too dazed to do anything but halt and try to recover their senses. It was Offer's chance to get away.

Lashley had never even eased his foot on the accelerator, though he was driving now with his head slewed round, gazing in awe at that tremendous pyre behind them. The Jeep was crawling towards the top of the ridge. Almost there. There. Going downhill and the wheels accelerating merrily. The armoured cars out of sight. Only the huge cloud of smoke over Telatha visible.

Safe.

They found O'Keefe and the other Jeeps half an hour later. Each spotted the other's dust cloud and homed in on it. They came together. They were very tired men.

Lashley drove alongside O'Keefe's Jeep, then switched off. Captain Offer looked into the strained red face of his sergeant-major. 'You did your work well, Angus, my friend.' He did not even need to jerk his head to indicate the burning Fort Telatha.

For a few seconds they sat, some of them watching the conflagration, others too weary even to be distracted by the giant pyrotechnics behind them. John Offer spoke again. He was tired, tired of all this running away and destruction at the end of it. He said, 'I think I've had about enough of the desert, sergeant-major.'

O'Keefe looked at him, but without understanding. So Offer pulled himself together, slowly hauled himself out of his uncomfortable seat and stepped on to the desert.

'Let's make Palfreyman more comfortable, then get on the move again.' No sense in staying where they were. For all they knew, vengeful armoured cars might be breasting that last rise right at this moment, though Offer doubted it. He thought, 'Fort Telatha doesn't exist any more. Those Krauts are more needed on the coast road. They won't hang around after this.' Seventeen awkward desert raiders weren't worth chasing.

The Jeeps were too crowded for comfort with the spare crews dispersed among the remaining five cars. John Offer, though, told them to hold on to their seats because they weren't going to travel for long. He set a course south-west for half an hour, then swept round and headed east again. His men, minds dulled by fatigue and long hours of tension, never knew which way they were going.

Before dusk John Offer found their place of haven. Black smudges danced for a time on the horizon, then gradually resolved into palm trees. The men took a greater interest at that, and finally they came into a fertile oasis and halted where there was water.

Someone had the strength to ask, 'Where are we, sir?'

'Telatha Oasis,' said Offer. The last place an enemy would surely expect them to be, right back on the scene of their last activities. Here he was certain they would be safe; and here they could camp and stretch their weary limbs and try to find peace for minds too long obsessed by nearness to death.

They had a brew up. Nobody wanted to eat. Rest, that was all they craved for. A drink satisfying their parched insides, they flopped to the ground and sparked out in seconds. Sally Salkirk, who hadn't laboured in that terrible heat on that mountainous rubble, alone was left on watch. Ward made Palfreyman comfortable, then slept beside his patient.

Tired though he was, John Offer could not get to sleep immediately. He made a last tour of their little camp, making sure everything was all right, and as he did so looking down on each of his men in turn. He saw the haggard faces of old, old men still taut even in sleep, still unable to relax, bodies twitching, sometimes moaning. Old men, every one of them, yet only two – O'Keefe and Wilborn – apart from himself were over twenty-five.

He thought, 'I'm no different.' The strain of this life they led would show on him, too. The ashes of disillusionment were in his mind, exhausted by their recent ordeal. He remembered his words to O'Keefe – 'I think I've had about enough of the desert, sergeant-major.' He had. Now he wanted to get out of Africa and its tormenting desert. He wanted an end to his involvement with war, and the sight of death, and his own part in destruction. War was for immature minds; all he craved for now was peace. Memory flooded back and he thought of St. Martin's Lane and its old theatres, of the Strand and more theatres, Shaftesbury Avenue and Leicester Square, and he wanted to weep from sheer nostalgia.

'I've had enough.'

Right then he made the decision that Africa was no place for him and he was going home. He lowered his tired body to the ground and went to sleep.

When the German forces regrouped, the last to drive in over the desert were the two armoured cars which had almost trapped John Offer's Jeep. From one of them descended a tall, hard-looking Hauptmann, who strode purposefully across to where his commanding officer was standing, and saluted him.

He made his report, little different from others the Oberst had received. He had made contact with the enemy and had opened fire upon one Jeep, but they had got away apparently unscathed.

Then the Hauptmann reported something further, which was interesting. He had trained his glasses on that fleeing Jeep and had recognized one man in the passenger seat.

'Those raiders are the ones known as the Glasshouse Gang, Herr Oberst. The man I recognized was their officer, Hauptmann John Offer.'

The Oberst was startled. He knew the name. Field-marshal Rommel had given orders that this particular gang of desert raiders must be captured almost at any cost, and their leader, Glasshouse John, was the man most wanted of all. Twice Offer had been in German hands – once he had given himself up in an effort to save his fleeing men, hampered by badly injured comrades. That time it was this Hauptmann who had held him prisoner, but on both occasions by brilliant resource the wily Offer had escaped from them.

It hadn't gone well for Hauptmann Braunschweig, that escape, for the field-marshal had been very unpleasant about the incident. Hauptmann Braunschweig's Special Task Force, recruited specifically to pursue raiders like the S.A.S., L.R.D.G., and the Glasshouse Gang, had been broken up. In fairness to the Hauptmann it would soon have been disbanded, anyway, because Rommel could read the signs and knew he would shortly have need for every man at the front to try to hold a rampaging Eighth Army.

The Hauptmann did not suffer demotion, but probably lost some opportunity of promotion. He was a fine soldier, the Oberst thought, and in spite of that black mark against him it wouldn't be long before the field-marshal improved his rank.

'A pity you weren't quicker and cut them off.' The Oberst was not reproving his Hauptmann; it was his own decision which was at fault. When the machine-gun post reported a hole blown in the north wall he ought immediately to have sent out his armoured units. Instead he had wasted time trying to decide if moving them would be a breach of the truce.

'I would like to follow them, Herr Oberst.'

The colonel shook his head. He quite understood his

Hauptmann's feelings – poor Braunschweig would want to kill or capture Offer in order to expunge that stain upon his reputation. 'We have our orders.'

Those orders were to take Telatha regardless of what might happen to any Italian prisoners. Destroy the enemy, garrison the fort with those Italians, then rejoin their Panzer division at Sidi Rezegh. Rommel, driving, thrusting man, had told them they had thirty-six hours in which to do all this and get back to Rezegh. No time, then, for any desert chase.

'I understand.' Hauptmann Braunschweig's face showed nothing of any emotions within. He had his orders and he accepted them. Within an hour the column was on its way towards the coast.

But as Hauptmann Braunschweig's armoured car pulled away from the dust of preceding vehicles, he turned to look back at the still blazing, smoking Fort Telatha, then his eyes travelled the short distance across the dunes to where the drooping palms of the oasis shimmered in the distorting heat.

Practically the whole of the native inhabitants of Telatha seemed to be grouped there on the edge of the oasis. They'd be staring in awe and fascination at the white man's powers of destruction, and when the Germans had departed and they had found more courage they would come up to the ruins to see what might be looted.

The Hauptmann, however, gave little thought to Arabs. His eyes for some reason kept returning to those palm trees. Some curious thought had come to him that perhaps right at that moment his old adversary might be comfortably esconced within the greenery. It was just the kind of effrontery which had given Glasshouse John his reputation with the Afrika Korps.

Hauptmann Braunschweig turned, scoffing at the idea, and yet somehow it lingered, somewhere in the back of his mind. When they crested a last high dune and saw Telatha Oasis before it finally disappeared from view, Braunschweig thought, 'Some day I'm going to return there.' He wanted to know if his hunch was right.

Captain Offer gave his men three days in which to recover their strength – time, too, for him to reconsider the decisions he was making – before he addressed them on the subject. In that time he had personally reccied the fort, or what remained, still burning, of it, and assured himself that the enemy had indeed pulled back to the coast.

The Arabs had found them, and were friendly when they learned they were British, having no great opinion of Italians as colonizers. Telatha Oasis was truly a safe place to be, and for men just out of the desert a most pleasant one. But soon they would get restless. John Offer spoke to them before that mood caught them – he talked to them while they were ready and willing to listen to his arguments.

He picked his time carefully. It was after their evening meal, the best of the day, a meal of chicken and fresh vegetables bartered for cigarettes off eager Arab boys. They gorged and then lay back, the less fastidious belching to show loud appreciation of Wise and Redpath's cooking.

It was the right kind of night, anyway, to talk men into a mood of wanting to go home. There was an early moon and a star-littered heaven above. Palm trees, ever a magical symbol to men of colder climes, drooped in graceful silhouette against a night sky of burnished serenity. Weybright had tuned in to London and there was a Cockney programme on, full of Old Kent Road, and Knees Up Muvver Brah'n, and then the lilting Lambeth Walk. John Offer had them half-way to agreeing to anything before he opened his mouth.

He talked to them, standing so that all could see him, his followers sprawling on sand silkily soft and still warm from the day's sun-soaking. In that light they didn't look so rough: some had shaved, others had trimmed vagrant beards, and all had dhobied their much-worn uniforms. They didn't smell so strongly now, either. And Palfreyman was there, sitting up and taking nourishment, liquid because of the smashed teeth and hole in his cheek. Must get him to an army dentist, Offer thought.

His first words made them sit up. He told them, very clearly, 'You're dead men, all of you. Dead, d'you hear? You died three days –' He peered at the luminous hands of his watch – 'five and a half hours ago.'

No one spoke, each man there too polite to say the old man had finally gone off his nut.

'You died when Telatha blew up, and some day – perhaps soon – it's going to be entered in your army records: "Believed killed in action at Fort Telatha".' His mood changed to one of briskness. 'All we have to do, chums, from now on is to keep our noses clean, keep out of the hands of Red Caps, and the army'll go on believing we are dead meat in the desert. Telatha may have done us a lot of good.'

It took time for his words to sink through the thicker minds of some of the men, like his gorillas, Busker and Cruiser, for instance, but eventually they all arrived at understanding. Then they sat up, keenly alert, seeing possibilities of turning this to advantage.

Captain Offer saw he had them, and cunningly changed tack.

'Chaps, I'm browned off with war. I don't know about you, but I've had it. It's been great fun, all this desert romping, and I wouldn't have missed it for anything.'

Or missed knowing this comradeship with these men of his. That was about the only good that came out of war, this marvellous sense of comradeship.

'But it's as if I've suddenly run out of steam. I now feel that I don't want to go through another desert safari, or another Telatha again.' He shuddered, thinking back. Telatha had nearly been the death of all of them.

'I'm homesick. God, what would I do to see London again!' The familiar streets, the barrow boys, the strolling crowds of pleasure-seekers, the odours of cooking around

Soho. And the wonderful English bints, better than this brown stuff tattooed down to their thingummies. He knew that his men, even the non-Londoners, right then were nostalgically dreaming as he was. 'I've had all I want of Africa and I intend to go home.'

Someone croaked, 'Count me in on that, sir,' and there was a stir and growling words of approval. John Offer relaxed, knowing he was carrying his men, even the desert-enamoured O'Keefe, with him.

'I've been doing a lot of thinking, these past three days. Once Cairo get the idea into their heads that we went up with Telatha the heat goes off. They won't be looking for us. We'll be dead, and you don't look for dead deserters. And what applies out here, applies to civvy life, too.' No cops looking for them.

They lay there, listening in silence, but their hearts beat faster when they thought of what it could mean to them.

'The desert war's nearly over.' Not one of them had a doubt about that. This time Monty's army was going to chase Rommel right out of Africa, and nightly the war news from the B.B.C. spoke of a rapid advance along the Mediterranean coast. 'Anyway, when the army hops over into Europe *we* can't stop here. Too damned conspicuous. We'll have to get out of Africa then, somehow. So I say, don't let's wait, let's clear out now and get back to Blighty.'

It wouldn't be quite straightforward, of course. In war-time England they'd need identity cards, clothing coupons, ration books – and new names. All could somehow be managed by these men, all were first-rate scroungers. Busker and Cruiser would disappear easiest, among their fairground brethren; Wise and Wilborn, wide boys, would go their happy ways unworried; Eddie Walker, Jack Redpath, Sally Salkirk knew how to look after themselves. Palfreyman might have problems because he came of a middle-class family. Pom . . . Pom with his yapping mouth could get himself and all the others into trouble. But that was one risk they had to take.

He told them his plan. 'We lie low here in Telatha until Monty captures Benghazi.' Offer had a loving French-woman in that city and before he left Africa he must love her at least once again. 'Benghazi will become our principal port. Ships will sail there with supplies from all parts of the world, and some will return to London empty. We're going back on one of them.'

'How?' asked Pom, niggly little bastard, and it annoyed some of the others. If Captain Offer said they were going back to Blighty in style aboard a steamship, they all knew he'd somehow fix it and it wasn't necessary for Pom to know the details.

Good-humouredly John Offer answered him. 'Right now I haven't a clue, but let me get down to the harbourside at Benghazi and you bet I'll dream up a way of getting us passage home!' If he could get them in and out of a Glass-house, talking his way aboard ship was as easy as falling off a log.

That night, then, became one of decision. From then on they were committed to leaving the desert. Now they listened avidly to every B.B.C. news bulletin, each day care-fully marking the progress of Monty's Eighth Army on their only much-stained map.

An aircraft with Allied markings, clearly on reconnais-sance, flew over the still-smouldering Fort Telatha two days after the men learned they were all dead. They watched it from the shelter of the palms, no man going out to wave to it. That night Weybright came to say that Cairo was trying to call up Captain Offer.

John Offer said, 'The aircraft's reported that Fort Telatha's no more. If we don't answer their signal, that's when they'll begin to assume we're no more, either.' So Weybright maintained radio silence thereafter.

In Cairo a big, lumpish major-general said, 'They've bought it.' He looked up at Captain Tansley from the fan of aerial photographs in his hand. 'Christ, someone did a right job on Telatha. No use to Rommel now.'

'Who bought it?' Tansley was not always able to follow the meanderings of his C.O.'s mind.

The major-general was irritated by Tansley's obtuseness. Very testily, 'Why, Offer and his gang. Who else were we talking about?' Tactfully Tansley forebore to say that Glasshouse John's name hadn't been mentioned in half an hour.

'You think they went up with Telatha, sir?'

'What else can we assume?' Tansley was interested to note that his superior's voice held a distinct quality of gloom. 'You know Offer by now. Tell me, if he had pulled off this one – blown up the fort – wouldn't he have been on the air in no time bragging about it? Has he ever failed to come through when he's done something big? He doesn't answer our signals, and I regard that as ominous.'

Some accident, the m-g was thinking. Someone careless and the whole bloody place going up in smoke, the Gang with it.

'He was in such good heart when we last heard from him.' Fierce eyes peered up through barbed wire brows. 'Remember, Roger? Told me to get stuffed, cheeky young sod.' But he reminisced without malice now, and his aide thought, 'The poor old chap's grieving.' What a love–hate relationship existed between the m-g and the impudent Offer!

'You almost had a stroke when that last signal came through,' Tansley could have reminded his boss, sagging over his desk. Now apparently all was forgiven by death.

'They've had their chips, Roger,' the m-g said, and he had to rise and go for a drink in the generals' bar. He needed it, for he had something on his conscience. That arrangement for the Gang to be flown out with the useless Mussolini – perversely the m-g had altered that plan. Shouldn't have finagled that immunity out of me, though, just to get a pal out of clink, he thought, but the excuse didn't satisfy him. In leaving them to get out of the desert under their own steam he had condemned them to death.

'He was a good chap,' the m-g finally, astonishingly, told

his fellow generals, alcohol bringing on the sentiment. 'Bloody good bloke, y'know.'

'Glasshouse John?' Thin lines of severity round the mouths of Brass sipping Tom Collins. 'A rogue, an undisciplined villain.' And finally the ultimate in condemnation, for if all soldiers behaved like Offer generals would be out of a job: 'A damned deserter!'

The m-g looked at them coldly, and then, not for the first time, delivered himself of a heresy. 'Give me men like Glasshouse John and I'd win the war before you could say bullshit and Brasso.'

He lifted his glass. 'To poor old Glasshouse John.' No one would drink with him. He knocked back his ice-cold drink. 'I'm going to miss him, the young bastard.'

There came a day in early November 1942 when suddenly the Desert Rats gained the heights above Sollum Bay. All at once they were there, swarming like locusts, fierce men who had long smarted under the indignity of defeat and were intent on retrieving their honour.

Before the ferocity of this mailed attack the Axis armies were routed and put into disorder; they pulled themselves together, however, and fought back with courage and parallel savagery. But they were on the retreat, relentlessly hammered by Montgomery's big new tanks and guns, and assaulted night and day by Allied aircraft, masters of the sky over the North African battlefields.

Close to Sidi Rezegh one of the most savage battles of the North African campaign was fought out to a bitter end. The land was a place of mangled men and vehicles, with black smoke rising in tall columns as far as the eye could see. Still there was no holding Monty's men, and once again there came a moment when the Axis force collapsed and disintegrated, small units racing from the field to save themselves if only to fight again. Some ran into traps, and died or were taken prisoner by the tens of thousands; others, luckier, stern in their purpose, pulled back, intending to regroup and make yet another stand south of Tobruk or Gazala.

The Hauptmann's regiment fought with all the skill and courage of the famed Afrika Korps, but finally it too was overrun and scattered. Braunschweig found himself having to turn and pull back, though fighting a rearguard action to enable other units of the regiment to limp away to safety.

When night came so welcomely the Hauptmann found himself with three other armoured cars only. He did not know where the rest of his regiment was. They went into leaguer for the night, making a fire and cooking a meal. Everywhere across the desert small flames flickered, other fires where other groups of men cooked food before sleeping the sleep of the exhausted. Some would be Allied, others German or Italian. No one bothered to find out. With darkness, the game ended, an unspoken truce existing between warring men which would end with daylight. We'll let you sleep if you don't bother us, that was the idea at such times, so everyone slept except Braunschweig.

He was the man who next day had to make decisions for his tiny unit. He sat for a long time looking at his map by firelight, pondering on their next move. His appreciation of the situation was that this time the field-marshal wouldn't try to hold Tobruk. If that were so it wasn't much good trying to head north for the coast. South of Gazala would more likely be the gathering ground, for here was a short cut across the escarpment to Benghazi and Agheila, the trail known as Trig-el-Abd. It would have to be defended. Bir Hakeim would be the next big battleground, he thought, and then his eye fell upon another name on the map. It was Fort Telatha, no more than ten miles south of their present position.

Telatha. Hauptmann Braunschweig sat staring at the dying flames in the fire-can. That name so strongly associated in his mind with Hauptmann Offer.

He remembered the curious instinct which had come to him, staring at the palm trees at Telatha, that John Offer would impudently return to the oasis. He remembered, too, his own half-resolve some day to find out if that instinct had been true.

It niggled in his mind, not letting him sleep. The longer he thought about it, the more obsessional it became to detour and see what he could learn in Telatha Oasis.

They weren't ten miles away; they were down on water, and there was plenty in the oasis. It wasn't all that out of the way to Bir Hakeim.

Suddenly he made up his mind. 'Tomorrow we'll take a look at Telatha.' After that he slept.

It was a cushy number, Telatha Oasis. Chicken every day. All the water they needed. Slumbering and playing cards and cheering to the heartening news on the radio, with guard duty only two hours on and six hours off.

Cushy, but wary Captain Offer was tight on discipline.

They had pitched camp a couple of hundred yards into the oasis, where the palms grew thickly and there was a depression in the dry sandy soil which hid them from view most effectively. The Jeeps were drawn up facing all directions, so that in case of attack the Brownings could go into action with the minimum of delay.

. . . Brownings? Four Brownings and one Breda now. Sergeant-major O'Keefe had fallen in love with the Italian weapon and had brought one out of Telatha with him.

Offer posted two sentries, one on watch on the open side across the desert, the other overlooking a well-worn camel trail that wound through the oasis. He stressed vigilance, for they were still deep in enemy country, and while they were on watch guards must not fraternize with natives. These could come to the edge of the camp, but O'Keefe chased them away when they went up to his sentries.

Vigilance was maintained, even off duty, around the camp. Captain Offer told his men they must be in such a state of preparedness that if need be they could leap into their Jeeps and drive off without any need for packing.

Everything went back into the Jeeps immediately after use. Even fire-cans remained slung on their vehicles, petrol too precious to be used for cooking, anyway, and dead palm branches providing excellent material for open fires.

And every day the Jeeps were checked to ensure mechanical efficiency, and the engines were always started and run for a while to top up the batteries. The Gang weren't going to be caught short for lack of a little care and maintenance.

And yet they were caught out, shortly after dawn, ten days after going into camp in Telatha Oasis. Perhaps it was because it was an awkward time – these days of ease, men lingered in their blankets, unlike the time of desert travel when it was best for them to be moving while the morning was cool. Breakfast was a leisurely affair, too, conducted over a period of time; for after all wasn't this a rest camp? So when Hauptmann Braunschweig came, some men were breakfasting off fried-up remains from the previous night's supper, while others were sitting up in their beds, yawning and scratching themselves.

The guard had been changed promptly at six o'clock, Sergeant Walker seeing to it himself. Jack Redpath was posted to watch along the winding camel track, while his oppo, Sally Salkirk, leaned against a tree and scanned the brightening desert.

An hour after daylight the Germans came. Redpath later swore that all in one second suddenly they were there within fifty yards of him. He said he'd been looking along the trail, then turned to look the other way, and there, hideously close, was an armoured monster, an Afrika Korps patrol car, and not a tin-pot Kubelwagen either.

But armoured cars made a noise, they objected afterwards. These came stealing silently up towards him, he averred vigorously, but that was nonsense. Either Redpath was a negligent sentry or the cars were a damned sight farther than fifty yards from him when he spotted them. Probably the latter.

Momentarily negligent or not, Redpath did the right

thing. He yelled, 'Oh, sod me!' and fired his rifle.

Every man in the camp went into action. No waste of time for mess tins and blankets. Startled shouts, half-naked forms leaping towards the Jeeps. Engines starting, guns swinging. Redpath and Sally racing in, Redpath with his face looking wild, still shocked by that startling sight. The Jeeps moving, but no one knowing which way to go or what to do, John Offer as much as his men.

Then Redpath came pounding up to where they waited, poised and tense, taking long strides down the soft slope of the depression. 'Armoured cars!' he began to yell as soon as he saw them. 'Krauts!'

John Offer for one moment looked to where Sally Salkirk was scuttling up. Sally looked startled but not panicky like Redpath and that told Offer all he wanted to know. Sally knew no more about the situation than he, therefore there was no threat from the desert.

'Pull out!' he yelled, and waved towards the open desert. He had just got out the order when machine-guns began to lace the trees around them. Something was moving above the slope, a steel turret turning. Twin guns rattled, making a furious din after the silence of the morning, tracer telling of the flight of deadly unseen bullets.

The Jeeps scattered, drivers going through their gears like madmen, wheels spinning before gripping and throwing up the dust. Their Brownings and the Breda beginning to rip off, all concentrating on that turret, lurching towards them, growing bigger. The armoured car stopped moving suddenly, as if the concentrated fire had done some damage to driver or vehicle – lucky shooting – but other turrets were showing, moving and lifting high enough to enable their guns to bear upon the startled Gang. And solid fire began to pour into the hollow.

Skidding furiously, the Jeeps rushed the slope. Four got to the top. The fifth took all the fire. Tiffy Jones' bandaged body caught a lot of it and he died instantly. Charley Crookshank was driving and he died, too, and the Jeep seemed to do a somersault on the slope and went rolling back down it, the engine cutting abruptly.

Arab Ward and Sergeant-major O'Keefe had scrambled aboard this particular Jeep and they were thrown out but had the sense to lie still because they knew they'd die if they attracted fire.

The other Jeeps were luckier, and went over the top and began to dodge at crazy speed between the palms. It wasn't any good firing back at that speed, with the Jeeps throwing them all over the place, so everyone just clung on. Then the armoured cars came on round the rim of the depression, their guns hammering furiously all the time. Bullets zipped sickeningly close to the fleeing Jeeps, and the Gang crouched lower, hearing them and seeing the splinters of wood torn out of palm trees that gave them protection.

The desert. The Jeeps plunged out from the trees and took to the open land. Instantly they scattered, no word of command being needed. Four dodging, swerving Jeeps tore at fastest speed over the depressingly flat desert. In every one men crouched and prayed, hoping they'd get out of range before the slower armoured cars broke from the trees and opened up on them.

They were six or seven hundred yards out into the desert when the first of the German machine-guns again came into action. Dispersing saved them, that and the evasive tactics each driver resorted to. Tracer shot after one Jeep – it was Offer's – and nearly got it first time. Offer, driving, threw the Jeep into a skid, pulled out of it and was twenty yards out of his original line of flight in two seconds. The machine-gun tracer swept after them, so Offer went into another skid and again the bullets missed and by now they had increased their range to eight hundred yards.

Then the other armoured cars must have cleared the oasis, for the fire became heavier, for some reason all concentrating on Offer's Jeep. Offer used every bit of ingenuity to keep out of the path of those deadly missiles, but in spite of this they raked the side of the Jeep and water and petrol poured out of mangled jerricans and Cruiser took some flying metal splinters in his face. Then a tyre went and the Jeep lost speed.

At this moment they ran into a shallow depression that wound a brief way across the desert, and the firing swung from Offer on to the other Jeeps. But distance had been made in that vital half-minute. They were all over half a mile out from the oasis now and still dodging and swerving and presenting a most difficult target for the German gunners. Another few seconds and they too were out of danger, finding cover amid some rolling ground. Only Offer and his Jeep were in danger.

John Offer thought, 'They're sure to follow us.' Of course they would, especially if they realized that one of the Jeeps was running on a flat tyre. So he kept his foot hard down on the accelerator, though it did no good to the wheel and its tyre, keeping up the best speed possible along that winding depression.

It began to peter out. Instinct told Offer that within seconds they would be riding up on top of the desert again, in full view of pursuers who would see their distress. Then they would be after them like relentless wild dogs.

He braked. The damned wheel must be changed. He didn't need to give any orders; his companions knew what to do.

Cruiser, his face pouring blood, leapt out and grabbed the back of the Jeep ready to lift it. John Offer suddenly realized he had another wounded man with him – Palfreyman had been manning the Browning in its brief burst of activity within the oasis.

Offer grabbed the tool kit and hurled himself at the offending wheel. Palfreyman swung the Browning to deter, even briefly, any armoured car which hove in sight. Not that their solitary Browning would do much to hold back steel-plated vehicles, he thought.

The nuts loosened, he shouted, 'Now!' and Cruiser exerted his great strength and lifted the back of the Jeep.

The wheel off, a replacement shoved on and the nuts tightening. Cruiser's strength suddenly running out and the Jeep dropping, but it didn't matter, the wheel was firm enough . . .

Armoured cars rolling up parallel to the depression, three of them, and simultaneously seeing them. Offer leaping back to the wheel, Cruiser, gasping, rolling in under Parfreyman's Browning. Palfreyman letting go with a long burst and undoubtedly hitting the advancing cars, though not visibly damaging them.

The Jeep starting again, ducking madly to escape the bullets, the chase on once more. Death raining round them for a few seconds, but missing because of the speed with which Offer took off. Offer desperately charging a long bank as their only way of escape. A bit of a razor edge and they flew into space and Palfreyman and Cruiser were both flung together and bled on to each other, Palfreyman's cheek bursting open again.

But safe. The bank of sand and earth behind them for a few minutes, and in that time the Jeep scudding quickly out of range. Lifting himself off the groaning Palfreyman, Cruiser peered back and saw three armoured cars breast the bare mound a long way behind. They opened fire at long range, but it was a futile burst and did no damage. The armoured cars stayed where they were on the ridge, making no move now to pursue the faster Jeeps. Cruiser tapped his captain on the shoulder, shouting, 'Ease up, sir! They're not following.'

With a sight of relief Offer let his foot come up off the accelerator and brought the speed down to something more controllable on that rugged surface.

Five more minutes running steadily south, to a point where a halt would be no incitement for armoured vehicles to resume pursuit, Offer let the engine die and pulled on the handbrake. Then he sat at the wheel, not moving for a few seconds, and tried not to feel disheartened.

The moment they stopped, the heat of the desert rose

around them; sweat came and bit acidly into the corners of their eyes, and blackened the belt-lines around their waists. Within seconds flies found them, perhaps having followed them all the while they fled from the oasis, unpleasant crawling things, unceasing in their attentions, and making their flesh twitch.

John Offer thought, 'We're back where we started.' Wanderers of the desert again, the cool, pleasant oasis denied them by the presence of a powerful enemy. Bang went all their plans to sit it out until they could bluff a passage to cool and civilised Blighty.

Only seconds did he sit there, easing the taut nerves shattered at that early hour of morning by this wild jousting with death. A groan from behind and a stirring of men. He turned swiftly. Big Cruiser was trying to get out of the little vehicle, the wounded Palfreyman helping him. Offer thought for one awful moment that the fairground bully was blind. Blood was all over his face and running off his chin. Palfreyman looked little better, the dressing on his face soaked with blood, too, yet he was strong enough to give a hand to Cruiser. A lot of toughness in that ex-solicitor's clerk, Offer thought.

The officer shot round and held Cruiser as he came unsteadily to earth. He stared anxiously into that bloody face. 'Eyes all right?'

'They're all right.'

Palfreyman found the first-aid bag and handed over a field dressing. Offer ripped it open, then used the dressing as a pad to mop up Cruiser's blood. He was relieved to see only skin wounds, but they were messy and the blood kept oozing out.

Suddenly another Jeep was alongside theirs. Two men only in this one – Busker and Pom, Pom yakking the moment his eyes set on them, his voice shrill from fear. Offer told him to shut up and handed Cruiser over to a concerned Busker for medical attention. Could do with medical orderly Ward now, Offer thought, and looked round hopefully. No other Jeep was in sight; neither, though, were any German armoured vehicles.

Offer said, 'We must find the others. Pom, back in that Jeep and we'll go looking for them.'

The solitary Jeep set off, deliberately throwing up a lot of dust, and ten minutes later they were spotted and a third Jeep came bumping over the desert towards them. Only two men in this one, too, Salkirk and Redpath, their morning's sentries. Offer began to feel uneasy, but a short time later again they spotted dust and headed for it, and finally it turned and came towards them and it was a fourth Jeep. Five men in this – Weybright, Wise, Wilborn, Lashley and Sergeant Walker. Four men and one Jeep missing. They cruised around for a time, but no one came walking up to them, and no cloud of dust told of a Jeep on the move. Finally, quiet and anxious, they returned to where Cruiser and Palfreyman, freshly bandaged, were knocking back a much-needed drop of char made by Busker. Char was ready for all, unhealthily stewed but good to their palates.

Offer asked, 'Who was the last to see the other Jeep, or any of the missing men?'

No one had much to contribute, flight being such a deathly scramble back in the oasis and every man thinking only of himself. Wise said, 'There was another Jeep behind ours, sir.' And Weybright, that thoughtful man, said he'd had some impression of one Jeep taking a lot of leather.

In time they began to accept that one of their Jeeps had failed to get away. They resisted the thought for quite a while, but finally, still with no one showing up, it did look as if four of their number had bought it.

Four men, comrades for so long, on so many desert forays – they were made unhappy by the thought of them dying back in Telatha, or, not much better, of them taken prisoner.

'What do we do now, sir?' someone asked Offer, standing on the spare petrol cans strapped across the bonnet of a Jeep. He was scrutinizing the desert through his glasses.

Offer lowered the binoculars. 'Do?' His tone was rather sharp, showing that even his nerves were on edge. 'You know the drill.' You never left an area until you were pretty sure you knew what had happened to missing comrades. That is, if it were safe enough to linger; and here Offer thought they were in little danger. Men made miraculous escapes under enemy fire, but it could take hours for them to crawl away. Their Jeeps must be hovering round if any survivors came walking over the desert.

Offer said, 'Two Jeeps will remain here.' If the missing men broke from cover Offer knew this was the way they should walk, following the trails left by their vehicles. 'I'm going to watch the Bir Hakeim trail.' Germans would most likely head towards the coast when they left the oasis, and there was only one track running north.

'You think they might have taken our chaps prisoner, sir?' Redpath, wanting encouragement.

'How the heck do I know?' Offer wanted to say, irritable again, but instead he shrugged and said, 'It's a chance. We might be able to spot them, if so.'

And if they did spot them? Offer's jaw tightened. The Germans weren't going to take any of his men into captivity if he could help it. Any of the Gang who fell into enemy hands was guaranteed a particularly rough passage, and Offer couldn't go and leave men to such a fate. Besides, they were 'dead', and Red Cross lists showing prisoners might resurrect the Gang in the eyes of G.H.Q. and their Military Police.

The two Jeeps went bumping off across the desert, making a wide circuit to keep out of sight of the oasis. No smoke rose now from the ruined Fort Telatha but the stink of it floated downwind to them, miles away, and was pungently unpleasant. It took them two hours to make the circuit, and all the time Offer was wondering if they were wasting their time. Already the invaders of their desert hide-out might have departed, bearing their prisoners with them. Or they might have departed without prisoners because there was no one alive to take out. Offer resolutely turned his mind away from that chilling thought.

Finally they found the trail, some tyre marks showing that sometimes motorized vehicles, almost certainly military, found their way into Telatha, along with slurred footmarks of camels, asses and horses, though not many of the latter. After a brief recce they tucked themselves behind a low mound covered with camel-thorn, and here they lay and watched, long hours of boredom, too hot at midday, but with the cold of winter coming over the land with unexpected earliness, hours before dusk.

At four in the afternoon Offer, thinking the Germans after all weren't going to leave Telatha that day, sent Pom off in a Jeep with Wise as his gunner. Contact had to be maintained with the other party. For that matter, for all they knew the missing men and Jeep might have turned up since they had parted.

'Tell Sergeant Walker to stay where he is if no one's shown up. Then return here at first light tomorrow.' The distance was too great for Pom to make the double journey before dark. Tomorrow would have to do.

Yet only half an hour after Pom's Jeep had disappeared over the cooling desert, four armoured cars emerged from the distant Telatha Oasis. Offer cursed. He could have done with Pom's Jeep now. Then he saw a Jeep with those armoured cars and cursed again, fearing the worst.

Lying under the prickly camel-thorns Captain Offer, Wilborn and Weybright watched the little convoy grow bigger along the trail. Finally, it came abreast of them. It was travelling slowly, and Offer had an impression that one of the armoured cars had suffered damage and the others were having to keep its pace.

But the object which riveted all their attention was that Jeep. *Their* Jeep. It led the way. A German soldier was driving, with an officer sitting beside him. Behind, squatting under a Breda gun, were Sergeant-major O'Keefe and Ward, still wearing his Arab headdress. The way they sat, Offer was sure their hands were tied.

The sight was immediately one of relief and then of concern. Relief because two of their comrades at least were alive; concern at the implications of seeing only two of them. Two – that was ominous. Four men were missing. Did this mean two were dead?

Under the camel-thorn they whispered together. 'They mightn't be dead,' Offer pointed out. 'If they're badly wounded the German's wouldn't want to bring them out.'

Then something about that officer concentrated Offer's attention upon him. He looked familiar . . .

John Offer suddenly exclaimed, 'By God, it's him!' and then had to explain to his companions what had startled him. 'I'm sure of it – that's the fellow who took me prisoner after Benghazi.'

Now what do we do, Offer thought in perplexity, and between them they discussed tactics. They would follow the armoured cars, of course – it never occurred to them to think otherwise – and given half a chance they'd attack them and release their comrades. But what about Sergeant Walker and his two Jeeps?

In the end Captain Offer wrote a brief message for Pom. 'S.S.M. O'Keefe and Ward are alive but prisoners. They are being taken by four German armoured cars towards Bir Hakeim. It is possible that Crookshank and Jones are wounded and have been left in the oasis, or they might still be hiding there. You will return with this message to Sergeant Walker, who will approach the Bir Hakeim trail via Telatha Oasis. Ascertain the situation there, then follow our tracks with caution.'

The note was put inside an empty tin and left on a little cairn behind the camel-thorns. Pom, wise to the ways of desert men, wouldn't miss it. Captain Offer led the way down the slope to their Jeep. Weybright took the wheel, Wilborn taking up his favourite position behind the Browning. They set off.

The enemy kept on the move while ever there was a

scrap of daylight to help them, and the convoy might have continued even then but there was no moon, and cloud had come up with the chill of night, obscuring even the stars. Offer had no difficulty in keeping tabs on the convoy, for armoured vehicles especially throw up a lot of dust. Because they didn't want their own, smaller, dust cloud to be detected, they kept their Jeep a good three miles behind the column.

As darkness began to fall, however, Weybright accelerated, closing the gap so as not to lose contact. Finally, above the sound of their own engine they began to hear the heavier beat of the vehicles before them, and then for some time followed the Germans by sound only. Abruptly the roar of armoured car engines died. Instantly Weybright switched off the Jeep motor, and they sat there motionless, listening. When they were sure this was no temporary halt but a camp for the night, Offer stirred his chilly limbs and said, 'You wait here, I'm off on a recce.'

He found some warmer clothing than his bush shirt and shorts – someone's kit was aboard and he helped himself to KD trousers, jersey and cap comforter. He didn't know whose clothing it was, but the way it hung loose upon him he thought it could have been Busker's or Cruiser's. Still, it kept him warm and he sloped off into the darkness.

When he'd walked for quarter of an hour he began to hear sounds of camp life. Mess tins rattled, and the growling notes of men talking floated to his ears. Then he saw a small glow as of a fire inside a can, and the smell of cooked food and coffee came tantalizingly to his nostrils. He wished now he had thought to have a bite before leaving their Jeep.

Offer did nothing so Boy Scoutish as to worm his way on his stomach closer to his quarry. He walked quietly but openly to within fifty yards of the camp and then stood with his back to a bush, confident he could not be detected. *He* could see the camp because he had a tiny fire to help him, but he knew that in that blackness even the sentry on watch wouldn't see anything beyond the radius of firelight.

Obligingly, but dangerously, some German soldier dropped a diesel-oil-soaked rag into the fire-can, preparatory to more cooking, and flames shot up immediately. For several minutes the camp was better illuminated, so that Offer, stepping behind the bush now, was able to get a good picture of it.

The armoured cars had leaguered in a hollow square, facing out with their guns. Within this defensive cordon the Jeep had been halted, and here they had their cooking fire and were preparing to bed down for the night. Two sentries, well-overcoated against the night's cold, stamped restlessly between the armoured cars. The officer sat with his men, but ate silently, eyes intent on the firelight, heedless of the soft talk about him.

The two prisoners sat apart from each other – the Hauptmann had learned his lesson from Offer's previous escape. They were tied, but not to each other. Sergeant-major O'Keefe had his hands fastened behind him, with a cord leading to the wrist of a Feldwebel. Arab Ward similarly had his wrists tied together and was tethered to another Feldwebel.

Offer thought, 'Not much chance of springing them from captivity.' Even so, his mind went over possibilities. Push the Jeep up close to the camp. He and Wilborn creeping up in the dark and quietly disposing of the sentries, then crawling on and just as silently quietening the Feldwebels. Tricky work, and if one sound was made the whole camp would be in an uproar. The Browning would have to open up then, and under cover of its fire they and the rescued men would race to the Jeep and all drive away before the armoured cars concentrated their aim upon them.

Offer stopped day-dreaming. There were two reasons why the plan was out from the beginning. First, he and two men couldn't pull it off. There was bound to be noise, these Panzergrenadiers were smart soldiers and they'd never get away from the camp alive. No good trying to rescue O'Keefe and Ward if it meant them dying in the process, and probably he and his companions, too.

The second reason was even more important. John Offer had never killed a man in cold blood and knew he couldn't do it now.

He stepped quietly away from the camp as the fire-can lost its glow. The Germans were holed up for the night. 'Might as well get some sleep ourselves,' he thought, and went cautiously back through the night to find his Jeep. After a while he thought he had lost his way, no sound or glow to guide his return, so he risked a little cough. Weybright coughed back within twenty yards of him.

They had supper then, hard tack and bully, standing in the dark, no knives or spoons or similar fripperies, but fingers getting greasy as they tore off hunks of unseen soft meat. No brew-up, either; no sense in risking a fire-can glow in such blackness. But water, flat and warm after days in rusting cans, was good enough.

Offer said, 'No need for a guard.' No one was going to romp around the desert in this blackness, so why not grab all the sleep they could while they had the chance? The Germans couldn't move off without starting their engines, and if such a racket didn't waken them he didn't know what would.

As it was he was awake from just after four o'clock, some time-mechanism telling him it was the moment to stir. He lay there listening for an hour. Because of the cloudy sky the morning was still black as Hades, and he guessed the Germans would be in no hurry to get away. This wasn't summer when night-travel under almost any conditions was better than driving through the heat of a burning hot day.

At five o'clock he wakened the other men. By this time the Germans were probably stirring, too. Daylight began to show about six-thirty, so they had plenty of time for breakfast; bully beef, hardened this time by the night's cold, the eternal tooth-breaking hard tack, and water chilly enough now to set their teeth on edge.

Long before dawn they had finished their meal and were

huddling together in the Jeep. Offer thought, 'About now Walker will be ready to move across to Telatha.' He began to work out times, Walker having to detour through the oasis. He doubted if the other party would catch up with them before late that afternoon.

Daylight. It came gradually at that time of year, very cold and grey, the sun only with difficulty penetrating the cloud. When it was just light enough to see each other, they heard the German vehicles start up. Time for them to move, also. When they were sure those other engines were making enough noise to cover the sound, Weybright started the Jeep.

The armoured cars began to pull away, their engine noise receding. Weybright shoved in the gear and went cautiously after them, trailing them by sound at first until the light became good enough for their quarry to be seen.

Suddenly the clouds went swirling away, sun shafting between breaks, warmth striking them welcomely straight away. Instantly the Jeep halted, the light suddenly too good now. If they were too close, even though they might not be heard, the Germans could spot them.

After some minutes they were able to see ahead the camouflaged vehicles crawling through scrub, not much dust going up now because the heavy dew of night had settled it. Offer decided to give them a good start before going after them again. When they were mere dots in the distance he told Weybright to push on once more.

The day grew warmer, the sky still cloudy but the sun hot upon them most of the time. Ahead, a broken line on the horizon, was the escarpment south of Tobruk. Very rugged there, but where they were the going wasn't bad at all.

As the day grew warmer, so the dust began to rise, and before eight o'clock the armoured cars were kicking up the usual cloud that betrayed their position for miles around. Driving carefully, and several miles to the rear, Offer's Jeep made less dust and it was unlikely that it was spotted.

Almost dead on eight the column ahead stopped moving, and Weybright brought the Jeep to a halt, too. At first

123

Offer thought it was a pause for a second breakfast, but when a couple of hours passed he said, 'They're in trouble.' A breakdown of one of their vehicles, and the Germans having to halt to repair it. He remembered how slowly the convoy had passed them outside Telatha, and even then he'd got the impression that one of the armoured cars was limping along.

Wilborn, erect beside his Browning, kept watch behind, sometimes looking back for their own following Jeeps. This long halt would give them chance to catch up. Still, it was a bit early to expect them, so when he said, 'Something comin' up behind, sir,' they were surprised.

John Offer hauled himself up beside his gunner and trained his glasses on the distant dust cloud. It seemed large for only three Jeeps. After a while Offer decided that, anyway, it was not following their tyre marks; it was crawling across the desert slightly north of their position. Just before the armoured cars moved on again, Offer's glasses were able to distinguish those other vehicles throwing up that large cloud of dust.

It was a convoy, mostly of tanks and tank transporters, though with some high, covered trucks among them. Offer didn't have to be told that these were enemy; Monty's tanks wouldn't be within fifty miles of them, he was sure.

Weybright interrupted his thoughts, watching that grim steel convoy travel with such slowness over the dry land. 'They're on the move again, sir.' The armoured cars.

But out of habit Offer had swung his glasses to survey the terrain all around them. He saw other dust clouds, tiny grey-white blobs of dust telling of the passage of other vehicles over the desert.

Offer spoke down to Weybright, 'Hold on a minute: we shan't lose them.'

He wanted a steady platform for his binoculars. Much more carefully this time he let the glasses traverse the wide expanse of arid land around them. He began to count those moving dust clouds. In time he realized there were dozens of them, widely dispersed across the desert. The longer he looked, the more he counted. Some were far distant, but others, appearing to emerge from nowhere, were only a few miles behind. Another column seemed to be coming quite fast dead along their tracks.

John Offer put down his glasses and looked ahead. The armoured cars, black specks fanned out so as not to take each other's dust, were just discernible to the naked eye.

'I'm going to surprise you,' he said. 'We're in trouble.'

Weybright and Wilborn looked mildly interested, Wilborn extracting the last smoke from a quarter of an inch of tab. Weybright said, 'Well, that's a change, sir.' They weren't the panicky kind, his ex-Glasshouse wallahs.

'I may be wrong. That lot out there might be Monty's Desert Rats.' His hand indicated those many tiny dust clouds behind and around them. 'But my guess is Monty's still back at Sollum, and we're right in the middle of an enemy re-grouping exercise. If we go on we'll find ourselves amid a concentrating enemy force of tanks, armoured cars – the lot!'

'You're suggesting we should pull out while we have a chance?' Weybright stood up and took a look at those menacing dust clouds.

'Not exactly. I thought you should know the problem. Personally I'm going on until I'm sure I can't do anything to help the boys escape.' If Weybright and Wilborn didn't want to go with him they could back-track on foot to Sergeant Walker's Jeeps.

Weybright said, 'Of course we'll keep going, sir,' as if misunderstanding Offer. Wilborn said nothing, busy flicking tobacco strands off the end of his tongue, but he didn't alight from the Jeep.

So they started up and went after the armoured cars, still moving cautiously so as not to attract attention. Wilborn, hanging on to the Browning, kept watch behind and at intervals reported the situation.

'Them tanks, sir, they're dropping back.' With tank

transporters in their midst that convoy wouldn't travel at a quarter of the speed of their Jeep, though the Jeep wasn't going fast, anyway, because the armoured cars ahead still travelled with caution, as if unsure of at least one of their vehicles. In fact, three-quarters of an hour after restarting, the armoured cars came to another halt. 'Trouble again,' said Offer. No one had three breakfasts in the desert. So they switched off and waited, and kept watch around them, and soon they were mightily disturbed.

As the day grew brighter there was increasing evidence of troop movement across the desert. Everywhere now motorized units, remnants of battered Panzer divisions retreating in disorder from a recent battlefield, moved independently towards some distant gathering ground. Because Offer's Jeep was halted, those variously-sized columns caught up with them, springing rapidly from insubstantial clouds of dust into the hardware of a warring army. Soon it seemed to Offer and his men that they were in the centre of a stampeding herd of moving artillery, armoured vehicles, and an even greater number of clumsy supply trucks. It was astonishing how quickly a desert, apparently empty at daybreak, was now thronged with moving columns all converging on that unknown point north-west of them.

At first there was a tightening of stomach muscles and a jumpiness of nerves, sitting there in the Jeep. Then they relaxed. The nearest enemy vehicles passed by at least a mile away, and close up against some bushes their Jeep was probably indiscernible. In fact, Offer began to muse, probably no one would take a blind bit of notice of them if they were seen. Who would expect to find one enemy Jeep bang in the middle of this retreat?

'I suppose we're as safe here as anywhere,' Offer told the others, but about noon, with the armoured cars still halted ahead, he changed his tune.

Wilborn's reports of one convoy became increasingly sharp. That was the one right behind them. 'If it keeps coming on this course, sir, they'll run right on to us.' Then the fur would undoubtedly fly. Jimmy cocked his gun and swung it to cover their rear.

The convoy behind came on at a rapid pace. In fact it travelled so fast it could only be enemy scout cars on the move, Offer decided, and they were ugly customers.

Offer gave an order. 'Let's get out of their way.' Let that damned convoy tear on past them; they weren't staying to argue with well-armed scout cars. They could still keep an eye on the halted armoured cars ahead.

So Weybright started the engine and with great caution drove at right angles to their original course, threading along low ground where they could find it, and finally halting half a mile from their last resting place.

Offer stood up alongside Wilborn at the Browning and got out his glasses again. That dust cloud was very large now, the fast-travelling convoy less than two miles away. There were a lot of intervening bushes and Offer could see the dust but never a glimpse of the cause of it. That meant, he decided, they were small vehicles, scout cars, it seemed to confirm. Possibly those tiny Italian jobs, nippy two-seaters, but mounted with heavy machine-guns. They must keep clear of them!

The unseen vehicles came on, no slackening speed, and Offer could have sworn they must have been following their tracks. And then they did halt, and now Offer could hear engines – several of them. They halted at exactly the place where their Jeep had stood for the last half-hour.

Offer thought, 'My God, have we left something to give the show away?' He couldn't think what. And then Jimmy Wilborn spat out his fag, swore coarsely and prepared to bring the Browning into action.

Those vehicles were on the move again. They had turned south, though, at right angles to their course, and once more were coming on at reckless speed.

Offer snapped, 'They *are* trailing us!' No other explanation. 'Get moving!' – to Weybright. Though what good was that? Before they could work up speed those hounding vehicles would run them down . . .

John Offer shouted, 'Stop!' He had seen the first of the pursuing vehicles. It was a Jeep. Weybright halted. Three Jeeps came racing up like eager foxhounds. Sergeant Walker had arrived.

Offer got down. The Jeep engines died, and everybody else dismounted and looked pleased to see each other. Walker came over, a big grin on his face, so pleased to have caught up with his O.C. so early.

Walker called out, 'Not bad, sir, eh? Lost your trail a couple of times, too.'

Offer said, 'I lost a stone in weight, not knowing who the heck was trailing us.' He shuddered. That had been a nerve-wracking moment, seeing their pursuers deliberately turn off the trail to follow them through the bush. He'd been so sure they were enemy.

But no Tiffy Jones with them, and no cheerful Charley Crookshank.

'You didn't find them?'

'They're there, sir, in the oasis.' Walker's face lost its smile. 'Buried, sir. We found their graves.'

Offer said, 'Oh,' and all the men were silent. Tiffy and Charley had been with them a long time. They would be missed.

Their captain sighed. 'Well, that's war.' The sooner they got out of it, the better. Just let them rescue O'Keefe and Arab Ward and there'd be no more fighting for him. The desert would hide them until they could head for Benghazi. But first they had to get O'Keefe and Ward out of enemy hands.

Walker was saying, 'Christ, sir, we thought we'd had it.' He gestured to where dust clouds moved steadily across the desert. Once or twice Walker's party had found themselves running uncomfortably close to columns of vehicles easily identified as enemy. But they had pressed on, no thought of turning back. Captain Offer had sent for them, and Walker brought them through.

'Now what do we do, sir?'

'We have a brew-up and wait until the convoy ahead moves off again.'

'And then?'

Offer shrugged. 'Just follow.' What else could they do? 'And hope.'

Of course the armoured cars moved off just as the char was made, so they had to down it quickly, scalding hot though it was, and then pick up the pursuit.

'Get a lot closer,' Offer ordered. With all this movement on the desert the dust of another convoy wouldn't alarm the Panzer Hauptmann before them. So Weybright picked up speed until they were running no more than a quarter of a mile behind the armoured cars.

It was now nearing midday, and the world well warmed up. The war was also hotting up. To the north of them, perhaps seven or eight miles away, there was quite a commotion. Guns had opened fire, short, swift but heavy bursts, then they saw black specks hurtling low above the desert and realized that Allied warplanes were strafing the retreating Axis force.

They could hear the distant rattle of cannon fire, and there was ground ack-ack – light stuff – going hastily into action, for sometimes they could distinguish tracer curling lazily into the sky.

Pom, very interested in that distant beating-up, said the cannon fire was from Spitfires, and tried to show how knowledgeable he was on the subject. The others in his Jeep weren't sure they were Spitfires, but it didn't matter so long as it was 'our' planes that were dishing out the punishment.

As they rumbled along, swaying to the lurch of their tiny vehicles, they kept watch on the aircraft swooping around the desert. For some time there were two only, then others came flashing in, guns strafing, as if they had been called to the kill by the earlier aircraft.

They were making a killing, too. Now, time after time,

following a swooping, low-level attack columns of smoke rose to testify to the pilots' accuracy with machine-gun and cannon. The Gang cheered a little, though rather subdued as if feeling that the nearby enemy might hear them, but pleased as each new fire was started near to the horizon.

'All right so long as they don't come this way,' Offer thought. He knew what it would be like across the desert at this moment. Those fighter planes scudding close to the ground at well over three hundred miles an hour, lifting into view with only seconds in which to put up protective fire. The aircraft would come flashing over the ground troops almost before the sound reached them.

Each time there was an attack men would hurl themselves out of soft transport and disperse, diving for cover. Machine-gun carriers and light ack-ack would lurch to a halt, barrels swinging frantically, gunners trying to get in a burst ahead of the aircraft and usually failing. There would be seconds of pandemonium, the deafening crack of guns firing and shells bursting, men wildly shouting as they often did when surprised and unnerved and no one hearing them. And then would come bigger explosions, vehicles blowing up as cannon shells ruptured fuel tanks or detonated ammunition, but by that time the plane would be receding, the sound of the over-taxed engine dying almost as swiftly as it had burst upon them.

Not all planes made it back to base, though. The Gang, watching from a safe distance, saw two of them go into the ground and blow up, brought down by unusually alert enemy ground gunners.

Interestingly, no Axis aircraft came to take on the intruders. 'We must have air supremacy,' Offer decided. So early in the Alamein break-out? Well, that was a good sign, for Monty if not particularly for the Glasshouse Gang.

On they rolled. There were other objects of interest to them now, too, besides the strafing. Maintaining an uncertain line across the desert was a column of soft transport. Sometimes it came quite close to Offer's Jeeps – on one occasion within a hundred yards – at other times it veered half a mile or more away, as if following ground more negotiable for their big, lumbering trucks. The armoured cars ahead, in spite of having one uncertain vehicle to reduce their speed, were moving slightly faster than the soft transport, but for some time they travelled almost abreast of each other.

In Offer's Jeep it was Wilborn who first noticed that several of the trucks in that other convoy were captured British vehicles. Then Wilborn came up with a guess.

'Sir, I think them chaps in them trucks are our lads – prisoners.'

John Offer became interested and stood up, hanging on to the Browning while they lurched over the bumpy ground. Now he could see the trucks and they were Fords and Bedfords. They appeared packed with soldiers, seen over the high tailboards, and some of them wore bandages.

'Could be,' agreed Offer. Something about the way they clustered under the canvas covers, forlornly looking back, said they were British.

'Poor bastards,' said Wilborn compassionately.

'Poor old sods.' Offer hated to see them being driven into captivity. God, how depressed they must feel, knowing it was a prison camp for them, perhaps for a long time. He wouldn't want to be in their shoes.

No chance of helping them, either. The convoy was well guarded, a scout car with twin Spandaus driving grimly along one side; on the other side two German motorbike-and-sidecars bouncing along, each mounting one Mg; while bringing up the rear was an open truck in which sat a dozen Panzergrenadiers. They'd have Schmeissers and other automatic weapons, and any man dropping over the tailboard wouldn't get far before being chopped down by their massed fire. Likewise, if Offer's unarmoured Jeeps tried to stage a rescue, the firepower directed against them would blow them off the face of the earth within seconds.

Sorrowfully they could only watch and do nothing.

Weybright had closed to within a hundred yards of the column now, plainly visible if anyone turned round in those armoured cars, but why should they? They'd feel safe, with all this movement of their own troops around them, and no one was going to look back.

In the Jeeps they were all jumpy, even so. It seemed to them that one moment they were alone on the wide desert, save for the armoured cars and O'Keefe's Jeep ahead. Yet now, bewilderingly, they were bang in the middle of a moving army, crawling along on every side of them. How swiftly they had appeared – stray units galore must have been bedded down out of sight in little hollows, and it was a shaker, the way they seemed to pop up out of the ground and fill the desert.

True, those enemy trucks and guns were scattered with wide distances between them, the nearest to Offer's party being the Fords and Bedfords with their loads of P.O.W.s. Generally there was no hostile presence nearer than half a mile, yet at that they felt unpleasantly close. The worst of it was, enemy columns would soon be running right alongside them, for all were on a converging course.

Quite quickly an uneasy John Offer began to think, 'We can't keep this up'. The sooner they pulled discreetly out from the retreating army the better. They had tagged on behind the armoured cars in the hope of something turning up, but of course nothing had happened. Nothing would; and they'd get no joy if they attacked those steel-plated vehicles before them.

Regretfully, they must abandon the idea of rescue and look to their own safety, yet Offer knew his men would be as reluctant as he to abandon their comrades to their fate. So they rolled on with the beaten, retreating Axis forces, Offer always on the point of pulling away and then deciding – 'Just another couple of minutes.'

When finally he made the decision to call off the chase, he found he had left it too late.

Having arrived at the decision, for the first time John

Offer was presented with the problem of how to accomplish a discreet getaway. It meant they would have to turn south, and this would send them cutting across the paths of many enemy units. While his Jeeps travelled along with German and Italian transport, no one would give more than a passing glance at them. The natural assumption would be that these were captured vehicles, like the Fords and Bedfords, and the solitary Jeep which clearly led the way for the armoured cars. In fact, they might even think the four Jeeps were attached to that armoured convoy, so closely behind were they now driving.

Offer had doffed his shirt with its British officer pips, and he knew Walker's sergeant's stripes would be out of sight, too. There was nothing to distinguish them as British, their bare brown bodies or KD shirts looking no different from bare bodies and shirts of fairly similar hue in every other vehicle grinding across the desert.

But that was all right while they went the way of the crowd. Let them try to go off at an angle to the general movement, and attention would instantly focus upon them. Then someone, less numbed by defeat, was sure to wonder why four unusual vehicles bearing enemy roundels weren't heading, like the rest, for the re-grouping area at Sidi Rezegh. Offer could just imagine some suspicious German officer driving up to them and barking out a fierce question which couldn't be easily answered.

The best thing to do was to halt, as if with mechanical trouble, the old dodge they had practised more than once. Halt and let the tide of enemy vehicles stream past them until they had the desert to themselves and could decamp.

The thing upsetting to that theory was the presence of a big column, seemingly springing from nowhere and settling on their tail half a mile back – a nasty-looking convoy, this, full of artillery and light armoured units and plenty of infantry carriers. If they halted it would flood all around them, for like all other convoys in the desert units drove dispersed to avoid the leading vehicles' dust. One of them was bound to stop to see if help was needed; and Offer could imagine a proposal to hoist the tiny offending Jeep aboard a truck or tow it on to a repair base. The Germans especially never left any vehicle or equipment in the desert if it could be brought into action again.

Awkward, he thought, his mind evaluating their chances of bluffing a way out of such pressing attentions. Damned awkward. Weybright's German would hardly stand up to the test . . .

The desert rose up and hit them. Pain crashed through their eardrums. Dust was exploding in a long line of gouts which went racing before them as the Jeep went turning over. A final crashing roar as John Offer felt himself thrown clear of the rolling Jeep, then a receding sound, but his ears ringing.

Dust in his mouth, his hands outstretched instinctively to break the fall, and he turning over and over, bumping on the hard dry ground yet not feeling a thing. Gun noise coming through his abused ears, becoming louder and identifiable as a roaring engine sound swiftly diminished – machine-guns rattling and cannon cracking off. Then the firing stopped though Offer heard no command.

Dazed, he sat up. The Jeep was overturned, wheels spinning, kit scattered around. Weybright was lying on his face; Wilborn was sitting up and rubbing the back of his head, though his other fingers already searched a breast pocket for a fag to console him.

Then Cruiser's battered face shoving before Offer's dizzy eyes, mighty strength lifting him to his feet. Cruiser's hoarse, coarse voice, but concerned for him: 'Fuck me, thought you'd copped it then, sir.'

On his feet the dizziness passed and Captain Offer snapped into normality again. 'We were strafed –'

Lashley, Sally, Pom and the bandaged Palfreyman were running up, urgency in the way they ran.

'Spitfire.' Cruiser nodded. Their own fighter plane, beating them up.

'There'll be more coming.' Offer remembered the many fighters which had swarmed earlier, north of them. Now this area was in for a pasting. But there wouldn't be just one Spitfire.

The men were shoving the Jeep on to its wheels again. It went over easily under the combined effort of strong men. There was a stink of spilt petrol, but Lashley hopped into the driving seat, switched on, and the engine, after a few coughs protesting against ill-treatment, roared lustily and moved a few yards when Lashley slipped it in gear. None of the other Jeeps appeared to have been hit.

Weybright was beginning to move. Wise and Busker got him to his feet, but he looked groggy. He'd lost his glasses and without them looked a blind and helpless man. Wise went back and found the specs and they were sprained but repairable.

Offer shouted, 'Disperse!'

Everywhere enemy vehicles were dispersing like mad, trucks lumbering as if in panic away from their fellows then, distance achieved, men leaping out and running away, going to ground wherever there was cover. Some immediately started to dig slit trenches.

He saw his men streaking for their vehicles, but the second Spitfire was on them before they could get moving. A devastating crescendo, an aircraft coming in so low it was on top of them before they could even spot its direction of approach. Machine-guns and twin cannons firing, shells preceding the wave of sound.

This time they weren't the target. That big convoy of artillery and armoured units on their tail had taken the brunt of this pilot's displeasure and then he'd pulled up into the sky in a tremendous climb right over the Jeeps.

'Another!' someone yelled, spotting a black spot low on the horizon.

Into their Jeeps, a frantic starting of engines, gears slamming home, movement and a milling around in confusion, trying to disperse but for precious seconds just running on to each other.

The third plane strafing them, cannon shells the worst because they stunned with the suddenness of their explosions, twin lines of sound going away and digging big ugly holes in the earth where they had landed. Each man thinking how his body would have looked if it had detonated one of those shells.

But all safe. John Offer looked round from his bumping Jeep. He had taken the wheel, neither Weybright nor Wilborn looked capable. His other Jeeps were on the move. Stopping. His men out and going like the clappers away from vehicles which were the target for those Spitfires. Down on the ground, trying to press holes in it as a fourth fighter came in strafing, then a fifth five seconds behind it.

Weybright and Wilborn fully in control of their senses abruptly, yards away, belting hard for some bushes, as if they were any good against shells and bullets. Offer standing, watching until he saw that all his men had found cover and no one was in need of assistance. Then he raced after Weybright and Wilborn.

They were shoving dirt with their hands into twin banks, digging deep into the ground between. John Offer dived in and worked just as frantically. When they had created a shallow depression giving some protection, they flopped on their backs, streaming with sweat, exhausted by their efforts.

A few minutes' relief, no attacks in that time. Then back came the planes, beating up the dispersed enemy transport once more. John Offer kept his head down and let them crash by without even trying to look at them. There was some safety in this shallow trench, but none exposed above it.

Other brave spirits, though, were exposing themselves. They were the gunners fighting back as each new attack was mounted against them. Lying there, Offer heard the aircraft as they came tearing in, guns blazing. Instantly around him came the fierce reply from German and

136

Italian ack-ack gunners. As quickly as it had started, all firing would cease as the Spitfire became a distant sound only.

Then came the sound of men shouting. Stretcher bearers would be running up, the enemy medical service coming into action to tend the wounded. Smoke rolled upon their shallow trench, and they could hear the fierce roar of fire as stricken vehicles went up in flames. Several times there were quite big explosions as if ammunition carriers had caught a packet.

The strafing went on over a period of about ten or fifteen minutes, then, satisfied, the Allied fighters shifted their attentions to another area of the desert. When they were sure they'd had their dose and it was safe to come out of hiding, men popped up like rabbits out of burrows and began to find their vehicles.

John Offer walked back to his, Weybright and Wilborn coming up behind. Offer's Jeep was close to an armoured car – fifty yards away, anyway. That was something Offer hadn't noticed when they bailed out from their Jeep.

He looked round, spotting out for his Jeeps, and waving when he saw them. They began to trundle towards him. Two Jeeps rather too close together to his right; another looking as if it had been run on to a thorn bush and might be uncomfortable to get out; yet another beyond the armoured car; and his own. That made five. All correct, Offer told himself, and then the alarm bells began to clamour in his mind.

He didn't have five Jeeps. Four only – the fifth was in enemy hands. He counted swiftly again. Five Jeeps. *That Jeep beyond the armoured car, it must be O'Keefe's.* It had a Breda mounted, not a Browning, anyway.

A harsh voice was shouting at them. Offer wheeled, a sense of acute danger overwhelming him. Soft transport south of them was coming together, a mere hundred yards away, including those Fords and Bedfords, the prisoners' trucks. A German officer was standing clear of those vehicles, shouting towards them. He seemed very angry.

Weybright translated, and by the way he stuttered Offer knew he was jumpy. 'He wants to know why we didn't open fire on the aircraft.'

Offer, though, was staring towards that fifth Jeep beyond the armoured car. O'Keefe and Arab Ward were being walked across to it. Their hands were tied behind their backs, but for the moment they weren't anchored to any massive Feldwebels. Offer's racing mind was trying to think how this moment could be turned to best advantage. A swift rush, O'Keefe and Ward hauled aboard, then a race for safety?

Then the moment of opportunity, if ever there had been such a moment, was past. The Feldwebels were there, right behind the prisoners and stepping into view attracted by the sound of that bellowing German voice, was another Afrika Korps' officer, a tall, hard-looking man.

Offer said, 'Tell him we have no ammunition for these guns.'

Weybright shouted back. The German officer seemed only partially satisfied, as if irrationally feeling they ought to have ammunition if they had guns, even captured enemy ones.

Then Offer lifted his arms to form a circle around his head. The other Jeeps seeing it would know what that meant. Scram! Danger!

That tall, hard German officer was staring at them. Offer had taken one look at his face and had recognized it. And if John Offer could recognize the Hauptmann, the Hauptmann would be able to recognize him, too.

John Offer slid easily into the driving seat, showing no sign of panic, for haste drew attention to oneself. The Hauptmann was still standing there, as if puzzled. His eyes were on four Jeeps. The sight must have been startling. Where had four Jeeps sprung from? Then he saw a bare-bodied man in the act of turning and getting into one of the Jeeps. Something familiar about that face . . .

John Offer saw the Hauptmann turn suddenly and knew the game was up. He started the engine and had it in gear in a flash. The other Jeeps would be moving now if they'd got his signal. As he drove he shot a glance at the Hauptmann. The German officer was shouting. Then O'Keefe, quick man in any emergency, brought him down by throwing himself, hands bound though they were, at the Hauptmann's legs. Nearly as quick in reaction, Ward ran amok, butting his *kefir*-ed head into the Feldwebels and hampering them even if they didn't fall to the ground. Priceless seconds being gained by those two comrades, and yet there was no chance of racing to pick them up.

Offer's Jeep accelerated towards the P.O.W. convoy, seeking safety in their midst. His other Jeeps were revving up, dispersing as they drove because there was no sense in coming together.

A turret swung and an armoured car came into action. Tracer went leaping across after one of the Jeeps, but it dodged among the soft transport and the firing died instantly. Alarmed Germans everywhere were leaping to their guns, but Offer guessed they wouldn't know what all the firing was about. They probably thought it heralded another strafing, and for moments took no notice of accelerating Jeeps.

Offer's Jeep came out through the soft transport, but there was a lot of enemy stuff ahead. They were going to attract attention, he thought, beetling away from Sidi Rezegh at such a time. Half a minute later Offer was sure they *were* going to attract attention.

Two armoured cars had broken clear of the soft transport, too, and now opened fire after them. Wilborn shouted a warning and Offer took wild evasive action. Wilborn fired back when he could on the armoured cars.

Offer, foot painfully hard upon the accelerator, saw a mass of transport before them, all moving steadily north. A German staff car had halted, and Offer saw an officer stand up in it and raise glasses to his eyes. Some scout cars had also pulled round as if interested, too. The only thing that saved Offer and his men at that moment was the startling suddenness of their appearance, for all the world like hares appearing in the middle of a pack of hunting beagles.

Again for vital seconds no one did anything, no guns were brought into action. And all the time Offer was closing on that convoy.

He went bull-headed towards them, the open desert offering no protection, anyway. True, they were out of range of the armoured cars, but they were well within range of gunners ahead. If they tried to escape across the desert every gun would bear on them and they'd be too long within range to escape unscathed.

So, the hell with it, dive straight in where the enemy couldn't fire for fear of hitting their own men, do a lot of damage and start such a confusion that they could slip away beyond the convoy and gain a lot of ground before the Germans knew what was happening.

Not, he thought, that they'd get away with it, even so. Soldiers weren't long taken aback, and they'd never make the mile to safety before guns and cannon found their range . . .

The officer in the staff car was turning his head, very quickly, as if in sudden aversion to their presence. The scout cars were turning away, too, guns elevating. And the whole convoy, eighty yards before them, had gone suddenly crazy.

They had lost order. Suddenly enemy vehicles were travelling in every direction and accelerating crazily, like a herd of stampeding buffalo. For one astonished moment Offer thought it was because of their approach, then one word shot into his mind and with it the implications. Dispersal.

As the truth dawned on him, guns ahead opened fire, but not on his Jeeps. A crescendo of sound, a sudden flash of silver and a Spitfire was there again, banking swiftly to avoid the ack-ack fire, then skidding away high into the sky.

But not before its bullets and cannon shells had done damage to the convoy. Offer saw the long double line of shell bursts crossing the desert, machine-gun bullets kicking up dirt around them. A gun-towing vehicle was stricken, hit and on fire in a flash and men tumbling out and running, and then the truck blowing up with a mighty rolling sound as ammo exploded. And other vehicles were hit but died less spectacularly.

Then the Jeeps were right in among the convoy, some enemy vehicles still moving around them, some stationary, guns still smoking as, oblivious of the presence of Jeeps in their midst, they maintained watch on the sky for further aerial attack.

And another R.A.F. fighter was almost on them, sound deafening, bullets and shells all round them again and guns frantically fighting back on all sides.

Their own Browning was in action, too. Offer thought, 'He couldn't resist it.' Wilborn. Taking advantage of the confusion, he'd be doing an act of destruction on his own. Offer saw another of his Jeeps ahead and the gunner on that one was firing, too. Looked like Wilborn's oppo, Wise.

Offer, avoiding one vehicle after another, thought, 'Now, why do they do that?' *His* only thought at that moment was of streaking off to safety. Opening fire like that must draw attention upon them, and raids were swiftly over. But shooting was instinctive to some of the men, men like Wilborn, Wise, Cruiser, Busker and some others. But not Weybright. Weybright would never use a gun unless he were forced to do so.

Oh, sod, another Spit, and they still in the middle of the bloody convoy. Once again the screaming crescendo of sound, the guns and smoke, the explosions and fire, and heat now rolling upon them from fiercely blazing enemy transport.

But nothing touched them, his Jeep, anyway. He shot out from the last of the dispersed convoy, the open desert before him. This was their chance while the enemy was occupied defending itself against strafing aircraft.

A hundred yards into the desert. Two hundred . . . four hundred, no shots fired after them, and beginning to breathe a sigh of relief. Looking round and seeing the other three Jeeps going like crazy over the rough ground. Six hundred yards. Eight hundred. Ease off the accelerator a little but still keep weaving. A thousand yards. Pretty safe.

But no more attacking aircraft and now all at once the crap began to fall around the Jeeps. They had rumbled them and come into action against this impudent enemy, German gunners trying to take it out of the fleeing Jeeps because they'd done no damage to the damned Spitfires.

Suddenly some enemy showing half a mile ahead, climbing out of a fold in the ground. Swing east a little and keep out of range. Nothing much coming near them from behind now. Three-quarters of a mile from the beat-up convoy, and some undulating ground that kept them out of sight of enemy gunners for seconds at a time, dodging and weaving, anyway.

A mile. Nothing ahead. Nothing to worry about. Bits of hills – mounds really – good cover and they could come together and ease off the throttles. The Jeeps began to converge. When they were together Offer pulled up in a nice depression where a man on a nearby hill could have a good view for miles around. They all came trundling down the slope, but dispersing even now, Jeeps facing out in case of surprise.

Offer slid from his seat. Now he noticed the heat, never conscious of it during the hectic moments of chase. And the flies were already crawling over his skin. He tried to remember if the flies had stayed with them during the noisy moments of strafing, but he'd been too busy to notice at the time. When you were close to death heat and flies seemed too unimportant to bother about.

The men, caked with dust on sweaty faces and bodies, came trudging over the hot dry earth towards him. He said the only thing a good commander could say under the circumstances.

'Get the shanker cans out. We'll have a brew-up.' Something to eat, too, if any of the men were hungry. He wasn't. Action like that always put him off food for hours.

They drank gratefully, when the tea was ready, nothing coming to disturb them. Offer thought, 'A pity old O'Keefe and Wardy aren't with us.' It would have been a real celebration. So close to them, yet unable to free them.

He felt a bit off, unhappy at the thought of his comrades going into the bag. Yet ten minutes later John Offer was bubbling over with ideas for their rescue.

Char came over in his battered enamel mug. Good stuff, did him good, sweet and thick, and almost sticky from the can of condensed milk poured in. But even drinking the brew brought a frown. They'd lost too much petrol and water in earlier fracas, and if they planned to stay in the desert until Benghazi was taken, how the heck were they going to survive?

Because he felt low and thought his men might be a bit under, too, he told them to get something special out of the food box. Pom found some canned Frankfurters and four tins of M & V, exotic rations. Added to their bully and biscuits it made an appetizing smell and cheered them, and perhaps put Captain Offer more in a mood for constructive thought.

Surviving in the desert. They'd attack small convoys of soft transport and take from them what they needed. Easier said than done, and tables might be turned and his men get shot up, he among them. He wanted to bring them all out of the desert alive – his men, his responsibility. Getting them back to Blighty wouldn't be hard if they could only last out the next week or so . . .

In the past days his mind had worked out a plan. So easy, when you got down to it. They'd knock off a big packing case at Benghazi, fill it to an impressive weight with scrap picked up off the desert, and drive it to the first ship leaving for England.

John Offer could see himself approaching the ship's captain, his big tough men with tommies and rifles standing resolute guard over the packing case, keeping everyone away and not fraternizing with anyone. A guard such as that would be impressive. And he would salute and produce documents – the old Field Salvage (Forward Area) Coy would be best – then tell the captain that the unit was a blind for very special Intelligence work.

He could almost hear himself saying, 'We're the chaps who get sent out for special recovery work, German and Italian top secret new weapons, you know. There's always a first time when one of them falls into our hands.'

And in that packing case he would hint – never say anything outright – they'd got the latest in Luftwaffe engines. Something hush-hush and right out of this world. Absolutely imperative that the boffins at Farnborough should get their hands on it right away. Intelligence? Boffins? Magic words. And how impressive, an officer of colonel rank – yes, he'd have to promote himself again – with a special company of men acting as guard to him and his hush-hush aero engine.

John Offer knew the Merchant Navy. Easy-going, friendly types. Help yourself, they'd invite cordially, we're going home nearly empty, anyway. He'd ask for a special storeroom and they'd put the case inside and his men would mount guard on it the whole way back to England, and that would be convincing in itself. In England they'd knock off a truck, drive away with the case and get lost, and that would be the end of the Glasshouse Gang . . .

Palfreyman, uncomplaining man, had mushed up his food and was spooning it into his torn mouth. Amazing bloke, old Palfrey, just kept going, though Christ, his face needed attention . . .

If he was a colonel it would look odd, not having another officer with him. Colonels were undressed without their aides or adjutants. What officer material had he within the Gang? Palfreyman, no one else. He brightened. Palfreyman must rise to the height of captain. His injured face – 'Stopped one when we were getting away with the aero engine, y'know' – would invite sympathy, and bandaged, he wouldn't be expected to speak much, so he wouldn't drop clangers.

Sure, it was all easy, getting them back to Blighty. Just one big weakness in the whole plan. They were dead and wanted to go on being dead. But in the end O'Keefe's and Ward's names on Red Cross P.O.W. lists would tell Cairo that not all the Gang had gone up at Telatha. So would the Gang be able to get lost in England, no cops on the look-out for them? What was the good of demobilizing themselves if in the end they were hunted and picked up for their army crimes and made to do time in a Glasshouse again? Offer shuddered at the thought. When he left the army he wanted to leave it for good.

O'Keefe and Ward. If only they could have sprung them from captivity, back there where the enemy forces still streamed towards Sidi Rezegh. Still so close to them that occasionally they could hear the strafing of ground forces by the R.A.F. fighters; yet there was nothing they could do to save their comrades.

He got out a stained and worn map and went carefully over this area where the next battle would be. Tobruk, Sidi Rezegh, Bir Hakeim, Trig-el-Abd. So few names, such vast areas without populations, his map mostly blank spaces of white. Bir Hakeim, a tiny collection of mud huts which might justify the title of hamlet in Britain – Trig-el-Abd, he had to laugh when he thought of it. How important it was, yet what was the reality? A centuries-old caravan route, a trail through the rocks and dust in no way resembling a road, and yet so important now because it shortened the distance by coastal road to Benghazi . . .

Captain Offer startled them all by saying, 'I've got it!' Suddenly he knew how to save O'Keefe and the Arab-loving Ward. Trig-el-Abd was the key to the whole situation!

They gathered round him, he spreading the map on the

ground, though they didn't need it, knowing the thing by heart, anyway.

'Remember that convoy of British P.O.W.s back there, poor bastards?' He'd recalled it for some reason, God knew why, just at one moment when his eye was dwelling on the words Trig-el-Abd. The two things had fused in his mind, and all at once he could see how rescue could be done.

'All right, suppose you're Rommel. Suppose you're re-grouping between Tobruk and Sidi Rezegh. You won't want to be hampered by P.O.W.s, so what will you do with 'em?'

'Get rid of 'em?' – Sally Salkirk.

'Okay, how?' They weren't on the right wavelength and just stared at him or the map, so he explained. 'They'll shove 'em in trucks and drive them to the nearest port where they can be shipped across to P.O.W. camps in Italy. And where's the nearest enemy port?'

Theoretically, Tobruk, but with the Eighth Army pressing hard up the coast road and already reported to be within a few miles of it, Rommel wouldn't use it for P.O.W. transport.

'Benghazi.' Rommel's main supply port for the moment, plenty of empty ships to carry P.O.W.s to Sicily and thence on to the mainland. 'And which way will he take them?' His finger stubbed at the trail south of the rugged Jebel el Akhdar, the Trig-el-Abd. It would be rough going, but Rommel wouldn't send unwanted prisoners the much longer way round the mountains just because there was a good coast road between Gazala and Benghazi.

Offer said, 'I'll lay a pound to a penny O'Keefe and old Wardy will be heading along the Trig-el-Abd tomorrow. Now, don't you see, that gives us our chance? Sure, P.O.W. convoys are guarded, but what sort of a guard?' Not four armoured cars to one Jeep containing two valuable prisoners.

His mind raced to the possibilities of rescue. He and his men could keep pace with the convoy far out in the desert, making their plans to come in to the attack. Their presence

146

wouldn't be suspected. The Trig-el-Abd was the last place the enemy would expect to encounter marauding British. They could lie up, keeping watch, as the convoy passed them, then swiftly overtake them and – well, he'd cook up something when he saw what sort of guard was over the prisoners.

They all got excited when they knew his plan, and now couldn't wait to get started. Hurriedly they cleaned their mess tins or plates with sand, packed them away and prepared to move out. Captain Offer's eyes fell again on those torn and empty jerricans, still uselessly strapped to the side of the Jeeps.

'First we must shoot up some soft transport,' he told them. They couldn't linger along the Trig-el-Abd without water for men and vehicles; as for petrol, he wasn't even sure they had enough to get them to the old caravan trail.

Field-marshal Rommel was there at Sidi Rezegh, a whirl-wind of activity, inspiring his disheartened soldiers and organizing them back into fighting units again. Yet in spite of all the work that fell upon him there were moments when even inconsiderable items were brought to his attention and decision were asked of him about them.

Such a moment occurred when he spotted a motorized column of Allied prisoners, and he halted his car and wanted to know if anyone important had been taken. His driver got out a thermos flask and pack of food, and Rommel ate and drank and felt he wasn't wasting time with prisoners as a consequence.

No, no one of exalted rank had fallen into the bag this time. Top ranking officer-prisoners were mere majors and colonels, and Rommel couldn't be bothered with them. Then someone told him they'd captured two of the notorious Glasshouse Gang, and that did command Rommel's attention. He wanted to see them. Weren't they recently responsible for depriving him of his base, so much needed at this critical time, at Fort Telatha?

O'Keefe and Ward, under heavy guard, were only a few yards away, squatting beside their Jeep. Hauptmann Braunschweig came stiffly to attention, heels clicking and saluting when the travel-stained field-marshal came briskly up to them.

Rommel looked at the prisoners who recognized him but made no effort to rise off their heels. 'They've been questioned? Nothing useful?' Braunschweig shook his head. 'A pity.' The field-marshal's lips tightened unpleasantly. 'They're a nuisance, that gang. They have done more damage to our cause than a brigade of Scottish Highlanders,' and the kilted men were a terrible enemy. 'I do not like to think of them operating behind our lines. We should have caught them and shot them long ago.'

'Sir.' It was Braunschweig, a mere captain calmly addressing his general.

'Well, Herr Hauptmann?'

'Only two hours ago the whole Gang made a very determined attempt to rescue their comrades.' Then he modified his statement. 'At least they appeared on the point of doing so but were spotted and escaped once again over the desert.'

'Escaped! They always escape!' Rommel growled unpleasantly. 'Tell me about it.' He was wolfing black bread and sausage. Three more minutes and he'd be away, his meal over.

So Braunschweig told him, and even the field-marshal was astounded by the effrontery of Glasshouse John's commando.

'You mean, they were there, travelling in the middle of my army, and nobody noticed them?' Rommel's voice echoed sheer incredulity.

The Hauptmann had to admit that that was the situation. He might have added that no one could have been more shocked than he, seeing those four Jeeps at that time. There was the Hauptmann Offer and his men, right on their heels, dogging them like jackals seeking to rob a predator of its prey. The colossal nerve of the man!

Rommel snapped, 'This can't go on.' Yet even Rommel seemed impressed by the gall of the raiders. He looked at Braunschweig shrewdly. He remembered the man well. Hadn't quite come off in his encounters with Offer's gang, but he was a first-class officer. 'Have you any ideas about the situation, Herr Hauptmann?'

'I have, sir.' Braunschweig had been running over them in his mind for the past couple of hours.

'Then tell them to me.'

'Sir, Hauptmann Offer seems so determined to rescue his comrades that I think he will not go away without making a further attempt to free them. He is a very clever man and will doubtless have worked out that the prisoners will be sent to Benghazi via Trig-el-Abd.'

'Very good reasoning, Herr Hauptmann. You think he will make another rescue bid on the Trig-el-Abd?' Braunschweig was cautious and said he thought it was possible. 'And how would you counter this rogue of an Englishman?'

Hauptmann Braunschweig told him. It was very simple. When he had finished Field-marshal Rommel said, 'Let it be done,' and started to turn away. Then he added, 'You will take command of the operation, Herr Hauptmann,' and strode off to his car.

Hauptmann Braunschweig stood rooted to the spot. He did not want to play nurse to Allied P.O.W.s at such a time; his place was with his regiment, with his comrades. For one bitter moment the Hauptmann wished he had never spoken of his idea then, good soldier that he was, he accepted the situation, turned and began to implement the plans he had made.

Glasshouse John wouldn't get out of this trap, if he was indeed foolish enough to stage another rescue attempt.

'Fuel and water coming up,' said Captain Offer. He did not need to use his glasses this time, either.

The Gang had worked out their plans, then had set off north again, but moving with great caution. Offer was pretty certain they would find without difficulty what they wanted. 'Two or three trucks together, that's what we're looking for,' he told them. Not many more because they didn't want resistance, and of course they weren't going to stick up any trucks if they were loaded with nasty Panzer-grenadiers.

They'd help themselves to food and water, and if necessary siphon off the petrol from the tanks. But they wouldn't take all supplies: Captain Offer wasn't going to leave men, even enemies, stranded in the desert without the means to keep alive.

There was still plenty of stuff crawling across the horizon, stragglers limping back to join their comrades. After half an hour they sighted a small column, but this was too strong for them to tackle. It was a German field recovery unit, apparently organized to tow in armoured cars only. They had powerful trucks which hauled disabled vehicles over the tortuous desert, and they had picked up seven cars, four heavier and three light ones. The trucks would have been easy meat for the Gang, manned by a driver and a mechanic, but in each of the armoured cars on tow was a driver and perhaps a gunner. No sense in taking on this lot, they all agreed, and when it had gone by they struck north-west looking for other prey.

There was another field recovery unit transporting tanks towards Rezegh – in fact most of the transport they were to see in the next hours were recovery units of some sort – but they weren't having anything to do with this armour, either.

Then, surveying the terrain from the top of a short bluff, his Jeeps neatly tucked out of sight, Offer saw two big canvas-topped trucks lurch into view. They must have been in a hollow, perhaps doing repairs or resting after many hours of travel; now they came up into sight and weren't more than a quarter of a mile away. Because the canvas at the rear was strapped down Offer knew there were no men inside – no one would travel in that heat with the back flaps lowered. So all they had to contend with were four men, two drivers and their mates.

Giving one last careful look around and seeing no other transport within miles, Captain Offer ran down to his Jeeps and gave the order to move. 'A piece of cake,' he told them, and led the way out of the hollow.

Lashley was driving for Offer now, Weybright still feeling the effects of being hurled from the Jeep earlier, and he went hard across the desert, so that the others had difficulty in keeping up with the Aussie. They attacked openly, driving straight up to the massive trucks – ammo carriers, they guessed – so that the drivers must have seen them even before they opened fire.

Wilborn, fit again apart from a big bump on his head, had received careful instructions. So had the other gunners. They must not fire on the vehicles attacked in case they ruptured petrol tanks or caused an explosion. No good destroying vehicles accidentally if fuel and water went up in fire.

Jimmy, a damp brown dead tab drooling, fired across the bonnet of the leading vehicle. Tracer, skipping by within twenty feet of a driver, was enough to make a man think twice before continuing. A big boot came hastily off the accelerator, and the truck reduced speed, though it still continued to roll.

The Jeeps were now scudding in a wide circle round the two ponderous vehicles, guns covering them, not coming too close in case there was more to these trucks than they had anticipated. There wasn't.

'Give 'em another burst,' ordered Offer, and Wilborn obliged, this time hosing tracer within ten feet of the leading cab. The German driver got the message and hauled on his handbrake.

Now the Jeeps came to a halt, but no man dismounted yet. Weybright stood up and in German shouted to the drivers and mates to descend. With every appearance of reluctance the men did so. When they were grouped together with their hands up, some of the men vaulted out of their Jeeps and ran, tommies cocked, towards them. They climbed into the cabs and shoved enquiring heads through the canvas to see what the trucks carried. Others checked for fuel.

Within minutes they were back with reports. Water was disappointing. Each truck carried barely enough to last their crews more than a day or two – nothing to spare for the Gang. The fuel position was even more disconcerting.

'Sir,' said Eddie Walker, coming up with the bad news, 'we picked a bad 'un in this pair. We shan't get much petrol out of them.'

'Oh?'

'Bloody diesels, sir.'

'Well,' said Offer with feeling, 'bugger me!' All that effort for nothing.

When they had recovered from their discomfiture Weybright was sent off to tell the Germans to pack their belongings, including food and water, and start walking north. It wasn't all that far to Sidi Rezegh, and long before they reached it they were likely to be picked up by one of their own trucks. The Germans seemed relieved at getting off so lightly, not much bothered by the prospect of a long trudge over the desert.

The diesels were going to be destroyed. That would be their contribution to the war effort. 'After all,' John Offer reminded them, 'we're British.' No one cheered, but all took enthusiastic part in the blowing up of the trucks.

Wilborn, their demolitions expert, clambered into both in turn to ensure the most successful detonation of the ammunition within. Satisfied, he and Redpath counted in unison up to three, then each slung a Mills bomb into the trucks. The moment the bombs left their hands they hopped into waiting Jeeps which took off at frantic speed. When they were a hundred yards away both trucks blew up with a tremendous noise, but by that time the Jeeps were all safely out of range.

They began to hunt for other prey.

Infuriatingly they hadn't much success with the next trucks, either – Italian transport. Full of land mines, not much water to spare because they'd been in the desert for five days, and two out of the five vehicles were also diesels. Disgruntled, they blew up the trucks – the biggest bang they'd heard since Telatha, but it seemed to attract no attention on that wide desert – and went on.

Third time lucky. Three empty trucks heading back down the desert, probably seeking further salvageable equipment. The Jeeps, their technique now well-practised, went roaring round them, the occupants whooping like Red Indians. Lots of shooting across the bonnet of the leading truck and out tumbled the occupants, men suddenly in a most obliging mood.

The vehicles had any amount of water to spare, and more petrol than the Jeeps could carry. They also had excellent food rations, including some good Chianti, so that the Gang's supply problems were ended for some time to come.

Again the trucks were destroyed and the Italians, looking very doleful, set off to walk back the way they had come. Captain Offer struck west towards the Trig-el-Abd.

They went in a hurry. Shooting up enemy transport took time, and by now O'Keefe and Ward might be well along the caravan route. By sun-down they came upon it, to a fork where a track led off to Msus and Soluch and eventually to Benghazi. Just the right place to maintain a watch, and John Offer was confident that the slower-moving P.O.W. convoy wouldn't have gone through before them.

Night. They got down in their blankets in some broken ground out of sight of the trail, one man on guard only. It wasn't likely that any transport would go through after dark, and so far behind the enemy lines was safety in itself. They slept the untroubled sleep of men who had angels on their side, and rose at dawn to have one of the best breakfasts they could remember in weeks.

Satisfied, they prepared to watch the trail all day. 'If they don't come through by night,' Offer told the others, 'I've guessed wrong.' The prisoners wouldn't be heading for Benghazi, after all.

He chose a position within fifty yards of the very broad trail, as close as they could get because there'd be problems of identifying O'Keefe and Ward if they came through in a crowded P.O.W. truck. It might become necessary, in fact, to stick up P.O.W. convoys in order to discover if his men were among them. He didn't want to do that because if they drew blank the first time it would inevitably create alarm and betray their presence on the route.

Offer's hope was that because they were dangerous men O'Keefe and Ward would be kept separate from other prisoners, and thus might be more easily identified.

Their place of watch was a narrow cleft in some eroded rocks in broken ground south of the caravan trail. The cleft gave them cover, and for most of the day they would be in shadow. It also had the advantage of giving them a back way out from the trail, for they could walk erect away from it, a turn in the cleft completely concealing them.

Captain Offer put two men on at a time, one to maintain watch if anything turned up, the other to act as runner to the camp on the other side of the broken ground. One hour watching, the rest trying to find what comfort was possible in a camp of few shadows. Most of the day Offer stayed with the men on watch, too impatient for action to doze with the Gang beside their Jeeps.

An hour after dawn transport began to move along the trail. Some came from the direction of Agedabia, south-west on the coast, but much was from Benghazi. Most of it was heading east towards Sidi Rezegh, with only light traffic westward-bound, empty trucks going back for supplies.

But the Benghazi traffic was interesting. A lot of new stuff was being pushed up to the front, just in off the docks from Sicily. Tanks on transporters, guns of all descriptions, and any amount of armoured vehicles and trucks laden with supplies for Rommel's army in the field. It came through in convoys, sometimes passing the hidden watchers for half an hour at a time. Then there might be a gap of up to an hour.

'That might complicate things,' Offer said to his men, frowning as he saw the straining transport lurch and grind over the dirt track, an incessant dust cloud hanging over the trail, choking them, when they went by. They could hardly stage a rescue attack if a convoy happened to be going through at the time. He shrugged, finally. No good worrying, they'd meet the problem when the time came. First, spot their men.

Transport going west passed by in irregular fashion, generally no more than three or four vehicles together. Each time they saw a cloud of dust to their right their hearts leapt, thinking this was it, but until well into the afternoon no trucks bearing P.O.W.s came through. John Offer began to think he had pulled a boner, that after all P.O.W.s weren't being sent via Benghazi.

Then a Jeep came into sight, emerging from its own cloud of dust. A Jeep!

Offer, his glasses on it, said incredulously, 'Stone the bloody crows, *our* Jeep.' His powerful binoculars focused on the occupants – four men. A German soldier at the driving wheel, that stern-looking German officer beside him, and squatting in the rear under the Breda were O'Keefe and Ward.

Behind the Jeep rolled two big canvas-topped trucks. They were travelling at a steady pace, yet kicking up the usual cloud of dust. But Offer had eyes only for the Jeep.

He lowered his glasses and turned to his fellow watchers. They were Lashley and Palfreyman, insisting on doing his stint. He said, 'There's something odd going on.' That Jeep wasn't what he had expected. He'd thought O'Keefe and Ward would be brought to Benghazi in some more suitable vehicle; for a Jeep was too small, it didn't, for example, permit of a proper guard on the two prisoners.

He raised his glasses again. He was prepared to lay a pound to a penny those prisoners openly paraded couldn't be got out of that Jeep in a hurry. They'd be shackled to the vehicle, manacled and maybe with gyves upon their ankles. To free the prisoners they would have to recapture the Jeep.

Openly paraded. He found himself considering those words which had sprung to his mind. They did appear to be paraded, so prominent in that unusual vehicle, sure to catch everyone's eye, and driving ahead of the big trucks. His glasses took in the trucks again. Bedfords. Probably full of P.O.W.s with a couple of armed guards sitting by the tailboard. Not much opposition there.

His glasses came back to the Jeep, now bumping along a hundred yards away, those faces very clear in his binoculars. He should have exulted; this was a push-over, only a few armed men guarding their prisoners, and the Gang with four Brownings to quell any opposition. But he was uneasy. Something smacked wrong somewhere. It looked too damned easy, that was the trouble.

He tried to reassure himself as the Jeep came steadily level with them. Why was he bothered? So far behind the fighting line the enemy wouldn't waste many men to guard P.O.W.s; the smallness of this P.O.W. convoy held no significance.

But the Jeep, his mind insisted, did. Why waste a Jeep just to carry two prisoners, special men though they were? Something jarred about the whole thing, and Offer was suspicious long before the Jeep drew level with them.

Ward, Arab headdress on, was facing him. The driver was looking ahead, and the hard-looking officer couldn't see Offer for his driver. There was a risk that the driver of the Bedford following might see him, but Offer took a chance.

He stood up, standing back in the cleft, and waved.

Ward seemed not to notice him for a second or so, as if his eyes were focused elsewhere. Then Offer saw him stir, and he thought he kicked O'Keefe, for the sergeant-major sat straight up.

And then both prisoners began to sing the National Anthem.

Offer dropped out of sight with his companions. As the sounds of two lusty male voices, only approximately in tune, came to their ears the three crouching men regarded each other incredulously. Nobody sang the National Anthem. Not in the British army. Men fighting for king and country would roar out *Lili Marlene*, the Horst Wessel song or improper words to the Egyptian jingle of a national anthem. But never *God Save the King* if they could get out of it.

Yet here, along this ancient caravan trail, two deserters from His Majesty's army had decided to break into patriotic song.

'Christ!' said Lashley. 'They've been tortured – gone fuckin' nuts!'

Offer said, urgently, 'Ssssh!'

He was listening. They were so close to the trail they could hear every word clearly, and John Offer couldn't remember this verse in the authorized version.

'This is a bleedin' trap
It is a bloody trap –
God save your skins.'

Offer, peering cautiously out, saw the big officer turn as if surprised, then resume his seat looking forward as if not understanding the deliberately raucous-voiced words.

'This is a bleedin' trap
It is a bleeding trap . . .'

The first of the trucks now came abreast, and the singing voices were lost in the sound of the powerful engine. Over the tailboard they could see men hanging by the roof support overhead. They looked British enough, P.O.W.s standing, staring back along the trail, faces wistful or dejected. No acting there. Two German guards sitting on the tailboard, Schmeissers slung from their shoulders but seeming on good terms with their charges, chatting to them.

The second truck much the same, P.O.W.s and two guards fraternizing amiably, because no one was likely to make a bolt for it, here in this awful wasteland. It all looked too easy, ten opponents at the most, yet there was that warning song – *it is a bleedin' trap.*

The time of watching was ended. Offer rose, saying, 'Come on,' and led the way at a run to the camp. When they saw them running, every man came up from the shadows, guns ready.

'Okay, okay,' called Offer reassuringly and the guns lowered immediately. He gathered them around him, and told them what had happened on the trail.

'It's a trap, all right,' he said with certainty. 'The Jeep's bait. O'Keefe and Ward, sitting there, are intended to bring us out from cover.'

But what sort of a trap? He'd looked back along the trail and there were no other military vehicles following. The two Bedfords? They seemed full of P.O.W.s. All the same, Offer thought, that's where the danger must lie, and he said so to his men. 'Can't be anywhere else.'

He let his words sink in. They hadn't much time to linger, if they were to stage a rescue bid, but he was still worrying over the problem, trying to decide on the proper course of action. Better to take his time now than do the wrong thing and come a cropper.

Finally Eddie Walker asked, 'What's the plan, sir?'

Offer shrugged. 'Only one thing we can do. Let's spring the trap.' He gave some brief instructions, then went to his Jeep. Weybright would drive because Offer might need his German; Wilborn automatically took up position behind the Browning.

They took off, bumping round the broken ground and getting on to the trail beyond. Here the rough country ended temporarily, though there were some ragged hills five or ten miles to the north, the Benghazi trail hereabouts crossing a plain of painful flatness and desolation, only rank grass and thorn bushes surviving, and that sparsely.

Offer led the way, Weybright with his foot hard down. Ahead rose the dust from the Jeep and two Bedfords. Offer gave a signal, and immediately two of his Jeeps took off fast east of the trail, while Offer's Jeep and the fourth one swung west of the tiny convoy.

So they overtook the three captured vehicles, two Jeeps roaring on either side of them, a good quarter of a mile out into the desert. They must have been seen, but the Jeep continued at a steady pace, leading the way for the two big trucks. Weybright eased off on the accelerator, so that now their Jeeps maintained pace with the slower-moving convoy.

The Germans ignored them, and continued at the same speed.

For five minutes all vehicles maintained their positions, the convoy between the Jeeps, and all throwing up dense plumes of dust. Abruptly John Offer said, 'We're going in.'

As the miles rolled by and Benghazi came closer Hauptmann Braunschweig began to feel discouraged. No sign of the Glasshouse Gang. Perhaps he had been too optimistic, his theory irrational when one considered it coldly.

These men, after all, were criminals, men of little loyalty or they would not have deserted their army. The Hauptmann's lips tightened as he thought of that military crime. Why would such men take big risks out of loyalty to comrades? It was asking a lot of anyone, particularly of army deserters, to plunge even deeper into enemy territory in an effort, danger abounding, to rescue these men with him in the Jeep.

By the time they came to the fork in the Trig-el-Abd, Braunschweig had resigned himself to a wasted journey. If the Hauptmann Offer had intended a rescue bid he would surely have mounted it before now.

The thought should have lulled him into carelessness, but Hauptmann Braunschweig could never lose his guard, his military training too strongly instilled into him for that. In any event, every time he told himself that the Glasshouse Gang wouldn't attack, and weren't the men to take risks just to save some comrades, he remembered something: they had already done so. Any men who could brazenly trail him and his prisoners in the midst of a retreating enemy army had nerve enough for anything.

So he jolted uncomfortably along, conscious of a cooling day, ever watchful, pessimistic about the outcome of the whole thing, yet never losing his vigilance.

Sometimes he turned and looked at his P.O.W.s, as if to make sure they were still there. Two experiences with Glasshouse Gang prisoners – both times John Offer had been one of them – had created a respect for their resourcefulness in emergency. Curious men, these army deserters, so contradictory in their behaviour. For instance, what had impelled them to sing their national anthem suddenly, back there where the trail forked? They were not patriotic, yet all at once they had sung, and sung very loudly, too.

. . . terrible singers, the British. Now, his Germans would have sung loudly, too, but they would have contrived harmony and would not have mutilated their words as these lower-class British did. He had not understood what they were singing, anyway; it certainly did not sound like the words of their anthem as he had heard others sing it. What did that word 'bleedin' mean? What had blood to do with saving their king, though he hadn't heard them sing that sentiment, he remembered.

Now the prisoners were talking together, sitting under the Breda made useless so that they couldn't get up to any tricks. Not that they could do much damage with their ankles shackled and wired to the floor of the Jeep.

Hauptmann Braunschweig heard a sound, an engine noise above the beat of their own Jeep. His head turned, and instantly his hair almost stood on end, the moment so electrifying.

Out on the desert, separated by a distance of a hundred yards, two Jeeps tore along, dust thrown back by the little spinning wheels. Another sound brought his head the other way. Two more Jeeps paced them on the desert half a kilometre east of the trail.

It was somehow awesome, the way those Jeeps had suddenly appeared out of nowhere. What men they were,

Braunschweig found himself thinking. What courage to come hunting here in the heart of enemy country just to help comrades. Perhaps these deserters were of a different breed from their own. And then he thought, 'Perhaps it's their Hauptmann, Offer.' Perhaps the Gang leader made all the difference.

Braunschweig's driver had seen the Jeeps, too, and he shot an enquiring glance at his officer. 'Just keep going,' Braunschweig told him, and they trundled steadily on as if the Jeeps hadn't been seen.

Behind them the two prisoners had begun to talk excitedly, and he guessed they were waving to their comrades across the desert. The Hauptmann made no attempt to quieten or restrain them. It made no difference what they did. The prisoners were the bait, and they had successfully drawn their comrades out into the open for him. Now it remained to be seen how the situation could be exploited.

Braunschweig wanted them nearer. At a distance of half a kilometre they were well within range of his guns, yet the Hauptmann wanted them to come closer, much closer so that he could be sure of hitting them. Firing from jolting trucks gave no guarantee of accuracy in aim, and he did not want to halt because why should that tempt them? No, keep going, let them lose caution and come in to the attack, then they would have a surprise. Very much a surprise, he thought grimly, and then wondered if the clever Hauptmann Offer hadn't thoroughly worked out what surprises might be in store for them if they did attack? Offer was as devious as the devil, and capable of any act of divination.

But how difficult for the raiders if they did come in to attack, Hauptmann Braunschweig told himself, and that was the strength of his position; for if the Glasshouse Gang used their guns on the convoy they risked hurting their own kind, prisoners in each of the three vehicles.

So, as if unconscious of each other's presence, seven vehicles trundled over the desert towards the distant ragged hills. Abruptly, though, the pattern changed. One Jeep came swerving towards the German convoy. One only. The Hauptmann was disappointed. He had expected them all to come driving in at them, guns firing in an act of intimidation. But without even firing, just one Jeep was nosing its way towards them, as if to smell out the danger, he thought.

Again his driver looked at him, but the Hauptmann just said, quietly, 'Carry on.'

The Jeep was still a cautious distance away, about a hundred yards to their left. Now the Hauptmann did not bother to pretend he was in ignorance of the other's presence. He turned in his seat and looked directly towards the other vehicle. His eyes were good and he did not use his binoculars. He could see a man crouching behind a machine-gun in the back of the Jeep.

Beside the driver was a passenger. The distance was still too great to be sure, particularly with the jarring effect of the truck on vision, but Hauptmann Braunschweig thought the man looked familiar. Was this their leader, the one called Glasshouse John? He felt sure it was.

And so they stared at each other across that intervening scrub desert, two men curious about the other, and neither hating their enemy. Finally the Hauptmann saw the man he thought was Hauptmann Offer lift his hand in salute. He found himself raising his hand similarly.

It was a curious duel.

John Offer said, 'Fire a burst across his bow.' He had to do something; they couldn't go on just pacing each other. Perhaps a few shots would bring out into the open the trap he knew was there waiting to be sprung.

Wilborn promptly let fly, the tracer scooting only a few yards ahead of the German-driven Jeep. The Jeep continued without pause.

Offer sighed. He was up against a cool customer. Weybright said, 'Something coming up, sir.'

Captain Offer looked ahead. In the hilly ground ahead a tiny dust cloud told of the approach of another Axis convoy.

'Plenty of time,' he said; then to Wilborn, 'Go for the tyres.'
Not of the Jeep – if O'Keefe and Ward were manacled to it
it was essential that it could be driven away, if captured.
No, the Jeep must not be immobilized. But the Bedfords,
yes. Halt them and see what advantage that brought. It
might turn out there was nothing of a trap, after all.

So most unexpectedly Wilborn opened fire on the leading
Bedford. They were close enough to ensure hitting the
wheels without risk to any P.O.W.s. A swift burst and the
front tyres disappeared in shattered rubber. A slight swing
of the Browning and the second Bedford had its front tyres
shot off almost simultaneously. Both vehicles yawed madly
as the tyreless wheels dragged into the dirt, then came to a
sudden halt. Obedient to an order, Weybright put his foot
down hard and went like crazy away over the bumpy
desert.

That, curiously, was something Hauptmann Braunschweig
hadn't considered. Flush the Gang into the open, that was
his first aim. The second, to have them come incautiously
near. He had expected that to happen, four Jeeps confident
in their own firepower closing in to halt them. But one Jeep
nosing forward to investigate had upset his plans – opening
fire on the Bedfords' tyres quite dumbfounded him for the
moment. That damned Offer wasn't behaving as he had
expected him to!

He rose instantly in his seat, alarmed, shouting back to
the Bedfords: 'Keep out of sight! Don't let them know you
are there!' But they wouldn't have heard him, and anyway
his hidden men had reacted instantly to the firing and the
abrupt halt of their vehicles. They thought the attack had
come, and now they came leaping out to teach these desert
raiders the bloodiest of lessons.

Bouncing along as fast as they could go, Captain Offer
looked back and saw man after man leaping out of the now
stationary trucks. Man after man, and none of them in the
familiar KD of the P.O.W.s John Offer had spotted before.
Panzergrenadiers. They must have been squatting out of

sight within, just as Offer had suspected.

'Sprung the bloody trap!' he roared with delight, shouting above the engine noise. But there seemed a lot of them and they came tumbling down dragging heavy guns between them. Get out of range, Offer urged himself, and hoped the other Jeeps weren't lingering, either.

The Panzergrenadiers were bringing heavy machine-guns into action, and then cannon shell came exploding to their right. Formidable stuff, and four Jeeps dodged and swerved and went like stink across the bumpy desert, tracer pursuing them, sometimes almost getting them, but those few seconds' lead were enough. Exasperated German gunners saw their targets growing smaller and smaller, sometimes disappearing from view for brief moments as the fleeing desert raiders found wadis and depressions and kept to them as long as possible. Violent German oaths did not improve their aim, neither did their speech grow less vigorous when they saw one of the Jeeps halt and they guessed they were being calmly surveyed out of gun range by someone with binoculars.

The Germans had stopped firing – pure waste of ammo, thought Offer, and watched them for a few minutes through his glasses. God, how simple it had all been, teasing the Germans into showing their hand. But having done it, having found they were there in strength, what good did it do them? How did it help them to rescue their oppos?

He saw the tall Hauptmann striding about, and felt sorry for the man. A bond had sprung up between them in their brief relationship. John Offer appreciated his opponent's courtesy towards him, that polite consideration when he had been the Hauptmann's prisoner. A good type, the Kraut officer, and Offer regretted that he had always to be in a position of having to outwit and defeat him, and in the process undoubtedly cause him to be humiliated.

He turned his glasses north. That cloud of dust was advancing. Offer made some calculations. The approaching

164

convoy would be close upon them by sunset. So? Offer shrugged. How did that fit into the picture? A convoy, probably wicked with armoured cars almost as fast as his Jeeps, hardly seemed an ally in his efforts to release O'Keefe and Ward.

One final look at the Hauptmann and his men. They were busy around the wheels of their disabled Bedfords. It would take some time to get them moving again, he thought, for heavy machine-gun bullets make a mess of nuts and bolts and they'd be the devil of a job to move.

Captain Offer said, 'Let's get cracking.' Weybright slipped the Jeep in gear but held the clutch down, looking at his C.O. to amplify the order. 'Just find a cosy hollow where we can sit and watch the Hun.'

Weybright accelerated. They retired a further quarter of a mile, then came to a nice depression, only a few feet below the surrounding desert and easy to get out of in any direction. Offer said, 'This'll do,' and looked round. His other Jeeps were widely dispersed and one seemed a very great distance away, yet he knew they would be watching him.

They went below ground, switched off, then slowly got out. The elation of that last brush with the enemy now drained away, leaving them with the usual feeling of emptiness, weariness stealing over them, a reminder that their day had been long.

Within minutes there was a roaring sound, then one after the other the remaining Jeeps came swooping down into the hollow, making a great row and throwing up the dust. Engines switched off, and men alighted, all looking to their officer for instruction.

'Okay,' said Offer, the drill most apparent for such an occasion. 'Brew up. Make a nosh. Just two men on watch.'

Sergeant Walker remembered his stripes and said, 'You and you,' and Pom, furious and dragging his leg to remind them of his tortured backside, and huge Busker climbed to the lip of the depression to maintain first watch.

John Offer went half-way up the bank, too, then got down

flat on his back. He wanted to be apart from his men, for he knew he had to do some heavy thinking. Besides, he was running down inside, that unwonted feeling of pessimism, rarely known before this last patrol, taking hold of him.

As he lay there he tried to analyse his feelings. He had never known such depression as he'd had in recent days. Even in the Glasshouse, suffering in the Punishment cells, he hadn't felt down like this. He knew what it was, of course: every man who kept on too long in the desert began to cave in within himself. Just like the R.A.F., he thought; too many sorties and the best of them began to crack up and had to be grounded for a time. Well, he had battle fatigue or desert fatigue, call it what you liked. He too wanted to be 'grounded', but how could a deserter find the relief his jangled nerves called for?

As he lay there he looked back on the previous months. He had never been a true desert-lover in the manner of Arab Ward and the sergeant-major, but all the same there had been a lot of satisfaction in traversing the vast waste-lands, however uncomfortable it might have been. Sure, he had done his share of moaning about the heat and dust, the flies and lack of water, but still there had been a lot with which to feel satisfied. He had never minded it half as much as he made out, he now realized. Even the jousts with danger he'd taken in his stride. Glad when it was over, of course, but getting stuck in when required and deriving an intense thrill and even, in some way, a kind of pleasure from the nearness to death.

Now was so different. He didn't want to have to risk his life again, nor to have another uncomfortable journey across the desert. His spirit at this moment craved peace and quiet, and an end to living in this awful state of tension.

'I've gone soft,' he told himself, the cold of late afternoon digging into his tired muscles. He wondered, 'Will it ever come back?' That fierce exultation with which he had gone forward to meet danger, the uplifting of spirit, the inspiration that excitement brought to him, his brain seeming to work on a higher plane than ever it did when fear of death no longer acted as stimulant to his imagination.

Now he wanted to stay in that hollow until all danger had receded, and he tried to make excuses to himself to keep them there. It did no good to hang around this dangerous Benghazi trail, he kept telling himself. What chance had they of releasing the prisoners? None – not a hope. So why waste time? Why not give up the attempt: they'd done their best and no one could point the finger at them. Just have their meal, then quietly steal away south into the desert, then west behind the safety of their own lines, anywhere to get away from the guns of those formidable Panzer-grenadiers.

Safety. The word lingered with him, making him stir uneasily. What in hell's name was he thinking about? What safety was there if they did attain Montgomery's lines? He stopped kidding himself, and it brought a further depression and despair to realize that nowhere in Africa was there safety for him and his men.

Weybright came trudging up with a mug of char. Offer took it gratefully, and felt better when he had gulped half of it into his parched throat. Then some quickly prepared hash came up, and again it helped, but slightly, to restore his spirits.

Finally Pom's thin voice came squeaking down to him – 'Sir, I think they're about to move off.'

Captain Offer climbed reluctantly to his feet at that, shivering and wishing he wasn't so damned lazy for then he would go and find a woollen warmer. He came to where his men were sitting, back to back so that each was responsible for half the world around them. Glasses out, he confirmed Pom's surmise. Indeed, as he watched, the Jeep began to move off again, the big Bedfords falling in line behind it. His glasses held on to the prisoners, O'Keefe and Ward, clearly visible, talking together. Still being used as bait, Offer thought, and still soundly manacled to the Jeep, so what chance had they of rescuing them?

Again the temptation was strong to call it a day and just sit there while they watched their comrades drive off towards an enemy prison camp. They could do nothing, so why not face up to it and accept defeat?

But when the time came John Offer was incapable of running out on his men. They looked to him to care for them, to do his best to help them in time of need and danger. He could no more run away now than fly, and though he hated to make the decision, when he made it it was not to desert his followers.

He sighed. He guessed that when they had to go into action something of the old zest would take over again, the excitement that had uplifted him before would sustain him again. That was always the pattern. The trouble was, each time it became harder to drive himself into making such decisions.

Again his glasses swung and picked up the advancing dust cloud, still miles away along the Benghazi trail. He thought in surprise, 'By Jove, it's a big one!' The convoy seemed to stretch for miles, throwing up an immense cloud of dust, so that it must have been abominably uncomfortable, driving in the midst of it. Miles away, but his glasses brought them close enough for identification, and that produced another surprise.

'That's a soft convoy,' he told his sentries, who remained uninterested by the information. His glasses sought through the haze of dust to find armour, but certainly at the head of the convoy there was none. He thought, 'Some ships have landed with fresh supplies and Rommel's rushing everything possible to his front.'

Of course he'd need supplies after the thrashing Monty's men had given him. The Axis armies had had to jettison so much in their hasty retreat, and now, if they were to be effective in the field again, they'd need ammunition, food, fuel and supplies on a prodigious scale. Here it was, coming the shortest way to replenish Rommel's battered army gathering near Bir Hakeim.

All soft transport, fuel tankers and big canvas-topped trucks. 'If Monty could get his bombers here now he'd win the next battle hands down!' But Monty could not have known of the vast supplies heading east along the old camel trail.

For some reason the soft convoy fascinated John Offer, and he kept looking at it, trying to estimate the size and giving up because there were so many grinding along and so much dust to obscure their number. The column, part of his mind calculated, would meet the Hauptmann's three vehicles within an hour.

He realized that all his men had come to the top of the rim to stare across at the Hauptmann and then at that advancing horde of enemy vehicles. Weybright was one of them. A knowledgeable man, Weybright.

'Tell me, do you think the Germans –' Offer's nod restricted his question to the Hauptmann's party – 'carry a wireless transmitter?' The Hauptmann's vehicles were moving quite briskly now.

'May I borrow your glasses, sir?' Weybright was a very polite man.

They were handed over. Weybright raised them and studied the three moving vehicles. When he lowered them he was emphatic. 'I wouldn't think so, sir. No aerials on any of the vehicles. I don't think they'd equip a convoy as small as this with a transmitter, anyway; we wouldn't, sir.'

So the Germans had no means of communicating over a distance, John Offer thought. For instance, they would not be able to signal information to that huge soft convoy ahead. At that moment John Offer had no plan in his mind, but was storing information, because information could inspire ideas, and when that idea came it could almost instantly dictate action . . .

It came, it did. Just watching that huge, advancing dust cloud put a thought into his mind. It always happened like that. One moment his mind was blank, the next there was something exciting there, an embryo idea to be licked into shape by later, more logical processes of thought.

He looked at the convoy, and one word hit his brain – confusion. With that word came a series of pictures of his Jeeps running amok like killer dogs among helpless sheep – just as they had done more than once before, he reminded himself, but never on such a scale. That picture was followed by others, among which O'Keefe's Jeep figured prominently. Dust and smoke and a bewildered enemy not knowing what was happening . . .

Captain Offer looked at his men. He thought, 'I ought to put it to them.' They had the right to say if they thought the risk of losing their lives was worth another attempt to save O'Keefe and Ward. His mind, anyway, was still grappling with his plan, and merely to express it in words would help to give it shape. But it would have to be brief; the Hauptmann with his prisoners would soon meet the convoy, and if the Gang were to accept his plan Offer's patrol had to beat the Germans to it.

He said, 'Look here, you chaps, I've got an idea but it's dicey and it's a question of volunteers only. If you don't like it, you don't need to come and I'll think none the worse of you for holding back. Okay?

'Well, over there is poor old Ward and the sergeant-major. All we learned from our last manoeuvre is that they are formidably guarded. We want to rescue them but how can we do it? Now, I've got a plan. I will admit it is a bit hare-brained but it's the best I can do at this moment. Very briefly, it's to go and attack that soft transport – bull in a china shop, you know. Run amok, give it hell, shoot up everything, get the dust rising and smoke pouring. In other words, create chaos, and under cover of all the confusion we might grab O'Keefe's Jeep and drive it away. The thing is, timing . . .'

He went swiftly into details, especially of a rendezvous later for any survivors. He spoke about survivors again at the end of his brief talk.

'Don't let us kid ourselves that attacking soft transport is without danger. Back of it all might be armoured cars, and they're things we're not equipped to tackle. So, you men, if we go into this op some of us mightn't come out alive.'

'But you think we've a chance?' Palfreyman was very alert and eager in spite of his bandaged face.

'If we hit 'em hard and fast and don't linger more than five or ten minutes we've a chance of getting away with it – all of us. The danger starts if they're given time to think and organize some counter to our attack, which someone's sure to do if we don't get in and out smartly.'

Palfreyman, the fire-eater, said, 'Well, sir, I'm game.'

Every man there growled approval, and some were immediately restless and wanted to be away, the idea of shooting up soft transport suddenly intoxicating to their destructive minds. Loudest volunteer was Pom. Pom always made the greatest noise when it came to volunteering, but was invariably the first to regret it afterwards and try to pull out as soon as the first bullet flew.

'All right.' Captain Offer felt guilty. He had been half-hoping his men would turn against his idea, and then there'd have been nothing for it but to say goodbye to O'Keefe and Ward and let them roll on into captivity. Things were getting bad with him; the sooner he got out of Africa the better. 'Christ, I'm cracking up,' he told himself, and began to lope down the sandy slope as if to make up with activity for the uncertainty within him.

The moment he hopped into his Jeep, however, the mood left him.

Pom, jealous of Lashley, often selected by Offer for dangerous expeditions, shot into the driver's seat and looked triumphantly at the slower Aussie. Wilborn got behind the Browning – no one ever disputed his position these days as gunner to their commanding officer.

Then they were off, four Jeeps careering up the sandy slope in fine style and heading north across the desert parallel with the old trail. The Hauptmann in their other Jeep would quickly see them, Offer knew, but that didn't matter now, so long as the German officer was indeed without wireless. If he could signal ahead it would be curtains for all of them.

They went like the devil, flat out over the bumpy desert, gradually overtaking the Jeep and two Bedfords but keeping well out of gun range as they did so. Ahead the dust cloud from the big convoy grew swiftly larger, and the black dots which were trucks took on shape beneath it. When Offer saw how swiftly they were closing on the column, the thought came to him that perhaps, after all, they hadn't enough time left.

'Faster, faster!' he yelled, and Pom did his best and the other Jeeps flanking him in that mad race were hard pushed to keep up with him.

Level with the Jeep and Bedfords but a long way to their right, the dust of their madly spinning wheels shooting back in huge jets, John Offer changed course. They began to close in on the camel trail.

Clinging to a vehicle which seemed intent on either throwing them out or of turning completely over, John Offer tried to glimpse the Hauptmann's three vehicles and calculate the time required to get in among the convoy before the German officer reached it. It was going to be a near do. Then he looked anxiously towards the west. That at least was in their favour, the sun a red rim on the horizon, darkness less than an hour away. In, out, then scurry away into the night, that was the plan. Then lurk deep in the desert until the B.B.C. obligingly told them Benghazi was in British hands, some smooth talk on a gang-plank and he'd be bedding it down with his old Chelsea girl friends in no time. He'd take a new stage name, of course, and no one among his friends would think it at all odd.

Thoughts racing through his mind as they roared on a converging course to gain the trail ahead of the Hauptmann. Time even for a fraction of a second to think of Hugh Atherton. Regretfully all those plans he kept making of writing his memoirs and living high off the proceeds would have to be shelved. If he was dead how could he write a story? Unless he employed a ghost.

They came bouncing on to the trail, rutted by the passage of many military vehicles, and no better going than the open desert. Looking back Offer saw they were perhaps half a mile ahead of O'Keefe's Jeep. Before them, maybe five minutes' run away, was the convoy. They had made it just in time.

Offer thought, 'Christ, it's a whopper!' There must have been close on a thousand vehicles stretching back along the broad trail. Well, size was not against his plan. On the contrary, the bigger the column the more confusion they were likely to cause.

Offer yelled, 'Easy now!' No need to keep belting along. In fact moving at speed would only draw attention to themselves and they'd be watched with surprise which could turn into suspicion. Yes, go sedately, just trundle along, so that the enemy would think them captured vehicles being returned to Benghazi for some reason, maybe with high-ranking officers intent on some high-level mission.

Keep to the west of the huge column on the prevailing wind side, because that was what would be expected of them. Come up steadily, and when the moment was right, turn and plunge in among them before they knew what was happening. But – timing, the Hauptmann with his Jeep had to be almost up to the column when they went berserk.

'Slower,' Offer ordered, and Pom took a reluctant foot off his accelerator. The Hauptmann must be given time in which to close the gap.

Wilborn, riding easily at this slower pace, standing and holding on to the Browning with one hand, called down, 'The Jeep, sir, it's left the Bedfords and is catching up.'

'Good,' said Offer and hauled himself up beside his gunner. Together they stood and looked back. Only a quarter of a mile behind them now the Jeep was coming along at a great pace, leaving the Bedfords with their Panzergrenadiers trailing in the rear.

Offer thought, 'It's a good job the Hauptmann isn't carrying a machine-gun.' At that range Offer's Jeeps would be in trouble. He eyed the diminishing gap between pursuer and his own Jeep, then thought, 'We've got him worried.'

It must have been alarming for the Hauptmann to see four enemy vehicles openly heading for that huge Axis convoy. He would suspect mischief, of course, particularly in view of the Gang's reputation for creating havoc and destruction, and doubtless he was rushing up to warn the column that these were enemy who so brazenly drove towards them.

'Just what we want,' Offer assured Wilborn, down to the last fraction of a tab end that further discoloured his upper lip. To Pom, 'Just a bit faster, son.' The Hauptmann mustn't quite overtake them. One last glance behind. The Bedfords were trailing but coming along at quite a lick now, not all that far behind their leader, and that was something John Offer didn't like. Those hidden Panzergrenadiers were men he didn't care for; *they* weren't going to be caught by surprise, and they packed a lethal armament. Must keep well clear of them, he told himself.

Suddenly they were level with the head of the convoy. It came along at a slow pace, little more than fifteen miles an hour, a huge herd a dozen or more abreast, spread out across the broad trail to reduce the discomfort of travelling in each other's dust. Captain Offer looked across at the lumbering vehicles and thought what grim hell drivers and passengers were suffering, hour after hour rolling through the dust of trucks ahead. He'd had the experience and it wasn't one he'd choose to repeat. Still, all this was in their favour. Men in such conditions sank into a protective mental torpor, deliberately dulling their minds so as to reduce this grim misery, and driving by pure automatic reaction only. John Offer needed an enemy who wasn't going to think quickly when he struck.

He struck. Exactly the right moment came. They were two hundred yards alongside the noisy convoy, their own dust rolling towards it. The Hauptmann's Jeep, so near now they could distinguish the bobbing heads of the occupants, was almost up to the leading vehicles, the German officer standing and waving as if to attract attention. Can't leave it any longer, Offer decided, then gave a crisp order. 'Get at 'em, boy!'

Pom hauled on the wheel. The other Jeeps caught the movement and came swinging round, so that suddenly, for a few moments they were line astern, all at once accelerating towards the soft transport.

Undoubtedly eyes caught the manoeuvre. Apathetic gaze must have seen those funny little vehicles abruptly turn and head towards them. No one took alarm. Why should anyone be alarmed? These were enemy vehicles, true, but to be here, deep behind the front line, meant they must be captured ones, in the hands of their own kind. Even more, size made attack seem impossible. Soft transport, yes, but who in their right senses would have expected attack by a few Jeeps upon a convoy numbering hundreds upon hundreds of vehicles? After all, in numbers alone there were thousands of men in that mighty column, drivers and passengers, and all carrying arms.

John Offer had one last glimpse of the Hauptmann, still standing in his captured Jeep. The German officer must have been astounded to see his enemy deliberately turn and head into the column. Then they were in the dust of the convoy, driving across the bonnets of mighty Italian and German transports, huge vehicles which loomed up through the bitter-tasting dust that crept under their goggles and made their eyes smart with pain and begin to run.

And noise. They seemed to have entered a world of heavy beating sound, all around them powerful engines adding to each other's volume, the noise deafening. Looking up from their tiny vehicles they saw flat-fronted monsters come bearing down on them through the choking fog, at the wheel goggled men like beings from another world, powdered grey apparitions who sat motionless, hardly turning their heads when the Jeeps flitted by through the enveloping dust.

Captain Offer lost his other Jeeps. They knew what to do. They were threading their own paths through the vast ponderous convoy. John Offer thought he heard one go almost immediately into action, but it was difficult to tell with all that noise assailing them from pounding diesels and revving petrol engines.

He picked a tanker. There were half a dozen moving like alien goats in a flock of soft-topped sheep. Pom was now heading against the tide, picking his way between the advancing vehicles, and still without apparent reaction from Axis drivers as they loomed out of the dust.

Offer gave the order. 'Go to it!' and he had to shout so that Wilborn could hear.

Wilborn sucked a tooth, no fag in his mouth this time, then crouched, depressed his gun muzzle and belted off a quick burst. The tanker was scythed open and Offer saw petrol begin to pour, but it didn't explode into flame – yet. They were racing now, Pom dodging expertly between the trucks, Wilborn raking a second tanker.

Offer had his Very pistol out and fired back at the first torn tanker. A quick flash of light as the incendiary leapt the intervening space, then an instant conflagration. Up went the tanker, fire roaring, a shock wave from the explosion batting them hard as they sped away, heat tremendous instantly.

The second tanker spilling open, holding fire for a second or so, then responding to a Browning tracer and blowing up. Debris raining down, heat upon them that left them gasping. A great yellow-red illumination which seemed to penetrate the dust cloud and leave all nearby trucks clearly identifiable; and heavy transport careering away in alarm, running into each other in their sudden confusion.

John Offer, almost in panic, the nearness to the second exploding and blazing tanker unnerving, clawed his way erect so that Wilborn could hear him. 'No more tankers!' God, Wilborn would be the death of them, going for petrol

176

at such short range! But by Heaven it must be startling, dramatic, utterly demoralizing to men dragged from convoy stupor by those sudden twin explosions in their midst.

Offer got back in his seat. Ahead someone else was having a go, for the enemy trucks were no longer coming along steadily in almost orderly lines. Now vehicles, as if in panic, were racing through the dust cloud, charging in blind haste to get away from some terrible pursuer. A mighty explosion amid the dust told of something big going up. His men would be having the time of their lives, scudding among the bigger vehicles, hosing them with heavy machine-gun bullets, halting transport, and setting them on fire with tracer. Up and down, five deadly enemies right in the midst of unprotected soft transport.

It was easy; it was murder.

But murder was one-sided only while the enemy was in panic and disorganized. Every minute brought increasing threat to the rampaging Jeeps. Time was against them. Got to get O'Keefe's Jeep now if ever it was to be done, Offer's thoughts insisted, and he told Pom, 'Find O'Keefe, you little bugger! Back you go!' Shouting because the noise level had risen to a height which was sheer pain to their ears, the roaring from trucks burning around them, the blazing of petrol tankers, and the revving of engines as Axis drivers strove frantically to escape this harassing enemy.

Abruptly Offer saw one of his Jeeps shoot into the light from a burning tanker. It was ripping off in quick bursts, incapable of missing at that range, racing from one big truck to another. Some trucks, even so, seemed to roll on, as if the firing had missed something vital; but others came to an abrupt halt, men tumbling out of driving cabs, one of the trucks taking fire instantly, the others just crippled.

The Jeep came skidding close to Offer's vehicle, yet the occupants seemed not to notice them, so intent at the moment on destruction. Captain Offer saw fiercely exultant faces, Private Redpath at the wheel, his oppo Salkirk in the passenger seat using a tommy, while behind, Wise raked all he saw with a thunderously roaring Browning. Just for a few seconds the Jeep was there, creating havoc, then it charged off into the dust and smoke but the Browning could still be heard hammering away even after the Jeep was out of sight. And that would be happening elsewhere, too, other Jeeps hounding a bewildered convoy and utterly demoralizing it.

Offer thought, 'They must think they are under attack by an army.' Men's imagination ran riot in times of danger. Their first thought would be that Monty's Eighth Army in some miraculous way had come bounding a couple of hundred miles across the desert to surprise them here on the Benghazi trail. Fear-distorted imagination would do the rest. They would see enemy everywhere; even their own trucks would be suspect, every other vehicle now a potential enemy. When men got into that condition blind panic took over, morale disintegrated, and they did absurd things, things they were ashamed of later.

Now Offer found himself in the midst of mechanized turmoil. Soft transport was charging everywhere, lost inside their own dust cloud, no driver daring to stop, and every racing vehicle a menace to all others. He saw two huge trucks come racing out of the shrouding dust and collide head-on like two rams locking in battle. He saw another truck swerve so quickly to avoid colliding with a tanker that it went completely over. Everywhere trucks howled in a crescendo of accelerating engines, ever on the move, none of them knowing what they were doing.

The enemy was at them! The feared Desert Rats had ambushed them and were destroying them! Escape! But how and where, when only for moments did they glimpse the enemy firing at them. Never had an Axis force been so utterly shocked and demoralized.

Pom was taking avoiding action as he threaded his way back to where he thought the head of the column should be. Wilborn happily continued his work of shooting up the panicky transport milling around them. The smell of burning was intense now; everywhere they went the heat closed around. Then they heard a roaring which told not of burning but of conflagration; and time after time they came upon huge fires, trucks being gutted in a matter of a minute or so, tankers in even less time. And still the destruction was going on.

Better than aerial strafing, was John Offer's thought, and then they ran into clean air. Pom had come out on the south side, the prevailing wind side, though there was little of it at the moment. It was a joy to get away from the blinding dust and smoke, but there was no time for relaxation.

Find O'Keefe, and they had only brief minutes in which to do so.

Offer's head swivelled round, quickly taking in the sight. As far as he could see there was dust and smoke rolling together, reddened where transports burned. Through the haze he saw lumbering vehicles still charging, some of them coming out into the open, probably by accident, as Pom had done, and these were the dangerous ones. In the clear, they could see and could collect their scattered wits. Such vehicles slowed, then came cruising together, not kicking up much dust, then halting, and Offer guessed their crews were exchanging information and thoughts. More and more vehicles were pulling out of the dust cloud and coming to their senses. Soon someone would organize men into attack . . .

He saw infantry come dropping out of one wagon and go running towards the dust and smoke haze, automatic weapons at the ready. Already the Gang's moment was nearly over, Offer thought. Surprise and panic were ending. Just a few resolute Panzergrenadiers could stop the slaughter caused by a mere five Jeeps.

Offer called to Wilborn: 'Don't fire!' Don't draw attention to themselves. The whole object of the exercise had been to create a diversion under cover of which O'Keefe and Ward could be rescued. If in the process they damaged the enemy and thus gave unexpected aid to Montgomery's army that was a by-product of their efforts, and the best of British luck to old rasping-voiced Monty. They had their diversion; now, where the devil was that other Jeep?

Offer rapped, 'Get to the front of the column, Pom' . . . where the Hauptmann in his Jeep had last been seen. Pom began to accelerate, keeping clear of the shifting dust cloud. They had to pass a group of trucks gathering together, but perhaps the German occupants were still too disorientated to spot the wolf in their midst and nothing was done, no shot was fired to halt them. It wouldn't be long, though, before these men too came to their senses . . .

It was a curious sight. The leading vehicles had scattered and then had grouped where the air was clearer, but the long column, like some mindless monster, kept pushing forward through the dust. Only when those behind came to where trucks stood abandoned or burned furiously did they become alarmed, and then the Jeeps were at them, too, harrying them, and snapping at their heels as they ran.

Two hundred yards clear of the column a group of vehicles had halted. Among them was O'Keefe's Jeep. Just coming up along the trail were those two decoy Bedfords with their camouflage of British P.O.W.s and squads of well-armed Panzergrenadiers. Offer guessed that in that group there was much discussion going on, the only man with real knowledge of what was happening amidst all that confusion being the Hauptmann.

He said, 'Blast!' seeing the Bedfords. That tore it, he thought. He'd hoped to find the Jeep isolated, preferably lost amid the smoke and dust, vulnerable to swift attack. Now O'Keefe and Ward were surrounded by an alerted enemy.

'Pull away,' he ordered. No sense in inviting suicide; no hope of charging in and nipping off with the prisoners now, not with the Panzers so close. Offer wondered if his Jeep had been seen, but thought not because no one made a move to come out to take them on. What to do now, time ticking away madly, the element of surprise reducing with every passing second?

He felt an urgency that made him almost frantic, and he was sweating profusely, staring over his shoulder at that distant, yet tantalizingly close Jeep. Yet even then he had time to think, 'Twenty minutes ago I was hoping my men would go against this rescue bid.' He had been in the grip of the jitters, those dreaded desert doldrums, not wanting to risk himself again in action, quite certain he would not have the nerve to go through with it if they did.

But now it was different – it was always different. Now the old recklessness was upon him, no counting the cost, just bursting to get stuck in and finish the job and drive away in triumph. He was not the same man; but how long would this synthetic enthusiasm sustain him, this blood-warming exciting challenge to death keep him going? He had a feeling this must be the last time, that never again would he be able to rouse himself to these heights of frenetic daring and activity.

John Offer suddenly saw an opportunity. The wind shifted a little. Suddenly that swelling cloud of smoke and dust, now rising hundreds of feet in the air, began to roll along the trail. Offer's quick mind realized that within seconds, before the Germans quite knew what was happening, that group of vehicles round O'Keefe's Jeep would be engulfed. This was their moment for a rescue bid.

'Back!' he roared, pointing. He was just in time to see the group scattering, then the fog of dust and smoke blotted them from sight. 'Find that Jeep! Keep your eyes skinned!'

Pom threw up a great spray of sand as he skidded the vehicle round, then sent the Jeep plunging into the smoke towards where last they had seen the Hauptmann. Choking fumes again, eyes smarting, peering through goggles which continually powdered with dust. Shapes looming up crazily, then careering away at sight of them, Wilborn happily snapping off a few rounds to keep the confusion going.

A Jeep. Offer's pulse raced. Then the Jeep laced a massive truck with a long trailer packed high under a taut tarpaulin. Not the one they were after, but Eddie Walker having a go at an ammo truck and trailer. 'Christ, if he sets that one off!' thought Offer, peering ahead. He began to cough, his lungs aching.

A parting in the smoke cloud. Abruptly three vehicles before them. One a Jeep stationary. Offer thought a man was leaning out of the Jeep, shouting up at a driver in a cab: a Bedford. He had a glimpse of O'Keefe and Ward sitting bolt upright, staring round them, two men on the alert knowing all this was for them and being ready for the moment when rescue came. That man half standing in the passenger seat would be the Hauptmann. Nice chap, but he would have to go, that seemed certain, when they went belting in, guns going. But they couldn't go in for the moment. Panzergrenadiers were leaping out from the Bedfords and deploying, guns in hand, taking up positions in a wide circle around the Jeep.

Offer uttered an unparliamentary word expressing exasperation and frustration, and told Pom to keep out of sight. They pulled back a short way, then halted. Now the dust and smoke really poured about them, and they were in great danger from huge trucks crashing by unnervingly close. Wilborn gave each careering vehicle a burst – 'Up their Jaxie,' as he said when they thundered by. Occasionally through the murk they glimpsed the Jeep, the Bedfords and the ring of armed men around all three vehicles.

'No good going in,' he shouted to Pom. A huge transporter almost got them at that moment, blundering like a crazed thing out of the densest patch of smoke – if Pom hadn't accelerated a few yards they would have been crushed.

Captain Offer hopped out. He had his pistol in his hand. 'I'm going in on foot.' Someone on foot mightn't be suspected, his uniform unidentifiable in that shrouding fog. If he could run in, top the driver and the Hauptmann, he might be able to start the Jeep and drive off with it. A lot of ifs, but Offer didn't pause to consider the dangers.

'Set up a diversion!' His hand waved towards the right of the group, then he went plunging the other way. Pom shot off. His Jeep must have been seen instantly, Wilborn firing at the three vehicles, but low so as not to hit the Jeep and its occupants or the P.O.W.s in the Bedfords. A brief appearance, not risking anything. Offer, closing in, lungs seared by the harsh smoke, saw Pom go racing away to be swallowed immediately in the murk of the fog. Wise man, but he'd done his stuff. Attention would have been momentarily attracted that way.

He saw uniforms, Panzergrenadiers', before him. They had Schmeissers slung from their shoulders and they were running, drawn away from their posts by an instinct to pursue the bold intruder. Not far, though; training would tell and soon they would halt, and then it wouldn't be easy; but Offer now was with them, running, and no one took any notice of him, thinking him one of themselves.

Quite clear now, thirty yards from him the Jeep. O'Keefe staring at him dumbfounded, then breaking into the hugest of grins.

The Hauptmann, in a curious pose of half-standing, where he'd been shouting up at someone in one of the Bedfords, turning and seeing him, their eyes meeting, recognition mutual and immediate. His mouth opening, calling a warning.

The Jeep driver. A round face swiftly turning towards the danger, John Offer racing in, a mere twenty yards away now. A face pink with youth which showed even through its powdering of dust. A young man at the wheel, unnerved suddenly by the sight of that grim, battered-nosed enemy almost on top of him.

His reaction was instant and automatic. He slipped the clutch and the Jeep jumped forward. Offer saw the half-standing Hauptmann go toppling backwards. He fell within range of O'Keefe's bound hands. Offer saw O'Keefe's lightning reaction. Bound hands swiftly raised, bound fists descending with cruel violence upon the Hauptmann's head, the German crumpling instantly.

But the Jeep was away, the driver beyond reach of O'Keefe's hands. Panicking because his officer was slumped in the passenger seat beside him and there was no one to give orders to his simple mind. All he could think of was of driving as hard as he could go, anything to keep him away from that terrible, murderous-looking figure bounding out of the fog. And so, obligingly, he left the protection of the Bedfords and those Panzergrenadiers.

John Offer was running alongside a German soldier who simply stopped when he saw the Jeep bolting. He heard harsh voices shouting in surprise. The Panzers would have halted, perplexed, but seeing no sense in chasing a Jeep careering off into the smoke. Captain Offer ran on and astonishingly no German appeared to notice anything odd about his appearance. No shout after him, no stream of deadly bullets.

Choking and coughing, Offer ran into the cover of the swirling murk. The Jeep had disappeared. It must be followed. Useless on foot, though. He stopped running, lungs aching, his body wet with sweat.

A Jeep just shot out of the muck. Pom's come back for me, he thought, but it was Eddie Walker's voice shouting, 'What happened to your Jeep, sir?'

'That way!' No time for explanations. Get after O'Keefe. He hauled himself under Wise's Browning and lay there panting, staring into the blinding dust and smoke.

Walker twisted in his seat. 'They're ganging up on us, sir.'

Offer remembered those other Panzergrenadiers whom he had seen debussing out in the clear and running into the smoke. Resistance was organizing. They'd had their chance. Where was that Jeep? So near, yet Offer knew he ought now to be pulling out his men.

Another Jeep careering up alongside. This time it was Pom's. Offer signalled for it to keep up with them. Their war was over. Keep going forward and hope to find the others – with a bit of luck they might even find O'Keefe's Jeep.

Another Jeep before them. It was involved in a fight and was retreating. The air was clearer here, almost on the edge of things, and eighty yards or so away crouching figures ran for cover towards a disabled truck. The gunners were putting the fear of death up the Germans, Brownings hammering at them, but doing little damage, their aim disturbed by movement of the Jeep. Offer saw figures pitch forward and go flat down, but whether they were hit or seeking safety on the ground he couldn't tell.

Offer yelled, 'Cease firing! Come on, let's get out of here!' They probably didn't hear a word of what he was shouting, but an imperious gesture with his arm was enough. They pulled out of battle, just when German guns were opening up strongly upon them. The smoke closed around them, acrid and choking, but at least it provided them with safety.

'Where's the other?' Their fourth Jeep. That was the thought in Offer's mind. Find it and then get the hell out of this inferno. No good staying any longer; they'd never spot O'Keefe's Jeep now in this fog. Well, they'd done their best and Offer's responsibility was to get his other men out to safety.

They had cleared most of the wrecks. Now they ran into vehicles which had merely halted, the drivers perplexed by all the noise and glaring fires ahead, waiting for the dust to disperse.

'Don't fire!'

Offer gave the order, pantomiming it across to the other Jeeps. Just keep moving and don't bring attention upon themselves. The Axis drivers would be watching them, enemy vehicles, but would be reassured if they took no hostile action, again thinking they'd be captured ones. No sense in shooting up any more trucks, not even to oblige Montgomery, Offer thought; just ease out of this and be satisfied with what they had done.

A Jeep came heading towards them. Walker stood up and waved, but the Jeep turned and bolted, and they knew then it wasn't their other one. This must be O'Keefe's, run on to by accident . . .

Another Jeep emerged from the murk. The fourth Jeep, it must have spotted O'Keefe's and given chase, driving it on to Offer's trio. Luck – good fortune – was on their side for the moment.

All Jeeps swung instantly into pursuit. O'Keefe's Jeep went dodging frantically among the Axis vehicles, trying to throw off his pursuers. It must have been a nightmarish time for that young driver, here amidst so many of his people, with armed Germans everywhere in those huge transports, yet he could not stop to call for aid because of the relentless Jeeps on his tail.

Goggled faces swung to watch them go by, skidding round the stationary trucks, vague faces, uncomprehending, watching the chase and doing nothing because no one had time to think of what to do.

The smoke behind them now, the dust thinning, the whole column coming to a halt along the miles of trail. Only their Jeeps kicking up a dust, and O'Keefe's incapable of losing them now because of it. Offer's drivers better than the German, anticipating and taking short cuts between the lines of vehicles, quicker on the turn, smarter at going through the gears when a sudden swerve in the soft earth almost brought them to a stall. Catching up, the distance between them rapidly closing, and the German knowing it because they could see his frantic young face turning increasingly often to look back.

Palfreyman's Jeep – Palfreyman's bandaged head like a landmark – somehow got ahead of the fleeing German and turned him. They were all so close now they could see O'Keefe and Ward, O'Keefe cheering uproariously though they couldn't hear a thing, Ward looking quite unmoved under his streaming *kefir*.

It was like beagles running down a hare, and their prey

186

was as helpless before them as that inoffensive little animal. All so swiftly done, Palfreyman racing across, the German hauling on his wheel and running before the line of other Jeeps. A swift pounce and the hare was snapped up. In this case another Jeep tore alongside the German, wheels threatening to lock.

Bullets were flying.

O'Keefe's Jeep tried to turn away again, but Palfreyman was riding him close on the other side. Three Jeeps ran straight for fifty yards, then the young German quit. A lot of bullets were flying. A skidding halt, the dust going up like steam from a halting engine.

Offer was out of Walker's vehicle in a flash. No time to give orders; do the damn' thing himself and get out of this place. Bullets.

He shouted and waved in case they hadn't understood. Lots of men were running away to his right. They were coming up between the halted trucks, and some were firing as they ran. Grey-green men with coal-scuttle helmets. German troops. And, God, what a lot there were, suddenly! All at once there seemed hundreds of them, and here little smoke and dust to shroud the Gang's movements.

Offer heard his Brownings go into action, then he was up to O'Keefe's Jeep. O'Keefe was shouting, 'Bloody good show, sir!' and Offer just heard it. Only a bloody good show if they made the most of the next few seconds.

A petrified face, the German with his hands rigidly aloft. Offer hadn't time for courtesy. He took one stiffly extended arm, heaved and the young chap came somersaulting out on to the dirt. O'Keefe cheering rapturously. Offer into the seat. Engine obligingly still running. Into gear. Out with the clutch. A neck-breaking jerk as the Jeep hurtled into motion. Bullets, bullets, bullets. Christ, how thick they were around them! They couldn't miss. Any minute something terrible was going to come through his backbone and out of his chest, bringing his ribs with it. Into second but no time for further gear-changing. Rev up and keep revving and if the engine stayed under the bonnet they might make it.

He had a feeling his other Jeeps were scattering but circling in order to give him protection, covering him with almost continuous fire from their Brownings. Some dust hanging ahead. Into it. Relief. Can't see me now, was his thought, and instantly hauled on the wheel and took another course.

The jerk threw a boot almost on to his clutch pedal. A German laced-up boot. That Kraut officer's. Nice chap, the Kraut. Poor sod, tables turned on him again. O'Keefe was shouting. Rommel wasn't going to be pleased with him. Wish his actions didn't always hurt the poor bastard. O'Keefe shouting. The hell with O'Keefe: he could keep his jubilation till later.

Lines of vehicles – irregular yet in almost continuous lines – almost halted, again the dust cloud dispersing. Offer shot across their bonnets, startling men in the act of descending. Open country, that's what he wanted. Christ, that had been a close do, those Panzer blokes suddenly catching them at a halt. Above the straining noise of the Jeep engine O'Keefe was shouting again, but he wasn't cheering.

Offer thought, 'What's happened to the others?' He twisted in his seat, but saw no signs of the other Jeeps. Well, they knew the rendezvous; they'd make their way independently towards it. He could only think of himself now.

The German boot stirred and lifted away from the clutch. Coming to, Offer thought, and should have thought beyond that reaction, but they were coming out through the last of the transports and armed men were standing on a sand dune, all turning to watch their flight. He needed Wilborn right now, or any machine-gunner, though the Breda was probably out of action.

Suddenly the group on the dune came to a decision. This was a hostile vehicle and they went down on their faces, rifles firing, and then a machine-gun swung into action. Mad, evasive turns, the Jeep skidding, dirt fanning up in huge sprays. Not out of the wood yet. Then going like a bat out of hell for broken ground beyond the camel trail.

And making it, and O'Keefe shouting in agony and exasperation. Oh, sod the man, hadn't he enough to think of!

Broken ground closing round them and the bullets no longer skipping uncomfortably near to them. Ease off the accelerator but keep going south, the sooner they were at the rendezvous the better. Engine not making so much row. Where were the other Jeeps? Had they all come through unscathed? He had a feeling they had.

O'Keefe bellowing, 'Look out, sir!'

This time he heard the words, and the urgency of warning. He swung in his seat.

The Hauptmann was sitting there, a rather groggy Hauptmann, but he was lifting a pistol as if newly drawn, and the hand did not shake which pointed it at Offer's middle.

Captain Offer did not halt. Instinct kept his foot on the accelerator, neither easing off nor increasing his speed. He could only stare at the lean-faced Afrika Korps Hauptmann, too shocked to think for a moment. Then he began to recover and his first thoughts were despairing.

Oh, God, no! he moaned inside himself. Not this, pipped on the post! All that hectic scheming and activity, O'Keefe and Ward finally lifted from right under the noses of the enemy, and now that pistol pointing, the tables turned on him for once by this Hauptmann. It was one of the bleakest moments of his life.

He could feel the sweat pouring out of him now, making rivulets through the caked dirt on his face. For one second he turned to look behind and met O'Keefe's grief-stricken eyes. He'd been trying to warn him, O'Keefe helpless to move because of the wire which shackled him to the Jeep, shouting but not being heard and understood over the roar of the Jeep engine. What agony for the poor bloody sergeant-major, tethered there, seeing the Hauptmann gradually recover, and all his frantic warnings ignored by his C.O.

'Sorry,' Offer mouthed silently, then looked again at the German officer. But shock was dissipating, Offer was recovering fast, his mind beginning to assess the situation for possibilities of reversing their positions . . .

A very ugly pistol pointing at him and the Hauptmann pulling himself firmly erect in his seat, hard grey eyes unwaveringly upon him. The pistol gestured; the Hauptmann said something in German which Offer interpreted as being, 'Turn.' Offer played dumb. He drove straight on, bumping over the rough ground. He wasn't going to do any turning if he could help it.

The tough face looking tougher, the pistol waving nastily, even more imperiously. And that command again, that solitary word which snapped out, an order from a man who lived by giving orders which had to be obeyed.

Offer shrugged. All right, he'd turn because that pistol said he had to. If he didn't he had no doubt the Hauptmann would shoot him through the heart, in the same movement dragging on the handbrake, kicking his dying foot away and throwing the clutch out. What pleasant thoughts, Offer told himself ironically, he terminating his own earthly drama with a bullet in the guts and dying in this damned place. Not likely.

So he turned. But he wasn't going to oblige by driving back to the German convoy, out of sight beyond these small hills. Meekly roll on into captivity, he, Glasshouse John of such terrible reputation, with the S.S. licking their chops and aching to get their hands on him? He remembered Walker and Busker and how they had looked after the attentions of the S.S., and he thought, 'No, I'd rather have a bullet through the old ticker.'

But he continued his wide circling, and in between watching the ground ahead he looked at the Hauptmann. He thought he had never seen a man appear so unyielding, so formidably lean and hard. It was no good playing with this fellow; when he did something it would have to be drastic . . .

He accelerated, and hauled hard on the wheel at the same time. He was thinking, 'The Breda mounting will save them' – O'Keefe and Ward. A stout thing, a Breda mounting.

Deliberately he turned the Jeep right over. The turn was too violent at that speed, the rough ground helping him. The quick turn and then the sensation of toppling over, Offer kicking himself up off the rising floorboards. He had a vision of the Hauptmann's startled face below him, the pistol going off but only tearing a hole in Heaven. Behind him O'Keefe's alarmed shout. Well, the best of luck to the sergeant-major and old Arab Ward.

The ground, cruelly hard, the breath knocked out of him, but he twisting his head instantly and seeing the Jeep above him, upside down, small objects cascading, O'Keefe and Ward seeming suspended in the air. Then the Jeep rolled right over them, the weight taken on the Breda mounting, turning again and rolling twice more, dust going up in a biting cloud. And finally it came to a halt, engine dead, astonishingly on all four wheels.

John Offer came to his knees. Instinct made his draw his pistol in the same movement. He peered through eyes which smarted from sweat and dirt, his dust goggles lost in the last few moments. Five yards before him the Hauptmann had just risen to his knees, his pistol still gripped in his right hand; it hadn't been lost in that tumble.

So two captains of war faced each other, their deadly small guns pointing. Stupid position to be in, Offer's mind raced; by Jove it must look comical, two men facing each other like dogs on all fours, about to blow each other's bloody brains out.

Yet neither fired. Panting and sweating, begrimed from the dust of the day, they held their position for several long seconds. Then Captain Offer began to recover his wits. No sense in getting killed now. Besides this was a bloody good

Hun, a much more charming chap than a lot of men fighting the British cause – he could think of several in Sharafim Glasshouse whom he would cheerfully have chopped. But not this Hauptmann. Old-fashioned word, and something he personally never aspired to, the Hauptmann was a gentleman.

Offer's battered face suddenly broke into a cheerful smile. 'Checkmate,' he said, and the German officer must have understood the word for he nodded and his face seemed ever so slightly to relax.

John Offer shrugged. He felt he had the measure of his opponent. Anyway, it was time to take risks. Deliberately he climbed to his feet, and just as deliberately shoved his pistol back into its holster.

Without hesitation the Hauptmann holstered his gun and rose, too, slapping the dust off him. Turning his back on the Hauptmann, John Offer walked towards the Jeep. Close by an engine was roaring. His mind identified it as a Jeep and it was coming up after them, probably following their tyre marks.

Ward and O'Keefe were sitting up, Ward looking as if nothing had happened, as if being rotated three times in a tumbling Jeep, and he tethered to it, was everyday stuff. O'Keefe looked groggy, though, as if his head had tried to do damage to something harder than bone.

'Okay, sergeant-major?'

O'Keefe focused his eyes upon him. 'Well,' he said doubtfully, giving the matter some thought, 'if you say so, sir.'

Offer had found the tool-kit. Pliers for the wire; an old-fashioned army knife, still with its tool for removing horses' hoofs from stones, for the roped wrists. The approaching Jeep almost on top of them, making a fearsome sound. The Hauptmann would be standing behind him, not running because a running German would be shot down instantly. Offer wondered if he had drawn his pistol again. If so he thought it would be aimed at his, John Offer's back. Not a nice thought. He carried on as if oblivious to such a possibility.

A bit of sawing on O'Keefe's bonds. Hard work, and Offer told him pleasantly, 'Better see that all knives are well-sharpened in future, sergeant-major. Never know when we might be having to cut you free again.'

'Yes, sir,' said that warrior and took the knife and set to work freeing his companion just as the other Jeep came to a halt beside them. Walker's: he'd found his C.O. again.

The Hauptmann hadn't drawn his pistol, but was standing there with his hand on the butt. Walker and his men were out of their Jeep like a shot, Walker with a tommy lifting to cover an armed German standing right behind their captain.

Offer saw it all, turning, a moment of high drama. Being Offer he immediately reduced it to anti-climax. Quite testily he said, 'Put those things away.' And severely – 'Don't you know it's dangerous to point a gun?'

'But, sir –'

Captain Offer had walked right in front of the German. Now if he wanted to the Hauptmann could draw his pistol and either shoot him – a bit suicidal, though, if he did, thought Offer – or use him as a hostage against his own freedom. He felt sure the Hauptmann would do neither. In that position of checkmate they had come to an unspoken agreement. Neither was to try to take any advantage over the other.

Walker looked very doubtful. He also looked big and ferocious, Offer thought, mighty grim behind his tommy, his comrades just as intimidating. The German must have thought his last moment had come.

Very courteously John Offer turned and spoke to him. 'Before you go, will you take a drink with us?'

And just as courteously the German officer said, 'I shall be delighted,' and quite calmly moved between Walker and his men and casually seated himself on the bonnet of O'Keefe's Jeep. Walker blinked a bit, then reluctantly

193

lowered the muzzle of his tommy.

Offer said, 'I feel the occasion demands something better than desert char, Eddie.' This wasn't his Jeep; if it had been he could have laid his hands on a precious bottle of Cyprus brandy. 'Anyone got anything stronger?'

Walker shook his head regretfully, but the question sent O'Keefe rummaging and saying, 'If the bloody bottle's not broken –'

It wasn't. And it was whisky, real Scotch. Captain Offer saw the label. 'Chivas!' he exclaimed, enraptured. The best Highland malt, just right for this occasion.

Mugs came up, the whisky poured out. The other Jeeps came homing in on them just then but too late; for them it was char, swiftly brewed. The last Jeep reported seeing armoured cars streaking up alongside the stationary column. Offer said, 'We won't hurry.' Don't spoil this beautiful moment. Their last mission accomplished. Never, never again would he risk his life in the desert. He was through, finished, and he was satisfied to know it.

'I never was a hero,' he thought, war being stupid, anyway. Look how friendly he felt towards this erect German, solemnly drinking from an enamel mug which had lost half of its enamelling. This tall Afrika Korps officer, standing there surrounded by sixteen enemies, had no fear of them now.

Enemies? In the way of the British soldier they had suddenly become embarrassingly friendly. *Kill him* was the first instinct. He's not to die? Then make a fuss of him.

The last drops from the bottle were insistently poured into his mug, though he politely tried to dissuade them from their generosity. A toast was drunk – 'To all of us!' – from Offer, and the Hauptmann nodded solemnly and drank with them. When the whisky was finally, unhurriedly downed, tea was ready and the men wanted him to share their brew, and he was a good chap and lingered over char just to please them.

Offer took tea, too – much more refreshing than Chivas.

He felt benign, his old self. So far as he could see none of his men had suffered in the recent action. Good. It would have weighed on his conscience if the last mad moments had produced casualties.

He began to feel a little light-headed – maybe he wasn't used to Highland whisky just then. A mood of euphoria wrapped warmly round him, so that the world about him, so harsh a moment ago, took on a golden glow.

Bloody good chaps, his men, his villains. And now it was all coming to an end; the inevitable parting couldn't be that far away for them. A few weeks – no more than two, he guessed – hiding out in the desert near to this trail. Not easy, especially with the nights as cold as they were, but they had ample water and food, and they'd take it all without much griping.

Then into Benghazi. He gave grave consideration to his next thoughts. Hop on to a boat immediately? Well, was there really all that rush? His men would like a glorious booze-up before they brushed the dust of Africa off them. Dangerous, of course, dallying around Benghazi, his men inclined to be boisterous when in liquor. A drunken brawl could invite the attentions of M.P.s, and he didn't want to have to use the major-general's letter of immunity to free them because that would give the whole damn' show away. They were dead, and it was better they remained dead.

Just two or three days, he decided magnanimously, a great indulgence upon him, beaming at his friend the Hauptmann, who smiled back and toasted him again with a battered mug of char. Wish there were more fellows like this one. What the hell were they doing, trying to kill each other?

. . . yes, a few marvellous days in Benghazi. His mind projected pictures of joy, the things he would do. They all contained a woman, charming French Marie. He saw her with her bright-eyed smile, coming in with the coffee. Saw her dimpling in his arms and making throaty little declarations of love. Saw her on the bed with him, happily naked and waiting laughingly, inviting his love, and for him, hungry man after his desert travail, those were the best pictures of all. That last one he held on to as long as he could.

Then the Hauptmann was before him, picking out his words of English. 'I must leave you, Herr Hauptmann.'

'You must?' Regret, genuine, in John Offer's voice. What a pity, such a good type. 'Then allow me to accompany you part way back.'

So courteous. A slight bow of acknowledgement from the Hauptmann, heels coming gently together. Then he turned and smiled at the desperadoes around him – a warm smile, curious coming from that lean hard face, the smile of a soldier with respect for others of his profession, even an enemy.

They crowded round; they all had to shake his hand. Pom even made a speech – 'For a Kraut, you're not a bad old fucker –' until the others shut up his tactless yapping.

Then the two captains were walking away from the group, heading towards the trail – walking sedately, no hurry, and talking amiably about London and Paris. Both had been to Paris. 'I must come to London some day,' the German said. 'We have great respect for England, you know, Herr Hauptmann.' No reminder now that Offer was a bogus captain.

'If you do, please call upon me. I shall be delighted.' But how could the Hauptmann find him if even he, John Offer, didn't know the name he would bear in the years ahead?

The trail winding between soft banks of sandy soil, tufted grass somehow growing from it. Lousy country, fit only for men to war in. John Offer came to a halt. No need to carry courtesy too far. The trail couldn't be more than a mile ahead, and Offer didn't want to run into any ferreting armoured cars, seeking them. His eyes alighted on their tyre marks. They could be followed. But he would hear the approach of armoured vehicles in good time.

'I must leave you here, Herr Hauptmann.'

They faced each other, regret genuine in both of them. Offer extended his hand. The German took it.

'Good hunting,' John Offer said lightly, and then thought, 'That's a daft thing to say.' Next time the Hauptmann went hunting it might be for him, their truce at an end.

The Hauptmann seemed to appreciate the inappropriateness of the remark, his face breaking into a smile. 'I think it would be better to say *auf wieder —*'

The Hauptmann jumped him. Shocked, John Offer felt the full weight of the taller officer hurl itself at him, bearing him down. 'You treacherous bloody bastard!' he raged inside, doing this when Offer had played straight at a time when he had had the German at his mercy, surrounded by his men.

A high-flying R.A.F. reconnaissance plane, *en route* to photograph shipping in Benghazi harbour, took a course which brought it across the Trig-el-Abd. The miles-long convoy coming south from that port attracted attention because of the smoke pall above it, and as a matter of routine the aircraft took pictures, at the same time signalling base the news of important enemy troop movements.

The wireless message, and later the pilot's report, created some puzzlement. The pilot signalled that the supply column appeared to be under attack, for big fires were raging, a dense cloud of smoke rolling from it, with every sign of attempts at dispersal by the transport below. There was no hint of R.A.F. activity, and the pilot automatically ascribed the action to that of ground forces.

Someone in Cairo got hold of the photographs and was interested. 'R.A.F. say they weren't responsible?'

Captain Tansley shook his head. 'Nowhere near the area at the time.'

'So everyone assumes it's the work of commandos, our forward line troops being a hundred miles away at the time. But you tell me everyone disclaims responsibility.'

'S.A.S., L.R.D.G., Free French, Popski – all are accounted for, sir. We just don't know who did it.'

Tansley's manner said, 'Anyway, what does it matter?' Monty was going like the clappers up the Mediterranean coast, and the boys of the R.A.F. had strafed that supply column within an hour of the signal and done appalling damage.

Who cared who got at Rommel's transport first! Roll on the end of the war; it couldn't come too quickly for Tansley now. He'd just met a girl in Cairo and had fallen to the disease called love. He wanted to marry her and get back as soon as possible to his home in Gloucester.

When they were introduced she had started to say she knew someone else called Tansley, but then blushed and shut up, he had noticed at the time. Beautiful Angela, angel by name and angel by nature, an infatuated Tansley sighed to himself. A nursing sister, too, noble girl. Tansley had got it bad.

The big stubby fingers again shuffled through the aerial photographs, the sharp eyes peering from under their barbed-wire brows. 'An important enemy convoy is attacked and badly mauled, yet no one claims authorship. Funny, mighty funny.' The eyes glared again at the pictures. Major-generals do not appreciate funniness of that nature, wanting everything always neatly labelled.

'Shall I tell you something?'

Tansley dragged guilty thoughts from Angela. He wanted to get her to bed, loving her so much, but he knew she just wasn't that kind of girl, and merely to think carnally of her made him feel a rotten bastard, unworthy of such sweet innocence.

'Sir?'

'If he wasn't dead I'd say this was the work of Glasshouse John.' He tossed the photographs on to the table, went off to the generals' loo, and forgot about the Trig-el-Abd, its mysteriously ravaged enemy transport, and bogus Captain John Offer.

John Offer kicked out and hurt because the Hauptmann gasped, then Offer struggled with the strength of a man outraged, fury total and irresistible. They broke apart, rolling away from each other in the dust, and John Offer, sweat pouring into his eyes, was hauling out his pistol.

Braunschweig was coming on to his knees. He wasn't attempting to draw his pistol. Instead his face was turned from Offer, looking back along the tread marks of Jeeps. John Offer, blind with rage, lifted the pistol, covering the Hauptmann. The German was waving to him, a gesture not understandable for the moment. Then Braunschweig was falling forward, flat on his face again. Offer should have fired then, and he had the excuse of treachery to condone a killing, yet at the last second his finger held on the trigger, not squeezing it. God, it would be murder, and he didn't want a death on his conscience, even though the bastard deserved –

Movement beyond the Hauptmann. Someone coming quickly but cautiously along the tracks. A man half-running, stooped, short gun swinging from a sling on his shoulder. Other men beginning to appear. Germans.

The Hauptmann twisted on the ground and looked at the British officer. His face was frantic, that hand waving for silence and telling him to get down. Then the German's eyes took in the pistol aimed at him, and it was his turn to register shock and recoil as if appalled at the appearance of treachery.

John Offer went down full-length, his pistol turning away from the Hauptmann, his head shaking regretfully, almost humbly, as if seeking pardon.

But no time for explanations. A lot of Germans now, at the most eighty yards away and coming along swiftly, and they lying across the Jeep tracks, certain to be discovered. Must have seen us go to ground, Offer thought, and sent out a stalking party. They'd have those armoured cars quietly in the background, ready to back them up. If he were with his men it would have been all right. Any second now the Krauts would be spotted by the Gang, and his Jeeps could race off, derisively cocking two fingers at the clever-clever Hun, thinking he could steal up on the Glasshouse boys without being detected.

The trouble was, he wasn't with the Jeeps, and if they sheered off they left him. And then? Too many Germans too close to. Suicide to make a fight of it. He looked at the Hauptmann. The big chap had wriggled alongside Offer, bodies almost touching. 'He's covering me,' thought Offer, protecting him, hiding his tell-tale uniform. The truce hadn't ended yet. Again he felt ashamed for having doubted the honour of this German.

Their eyes met. Offer's asked a question. The Hauptmann shook his head. The Krauts were coming along faster now, sixty yards away. Offer felt the Hauptmann stir, gathering his strength, and knew he was going to rise. He didn't envy the fellow. Trigger-happy Panzers, startled by his sudden appearance, might blast off and the German officer could be dead before they recognized his uniform.

Offer was thinking, 'I'll have to stand up with him, too' – when it was safe to show himself. Then they'd take him prisoner. The question was, could the Hauptmann insist on Offer being freed, just as Offer had seen to it that the Hauptmann got away from his Gang? He had a feeling that conditions mightn't be the same. These Germans were regulars: his own men felt no bounds in the rigid codes of military conduct. If there was an officer with the Krauts Offer couldn't see him allowing the Hauptmann's companion to be permitted to stroll off, not after the devastation to the convoy.

Then a Browning filled the evening with a sudden, hideous row. The Krauts had been spotted. Captain Offer wasn't in the line of fire – probably had disappeared from view of the Gang's sentry – and instant reaction was to get the Browning going. Almost at the same second Offer heard engines start up, probably half a mile away, perhaps on the edge of the trail. The armoured cars. They'd brought the infantry, set them to trailing on foot, and now were coming along to rout an enemy, flushed into the open.

Other sounds of engines, the Jeeps' starting, a couple of hundred yards behind them. More gunfire from the Brownings, savage bursts, tracer zipping over their heads as they clung close to the ground. Offer caught one last glimpse of the German Panzergrenadiers, scattering frantically to find cover, then the Krauts were replying to the Brownings. The heavy beat of armoured car engines became louder; they were closing in at speed.

John Offer found his eyes caught by the German's. He shrugged, then smiled wryly, and the Hauptmann smiled back and also shrugged. Both knew what the other was thinking. This was the craziest moment of the last half-hour. Here they were, deadly enemies, kept together by the crossfire of their own men, and neither would betray nor harm the other.

'Damned incredible,' Offer thought, and decided that if ever he were to meet Atherton again he'd tell him about this moment, though it could never be published, he remembered, because it had happened after he was dead.

Both lifted their heads cautiously. Offer's first glance was towards his own men. He could hear the Jeeps but couldn't see them, but he could see dust going up against the setting sun, and could tell a lot by the agitated way the Jeeps were being driven. They were clearing off to a safe distance, retreating before the menace of the advancing armoured cars; but they did it reluctantly, and he could hear them halt at times and rip off with the Brownings, lingering, unwilling to desert their officer.

The armoured cars. John Offer's head turned towards the advancing noise. He found himself staring over the shoulder of the Hauptmann, the man's back to him, a testimony to his trust in Glasshouse John even at such a moment.

He saw a turret only a few hundred feet away. He also saw more German infantry scuttling from cover to cover, rifles trailing. He thought, 'It's a question of time.' One of the armoured cars was sure to come bouncing along straight towards them; either that or a Panzergrenadier would come running round the corner of this dune.

John Offer had visions of the bag at that moment. Hands up and march away, and they'd take no notice of the Hauptmann and Offer wouldn't plead or try to bring the German into it. Braunschweig had done his best and had played straight. It wasn't his fault that Offer was within minutes of becoming, yet again, a P.O.W. Or would he simply be shot out of hand when they saw he was British?

There had been noise at that moment, Jeep and armoured car engines, the far distant sounds of the convoy perhaps on the move again, and an occasional shouted command from somewhere close where the Panzergrenadiers were deployed amid the dunes. Noise, but not much of it. Nothing, for instance, like the noise waves which battered them seconds later.

All at once the sky seemed filled with aircraft which flashed at low level the length of the distant Axis supply column, noise coming in swift and frantic crescendo, then beginning to die only to be swamped by the noise of following planes.

John Offer raised himself on his arm and stared towards the trail. Fighter after fighter was power-diving towards it, guns and cannon going, mercilessly strafing the unseen vehicles. One after the other, twenty or thirty of them, down on a level course for a few seconds, guns hammering, then pulling away, some of them right over where Offer and the Hauptmann lay, then circling to make another dive attack.

New fires began to rage and there were explosions on the trail, the ground tremoring. And then the fighters flitted away and the bombers came in. Medium bombers, at first, Wellingtons, bombing from a height of no more than five thousand feet. Then other bombers, and they could hardly miss.

The dying sun, the last red rays, long shadows and the

world being torn apart by that rain of high explosive. A long line of fires now, and a pyre of smoke that must have risen thousands of feet above the blazing wreckage of Rommel's precious transport. The smell of burning was all over the land, and both captains, watching fascinated, got the stink in their nostrils.

There was resistance, though, streams of tracer going in long lines of decelerating light towards the aircraft, and missing by a mile. Then some bigger guns were thrown into action – 88 mms – and one bomber caught a packet and then the others played safe and bombed from a higher altitude, but less accurately. One stick, in fact, fell within two hundred yards of the captains, and Offer was sure it knocked out one of the armoured cars.

The cars had stopped their advance the moment the fighters came with their strafing, the armoured cars seeming no longer interested in elusive Jeeps; instead they dispersed and opened up on any aircraft which came flashing close enough to them.

The threat to Offer had been removed; the R.A.F. had momentarily put an end to the hunt across the desert. But for the presence of the Panzergrenadiers at that moment John Offer could have risen to his feet and walked boldly away. The Krauts were there, though, still around him, for once or twice he heard voices calling. Better wait a few more minutes for complete dark, then he wouldn't be identified if he did run into anybody in the night.

There had been casualties where that nearby stick of bombs had landed; for against the glow of a great fire on the trail beyond, Captain Offer saw stretcher-bearers in silhouette and they were making several journeys to a box-like vehicle which could only be an ambulance.

He wished black-dark would come and he could be away, trudging over the desert towards the rendezvous they'd established earlier. A hell of a long walk, but he'd make it, though he suspected the alert Sergeant-major O'Keefe would be out looking for him at daylight.

He thought, 'Our truce is nearly over, my dear Haupt-mann.' They would part, probably with a handshake, and he would have regrets, for it wasn't often one encountered a man of such incorruptible honour as this German. He only hoped that Braunschweig held the same high opinion of him . . .

Braunschweig. Hell of a mouthful. Meant Bruns-wick, according to Weybright. Brunswick. Nice name, really. When he went back on the stage in London perhaps he would call himself John Brunswick. He thought of telling the Hauptmann, then didn't bother.

He wished the bombing would end, but it went on, the aircraft homing in on those huge fires below and plastering the area with stick after stick of 50-pounders. Now, because of the gathering night, the pilots wouldn't be able to see the convoy on the trail, only those flaming wrecks, and bombing was becoming increasingly inaccurate. More and more bombs were now landing uncomfortably close to where the two men still crouched together.

Offer sat upright. Time to move, he thought, not quite dark enough yet but the bombs screaming from the dark sky above were a bit unnerving. He put his hand on the German's shoulder preparatory to saying, 'I'm on my way, my friend. The best of British luck to you.' Or German luck, or any luck to enable a good bloke to survive this stupid bloody war. More bombs making their terrible row . . .

The earth came up around him and buried him alive. Concussion from some great wave-force smote his head and body and left him stunned and incapable of thought. Then he began to suffocate, his mouth full of dirt, his lungs gasping for air. His eyes opened and he saw light but it was only a crack. His mind, sharpened by approaching death, understood everything – a bomb hitting the ground close to where they crouched against that dune, the earth and sand being piled over them. If he couldn't free himself quickly he would die.

He shook his head vigorously, and the earth, thank God,

fell away from his face. He spat out the dirt from his mouth and blinked away the muck from his eyes. There was still enough light, and he saw that the Hauptmann hadn't been buried; instead the explosion had hurled him ten or more yards away.

Gasping, risking being overheard by some lurking Panzergrenadier, John Offer called, 'Get me out of here.'

The Hauptmann didn't move. He was knocked out, Offer realized, either that or dead. If Offer got out of this grave he would have to do it himself. Thank heaven his head was clear.

He was buried in an almost erect position, the shock-wave having thrown him up from the ground with the dirt. His arms were apart and imprisoned by a weight of earth upon them. When he realized how helpless he was he began to panic and struggled frantically to drag himself out of the ground, but it did him no good, so he pulled himself together and instead began a more rational effort.

He could move his arms just a trifle, the earth loose and sandy upon them. By wriggling and twisting he found he could worm his right hand inch by inch towards the surface, so for a few minutes he concentrated on that. Then with surprising ease the hand came up through the last eighteen inches of soil, almost with no effort at all.

The Hauptmann had begun to groan. John Offer thought, 'That might bring someone over to see what's happening,' and he began to work harder to get out of his predicament, for it wouldn't do to be caught like this, helpless in his own grave. All the same, he was glad the Hauptmann was alive.

'Hang on, old boy,' he called softly. 'I'll be with you in a jiffy.' The moaning stopped. Perhaps the Hauptmann heard and understood.

Using his free hand as a shovel, John Offer scooped away the dirt from before his chest. Another stick of bombs came down, the earth shaking, shrapnel flying, and dirt cascading into his unprotected face. But it didn't set him back in his efforts to free himself. Instead, with redoubled vigour Offer got his left hand clear and after that it was only seconds before he finally hauled his legs out of the ground.

A pause, recovering. The growing darkness a pandemonium of noise, guns and bombs and occasionally the shouting of men somewhere near at hand, or the starting of an engine, as if dispersal hadn't been deep enough and some courageous truck driver had decided to drive his truck still deeper into the desert. Then Offer, panting, plunged across to where the Afrika Korps captain lay in silence.

'What's wrong?' Offer went down on his knees beside him. The Hauptmann stirred a little, as if the voice got through to him, but that was all. He's in a bad way, Offer decided, his eye upon the Hauptmann's right leg. The leg had been smashed, perhaps by a piece of flying bombcasing. John Offer's eyes could still see, though the light was bad, and he saw blood. There was a hole torn in the flesh just below the knee and blood was pulsing out in big spurts.

'Oh, Christ!' thought Offer. Arterial blood. And the Hauptmann had been steadily bleeding to death in those minutes while he dragged himself out of the ground. A tourniquet. His eyes fell on the German officer's laced boots, and in seconds he had one of the laces out and tied below the knee, a long splinter of stone picked up in the dark as a means of tightening the tourniquet.

It was done, and Offer rose. He looked round. This was his chance. The world was now dark enough for him to go walking away to freedom. The bombing and explosions and fires on the Trig-el-Abd were sufficient distraction to occupy any Panzergrenadier's attention, lying amid these dunes, at that moment. He'd done his best for the Hauptmann; now he should think of himself and clear off.

But Offer couldn't go. If he walked away the Hauptmann would die. That tourniquet must be released within a few minutes, and if he left him no one would find him perhaps until daylight next morning. Offer wasn't going to let the chap die if he could help it.

He remembered the ambulance and the stretcher-bearers. Offer turned and went stumbling off into the dark. His sense of direction was good. Suddenly the squat vehicle was there before him, men working and he knew they were loading another stretcher into it. Other forms were standing around, watching the huge fires less than half a mile away.

Offer put excitement into his voice, bursting in among them. '*Avanti! Avanti!*' he cried. He grabbed an arm and started to pull on it. '*Offizier*,' he kept saying, pulling out the few words of German he knew. '*Deutsch!*' Then that insistent, '*Avanti, avanti!*'

The German began to come with him, then a second one joined the agitated 'Italian'. Offer was trying to run, and the Germans sensed the mood of urgency and ran with him. Offer's awful thought was that in the darkness he would fail to find the poor bloody Hauptmann, but to his surprise they came upon him first time. One of the Germans flashed a torch and saw the blood and broken limb. Then he saw the tourniquet and quickly released it.

John Offer had seen enough. He had done all he could for the Hauptmann, and now, under the circumstances, he was in the best possible hands. While the two German orderlies attended to him, Offer began to walk quietly away. One of the men must have heard him go and lifted his head and barked something in German. Offer said nothing but continued to walk off. The man peered after him for a moment, then got back to work.

Offer trudged for an hour across the rough desert, using the stars to maintain a course south. It was rough going, starlight only to aid him, and he kept falling, but it didn't matter; this night he was beyond feeling hurt. After all, wasn't he a dead man, recently digging himself out of his own grave? Dead men can't feel bruises.

At the end of an hour he judged himself to be beyond the radius of any wandering German or Italian, and he dug a hole and crouched in it because he was cold and wanted to be out of the chilly night breeze. When the moon came up he dragged his stiff limbs out of the hole and resumed his way.

He was a tired man, weary in every muscle of his body, yet he felt strangely content. He had performed his last act of war, here in the desert. As he walked he had the curious feeling that he was walking out of the army.